THE BLACK CASTLE

ALSO BY LES DANIELS

Living in Fear: A History of Horror in the Mass Media

Dying of Fright: Masterpieces of the Macabre

THE BLACK CASTLE

A Novel of the Macabre

LES DANIELS

CHARLES SCRIBNER'S SONS ✦ NEW YORK

Library of Congress Cataloging in Publication Data
Daniels, Les, 1943–
   The black castle.
   I. Title.
PZ4.D1878Bl   [PS3554.A5637]   813'.5'4 77-28235
ISBN 0-684-15533-8

1 3 5 7 9 11 13 15 17 19   O/C   20 18 16 14 12 10 8 6 4 2

PRINTED IN THE UNITED STATES OF AMERICA

THE BLACK CASTLE

1. Five Gold Coins

FIFTEEN men and women, naked to the waist, marched through the streets of the city. Each of them held an unlit green candle. Behind them walked men with whips, their faces hidden by black hoods. The leather thongs flailed at bare and bloody backs, and every stroke was answered by stifled cries and groans, yet the penitents never ceased their mumbled prayers.

Carlos Diaz watched intently as he leaned against a whitewashed wall warmed by the bright morning sun.

"Jews," he muttered, and spat in the hot dust at his feet.

This was his epithet for all heretics, but he knew that the people who passed before him could hardly be guilty of practicing the forbidden religion or they would not have escaped with a punishment as light as the Shame. It had been four years since Torquemada, the Inquisitor General, had persuaded the king and queen to expel the Jews. Those who had not fled Spain had become New Christians, and any sign of backsliding meant not just public humiliation but almost certain death.

Death. Carlos licked his thick lips at the sight of the half-naked women, and thought of the future.

This was Friday; in nine days there would be something re-

3

ally worth seeing. The Inquisition had announced an *auto-da-fé,* an act of faith, and that meant a real spectacle. Not a passing glimpse of pain like this, but a full Sunday of processions and penances climaxed when the worst of the sinners were consigned to the flames.

And some of them, thought Carlos with the satisfaction of a job well done, would be there because of information he had supplied.

The penitents and their tormentors passed him by. Carlos was tempted to follow, to join the crowd that jeered and gaped, but he had other business that was more important. There might be money in it.

He looked across the plaza, but the man he expected was nowhere to be seen. But the Grand Inquisitor would surely cross the square soon, and he would surely be pleased to hear what Carlos had to say. Discovering a dozen heretics would have been enough for Carlos, but he suspected that he had done even more. His foot tapped impatiently.

A fly buzzing overhead dropped and began to crawl across his bald pate. He brushed it away with fat fingers.

Two figures appeared in the entrance of the gray cathedral across the way. They were dressed in the habits of Dominican monks, with black cowls, and white robes tied at the waist with lengths of hemp. As they descended the marble steps to the street, Carlos approached them with studied nonchalance.

The younger of the two monks raised his eyes from their modest contemplation of the ground. Before him stood a short, heavy man of fifty, his face red and his jowls quivering with agitation. His clothes were soiled and he stank of wine.

The young Dominican turned to his superior. So did Carlos Diaz.

"Friar," said Carlos, "I must speak with you. I have seen something."

Diego de Villanueva, Grand Inquisitor, cast a cold eye on the informer.

"Not now," he said. "You should know better than to talk to

me like this where anyone might see you. Your own safety is at stake. Come to me this evening, and do not serve yourself so generously with the wine you sell or I may be forced to doubt the tale you tell me."

Carlos opened his mouth to reply, thought better of it, and hurried away, glancing from side to side as though expecting an ambush.

"Not a pleasant fellow, but a useful one," observed the Grand Inquisitor as they continued down the street. "He keeps a small inn and drinks most of the profits, but he has a sharp eye, and sometimes he hears the loose talk his business breeds. Now that you are my vicar, Miguel, you will doubtless see him many times again. His word has sent more than one sinner into the Holy House, and he must be counted a servant of the faith."

The Grand Inquisitor paused. "Yet sometimes I think it is not piety that prompts such service. Carlos Diaz is a good Christian, I suppose, certainly a careful one, and perhaps he seeks to make amends for the small sins that he commits. But he seems to take a strange delight in the suffering that must be the lot of the unrepentant heretic. There is some malice in him, not just the unsullied desire to rid Spain of heresy and save what souls we can. Still, his information has always been accurate, and we cannot expect each man to be a saint. He contributes in his own way to our glorious endeavor."

Miguel Carillo, lately appointed vicar to the Grand Inquisitor, nodded gravely but did not speak. Silence seemed best in the presence of such a man famed for his sanctity and feared for his severity. Miguel himself was still a bit afraid of him, even after almost a month in his service, for Diego de Villanueva was no ordinary Inquisitor. The man who walked beside Miguel had studied under no less a teacher than Tomás de Torquemada, the founder of the Inquisition, and had been received at the court of Ferdinand and Isabella.

In fact, it was remarkable that Diego de Villanueva had sought a post in a district as small and remote as this one. He was of a wealthy and powerful family; his lineage alone was suf-

5

ficient to guarantee him comfortable employment in one of the great cities of Spain. For a man of his background and ability to be so far from the centers of power was little short of a scandal, yet the choice had been his own. Perhaps a sense of duty had sent him back to the city of his birth, for he watched over its people as surely as did the ancestral castle of the de Villanuevas, which had stood empty since the death of his elder brother.

Such a man was to be Miguel's instructor in the mysteries of the Inquisition. Miguel glanced at him furtively. The face of the Grand Inquisitor was almost entirely hidden by his black cowl, but Miguel needed hardly a glimpse to remind him of the expansive brow, long straight nose, and thin lips. The face haunted the young vicar, yet the features themselves did not disturb him. It was their expression, or rather lack of it. The face might have been a mask; only the large, luminous eyes seemed alive.

Miguel kept his eyes on the Grand Inquisitor's long shadow as they walked together toward the Holy House. Diego de Villanueva towered over Miguel as he did over most men; he was tall and strong enough to have been a soldier like his elder brother.

As Miguel thought of the soldier, he wondered whether there might be armor beneath his superior's robe. He had heard of one Inquisitor who had saved himself from assassination with such protection and of others who had died for lack of it. Of course, he could find out easily enough—all he had to do was reach out his hand . . .

No. He could not do that. Besides, there was no need. Miguel believed that the Grand Inquisitor was above such devices, and his belief was sufficient. It was as ridiculous to picture armor beneath that habit as to imagine the silk undergarments that some monks were rumored to wear to protect their skins from the coarse cloth of their robes. Miguel did not need to know what lay beneath those dark folds, or behind that dark mask . . .

Where did such thoughts come from? They could not be his own; they were too close to blasphemy. Miguel felt that he was plagued by demons, yet he hardly had the pride to imagine that agents of the pit would bother with him.

Still, there was no need to consider the source of the attack; it was enough to know the best defense. His lips moved silently. He did not merely chant but prayed with his whole being. The sonorous Latin lines were soothing in themselves, but they served their purpose better when he remembered what they meant, when he spoke to the Savior and the Blessed Virgin, and his doubts drifted back into the darkness from which they had come.

"Miguel!"

The young monk started at the sound of his name. He turned and saw the Grand Inquisitor standing before the Holy House. Miguel's thoughts had carried him past his destination.

"I'm sorry. I was praying, and I didn't realize we were here."

"Such devotion is laudable, no doubt, yet we are here not only to dream of Heaven but to do Heaven's work. There is much to be done. Come."

They passed down a long row of pillars and through a massive door carved with images of sad-eyed saints.

Once out of the sun and in the cool, damp, musty building, Miguel felt more at peace with himself. Something had disturbed him, perhaps the manner of the innkeeper Carlos Diaz, but Miguel would have no time for suspicion or skepticism while he labored over the records of the Inquisition. Work was more than a duty; it was a remedy.

The last rays of the dying sun pressed through the stained-glass window, casting cold colors on the walls of the room where Miguel sat at the end of a large table. His left hand supported his head and the fingers of his ink-stained right hand were cramped around a bedraggled quill pen.

He had been there for hours, and the peace of mind that his efforts brought had gradually given way to dull exhaustion. His

7

day began at dawn, and an afternoon spent poring over transcripts of sin and its punishment had left him feeling numb and stupid. His only desire was that his superior should come to dismiss him.

But when the Grand Inquisitor entered, it was for a different purpose. "The innkeeper, Carlos Diaz, has come to see me," he announced, "and I want you to hear what he says. Your duties involve more than studying and recording what has already been done, and this may well be your first chance to follow a case of heresy from start to finish."

He glanced almost contemptuously at the records scattered over the long table while Miguel pulled himself to his feet, as if to offer his superior the chair. The Grand Inquisitor remained standing, however, and waited quietly until an anonymously hooded figure ushered Diaz into the room.

"Sit there," said the Grand Inquisitor, and the informer sank into the seat, visibly agitated. He was obliged to look up at the two standing monks, and Miguel wondered whether it might be part of a useful technique to tower above witnesses, thus increasing their sense of inferiority.

"Now speak," said Diego de Villanueva.

Carlos had changed his clothing and appeared to be reasonably sober, but he was hardly composed. He squirmed in his chair and cleared his throat before he began to talk.

"I have heard that you are concerned; that is, I have heard you talk of a special heresy—not just these Jews and freethinkers, but something more dangerous—and more evil. I have tried for months to hear some hint, but there has been nothing. But then last night—it was quite by accident, I assure you!—I came upon this ultimate blasphemy. I tell you, Friar, and may God be my witness, I have seen the Anti-Christ!"

Miguel crossed himself hurriedly and stepped back to lean against the cool wall behind him. He had no wish to know of such a horror. And yet, as he looked at his superior, he noticed a gleam in those dark eyes that he had never seen before.

The room was growing dim and the world outside was silent. Carlos wiped the sweat from his face with a fat hand.

"Continue," said Diego.

"Well, you know I have a weakness for wine. I will not lie to you about it, though I hope to reform. I drank too much last night, and there was a quarrel at home . . . no matter. So I went out, and I was drunk. I wandered through the streets. Thank the saints I was not set upon and robbed. Yet that might have been better than what happened. I had a wineskin with me and I walked clean out of the city. Finally, I fell asleep under a tree somewhere."

"Is this but a drunkard's dream?"

"No, Friar! I swear it! I was asleep, but something woke me. My head ached and my ears rang with the noise, but it was no dream. I wish to the Lord it had been. And yet, if I had slept on just a little longer, I think I might have died for it and been dragged straight to Hell by the fiends I saw. It was horrible.

"Oh, I know you despise me for being drunk. I saw the way you looked at me this morning; but if you had seen what I saw, you would have had a few yourself. I mean, not that you would, but Christ, it was horrible. It's hard enough for a man to be a spy and fight against these fools with their false beliefs, but this was something different. I have seen the witches at worship and I have seen the Devil himself."

Carlos Diaz looked up at the Grand Inquisitor and waited for some reaction, but there was none. Diego de Villanueva stood quite still and simply said, "Go on."

"I think it was the music that woke me. There was a beating of drums and tambourines and I heard shouting and singing, but most of all there was the sound of pipes, loud shrill pipes, playing a wild tune like nothing I had ever heard before.

"I didn't know what it was, I was still half-fuddled with drink, but I peered round the tree and there in a hollow I saw the witches at play. There must have been a dozen of them, dancing naked in the moonlight. And seated before them was a

9

creature with the head of a goat. It had two great horns, and a flame burned between them.

"I just stood and stared for a moment—I couldn't believe what I was seeing. And then I turned and ran back to the inn, and roused the boy to open the door. This morning I came to find you."

"Is that all, man? What else did you see? Where was it?"

"I swear before God I don't know. I came there in a fog and left in a panic. I don't know how I found my way home—some saint must have guided me—but I know that I could never find that place again. It was somewhere in the forest, near your dead brother's castle, rest his soul."

"You need not concern yourself with the soul of my brother Sebastian," said the Grand Inquisitor. "I want to know about the souls of those involved in these devilish rites. Did you recognize anyone? Can you give me a name?"

"I did see one," Carlos confessed, "otherwise I might not have come. I might have been too frightened or have convinced myself it was only a dream. But I saw her face and knew it was my duty to tell you, even though I have no hope of reward this side of Heaven."

"Our rewards sometimes come sooner than we expect," said the Grand Inquisitor evenly.

Carlos felt his pulse quicken. That might have been a threat, a hint that his life would not be a long one, but it might have been a promise that his tale had some value. In any case, he could hardly expect to hear more. Still, he had known from the beginning that he would have to give the name, and only some delight in his own importance kept him from blurting it out at once.

"They were masked," continued Carlos. "All of them were naked, but their faces were covered. For an instant I took them for monsters, but then I saw that they wore false faces. I'm not sure I realized it till this one took off her mask.

"Most of them were women. There were a few men, but most

of them were women, and old hags at that. They danced together strangely, back to back, and thrust their hands between their legs to hold their partners. This one danced alone, though, and she was young, so I noticed her especially.

"She had long black hair streaming out from behind the face of a monster. She ran up to the goat-thing and embraced him, then tore off her mask to give him a kiss. I could see her clearly in the light from the fire between his horns.

"It was Margarita de Mendoza.

"When I saw that, I turned and ran. She was kissing that thing! And that is all I know, Friar."

Carlos Diaz sighed and sat back with the satisfaction of a man who has completed a heroic task. By now the room was almost dark. He was suddenly anxious to be gone, to retreat to the security of his inn and the wine waiting there, but he sensed unhappily that the Grand Inquisitor was not yet ready to dismiss him.

"Margarita de Mendoza," repeated the Grand Inquisitor. "You say you recognized her. How do you know her?"

"Oh, you must know her too, sir. She is a Conversa, a New Christian. Her mother was a Christian but her father was a Jew, and when the king and queen signed the edict outlawing the Jews her parents fled Spain, as did so many others.

"That was in 1492, when this Margarita had just come of age, and she chose to stay here and be baptized into the Church. She was a beauty and had just become betrothed to a young man from a good family. No doubt she thought she had reason to stay, but she was fooled." Carlos laughed and slapped his thigh.

"The young man, or perhaps his family, reconsidered the matter of Margarita's tainted blood and she never became his bride, nor anyone else's, for that matter. Of course, her father's property was confiscated and she was left with nothing."

"I don't know if I remember her family," said the Grand Inquisitor. "So many fled four years ago, and of course those

Jews who chose exile are no longer the business of the Inquisition. But with no family and no property, how does this woman live? And how do you know her face so well?"

"Well, as for that, she was saved from the streets by some relative of her Christian mother who gave her a little plot of land. It might have been only to prevent her disgrace from becoming too public. She lives outside the city in a hut and raises sheep. She lives like an animal, though once she thought herself some sort of lady. What made me sick, though, when I saw her face, was the thought that I buy my mutton from her for the inn. God knows what kind of meat I have eaten!"

The Grand Inquisitor regarded Carlos sternly. "You are, then, prepared to testify that this woman has been seen engaged in these obscene rites?"

"I am, yes . . . in secret, of course, that is," mumbled Carlos.

"You know that you have nothing to fear on that account. The Holy Office has no wish to expose its friends to its enemies. Margarita de Mendoza will never learn the name of her accuser."

"But there must be two witnesses, must there not?"

"I will attend to that. If what you say is true—and God help you if it is not—there will be evidence, and the one who finds it will be able to testify. You need not concern yourself further. Miguel!"

The young monk emerged from the shadows by the wall.

"You will prepare a deposition," Miguel's superior said, "setting forth the facts in the proper form; do it this evening. And you, Carlos Diaz," he said, addressing the informer, who had risen from his seat and was moving as imperceptibly as possible toward the door, "you will return here tomorrow to sign it. I need hardly caution you to mention this matter to no one. And beware of the wine."

Carlos was as startled by this last suggestion as if the Grand Inquisitor had read his mind. Perhaps he had. Carlos stood nervously, half bowing and half backing out of the room, until a gesture of dismissal sent him through the door, moving at last with undisguised alacrity.

Outside, a moment later, the pleasure Carlos felt at escaping that penetrating gaze began to give way to another sort of anxiety. He was no longer in the sanctuary of the Inquisition but was alone on a dark street far from home.

A sudden clanging broke through the silence and Carlos jumped, but he realized at once that it was only a bell calling the monks to evening prayers.

The street was full of shadows. It was always unwise to be out at night, but more so, thought Carlos, for a man who bore witness against witches. He pictured again that midnight scene, the horror of it tempered by the vision of a lithe and lovely figure lost in some wicked ecstasy, throwing her arms around a horned monster. He began to wish he had not run so soon. What would he have seen if he had stayed?

Some faint flame of lust gave him courage as he walked. It was not the first time he had felt this way about Margarita de Mendoza, who came often to his inn, but only for business.

A year ago he had tried his luck with her. After all, she was only a peasant dressed in rags, and he would have been generous to her. But she had snatched his fumbling hand from her bosom and buried her strong white teeth in his thumb, almost to the bone.

God, she was strong for a woman! While he had stared astounded at his bleeding hand, she had kicked him twice, then knocked him to the ground with a hindquarter of mutton. She had spat upon him and called him foul names. Carlos had been afraid that she would kill him but more afraid that his wife might hear the commotion.

Still, the whole affair had taken only a minute, and Margarita had stormed away without waiting to be paid for the meat. On the whole, Carlos had come out of it fairly well. His thumb had not become infected, despite his fears, and business with Margarita had continued as before. Her mutton was cheap and she needed his money, but he did not like the look of contempt on her face when they met after that day.

It would be a pleasure to see the slut do her last dance in the flames of the *auto-da-fé*. There were other shepherds.

He hoped that incident would not come out when Margarita was put to the Question. He knew the accused were always asked to name their enemies, and it might mean a bit of trouble if she named him, since it could cast suspicion on his testimony. Did the Grand Inquisitor suspect already? What else could have made him so cold and ungrateful? For this sort of information Carlos expected praise and thanks, and perhaps something more. He would have sworn that Diego de Villanueva wanted a witch, and now he had one.

Carlos Diaz, though, had nothing, and he had put his life in danger. He hoped Margarita would be arrested before he saw her again. He did not know if he could face her. He wondered what kind of magic she possessed. Would he be safe from her spells? He pictured her laughing as she slaughtered sheep, her hands red and reeking.

A huge figure loomed up out of the darkness in front of Carlos and blocked his path.

Carlos gasped and started backward. He tried to speak, to protest his innocence, but no words came. He thought his tongue might be bewitched, and he fell on his knees before the shadowy giant.

Then he saw who it was. Carlos crossed himself in a prayer of thanks for his deliverance and rose unsteadily to his feet.

The man before him was Pedro Rodriguez. This massive old soldier, now a civilian, served the Inquisition and Friar Diego de Villanueva in the war against heretics. He was no stranger to Carlos or his inn.

Carlos started to speak, but Pedro pressed something into the informer's hand and turned away without a word.

Carlos was left alone with his thoughts and five gold coins. He should have known that the Grand Inquisitor would not forget him. It would have been undignified for the holy man himself to reward Carlos, but it was for such purposes, and for less pleasant ones, that civilians like Pedro were employed. These secular servants of the Inquisition were called familiars, Carlos knew—and didn't witches have familiars, too, imps in animal form that were also servants of Satan?

Carlos glanced around as though he expected to see one of the creatures, then cast the idea from his mind and scurried off toward the shelter of his inn.

2. Two Brothers in Black and White

THE candles were lit now in the dark chamber of the Holy House, but they illuminated no more than a small area of the table where the young monk sat again, preparing to write the testimony of Carlos Diaz accusing Margarita de Mendoza of the crime of witchcraft.

Behind Miguel stood the Grand Inquisitor. Miguel bridled inwardly at the thought of being under observation, partly because he realized that he did not really know what to do next. His awe in the presence of his superior was giving way to fatigue and to fear of what he had heard. He did not want to write anymore, particularly about witches. His head ached. He had never transcribed such a deposition before and could not think of the proper form to begin it, though he was certain there must be a good example in the records piled in front of him.

He turned toward the older man. He wanted either to register a protest or ask for advice but was prevented from doing either by the sight of a large leather-bound volume that the Grand Inquisitor held out to him.

"Here," said Diego. "Take this and study it. It will help you to prepare for the work we are about to undertake."

"But the testimony of the witness Diaz . . . you said I should have it ready for tomorrow morning."

"That will be attended to in due course. In truth, the evidence must be given again when Diaz returns tomorrow. I did tell him we would need only his signature, but it is sometimes necessary to veil the truth when dealing with nervous informers. We must adhere to the proper procedure, especially in such an extraordinary case as this. The testimony must be given before assembled officers of the Inquisition, taken down verbatim, and subjected to rigorous cross-examination. There must be no room for error. I am sure that Carlos Diaz knows all this—he has been a witness before—but it reassures him to think that he can escape his responsibilities so easily, and this assures his prompt appearance. There must be no delay."

Miguel took the heavy book in his hands and set it down upon the table. Opening it carefully, he saw that it was printed in Latin, in the black letters of the German presses.

"Malleus Maleficarum," he read. *"The Hammer of Witches?"*

"It was first published ten years ago in Germany. It is sadly lacking in some areas of the greatest interest and importance, but at the present time it is the most complete study on the subject of witchcraft, especially its investigation and suppression. Its authors are two Germans, brothers of our own Dominican order, Heinrich Kramer and Jacob Sprenger.

"Their work has brought them recognition and influence throughout their native land and far beyond. The book has been published in Germany, France, and Italy, and it includes a bull of Pope Innocent VIII commending their efforts and granting them extraordinary jurisdiction to prosecute witches throughout Germany."

"Then are there so many witches?" Miguel asked apprehensively.

"More than any man knows. This most devilish and damnable of heresies rages throughout Europe. Thousands of witches have been detected and destroyed. Yet here in Spain, where our Inquisition is so zealous in protecting the faith, not one witch has been taken."

"Then is this woman the beginning of it here?"

"Who knows? Some say this is a new evil which Satan has unleashed upon our weary world. It must have begun somewhere; perhaps it has not spread far into our land. Yet it infests France, and here in this district we have only a few miles of mountain ranges between ourselves and that bedeviled kingdom. The Pyrenees are hardly high enough to protect us from this spreading infection. I knew the cult would spring up here—it was the reason I requested jurisdiction here—and now it has come. And I am ready. What glory there will be in exposing this evil, and in purging it!"

Miguel viewed the prospect with less enthusiasm. He was glad enough to learn that he would not have to spend the evening transcribing the informer's testimony, but he took no pleasure in the idea of battling black magic. It was one thing to seek out those who were not good Christians and punish those who would not repent, but what sort of business was this? These witches might be more than fools and infidels. Who knew what powers they might possess? The answers, he feared, were in the massive volume that Diego had entrusted to his care.

Sometimes he wished he had not become a monk, or at least that some half-hearted ambition had not led him into the service of the Inquisition. Yet how many choices were there for a younger son who had inherited nothing?

He reflected on the fact that Diego de Villanueva had been in the same position but had nonetheless risen to eminence. Perhaps in this coincidence Miguel could find a topic for conversation, for he was undoubtedly expected to reply to his superior's unwonted enthusiasm but had no wish to talk of witches.

"He said he saw them near your brother's castle," ventured Miguel.

"What? Yes, somewhere in the forest outside the city. Some of them, perhaps, dwell in the mountains nearby."

"They say he was a great soldier, your brother," Miguel persisted.

"Yes," replied the Grand Inquisitor with an air of doubtful pride. "A great soldier and a great scholar, too."

"A scholar? I never heard that said of him."

"There were few who knew him well," said the Grand Inquisitor. "He was much alone. The castle was never a manor house surrounded by the homes of serfs and vassals; it was a true fortress, built to guard the French border. Troops were quartered there years ago but there never was an attack from the north, and the commander, my brother Don Sebastian, spent much time among his books, especially after the death of his young wife. With her died our family, for she bore no sons and Sebastian never wed again. Instead, he shut himself up in the topmost room of the topmost tower and there pondered the mysteries of creation."

"He studied natural philosophy?"

"Among other things. No one really knows. His aim, it seems, was not to add to the wisdom of the world but only to satisfy himself regarding some secrets of his own soul. It was a fruitless quest, and he seems to have realized as much, for when there was a call to arms he answered it. And so he died."

"Fighting the Moors, was it not?"

"At the siege of Malaga in 1487. They say it was a glorious day for Spain, a great defeat for those pagan invaders who had occupied our lands for centuries. It was an even greater day five years later when Granada surrendered without a fight and all of Spain was Christian again, but the reconquest began in earnest at Malaga."

"Malaga," echoed the young monk, filled with vague visions of half-remembered glories.

"You must have been little better than a boy then, Miguel, but the stories of the siege should be familiar even to you: how the king led the soldiers into battle and how the queen, with all the ladies of her court, attended the troops and urged them on to glory. In the front ranks was Don Sebastian de Villanueva, who traveled the length of Spain, from this northeastern corner to the plains of the southwest, there to meet his death."

"But was it not a noble death?" asked Miguel.

"Not, I think, what a true knight might have wished. I have been told, by those who claim to know such things, that this was the first battle in our land where guns and powder were well employed. I know nothing of that, but I do know that one cannon had some flaw in its construction and exploded in my brother's face. Without their leader, his men were easy prey for the Moors, and most of them were slain. Sebastian, with his shattered face, lingered raving for days. He was carried from the siege by the most steadfast of his followers, Pedro Rodriguez, but it was in vain. I never saw my brother alive again."

"Is this the same Pedro . . . ?"

"It is. He now serves me in the army of the Lord, as he once served Sebastian in the army of the king. It was he who brought my brother's body home and entombed him in the crypt beneath the castle."

"But is there no heir?"

"I might have been the heir had I not become a monk. Or the Crown might have confiscated the estate, but that would have been an ill reward for Sebastian's service. As things stand, it is a matter for the courts and magistrates, and their deliberations are rarely speedy. I believe there is a distant cousin somewhere who has a claim, but he has not been easy to find and no one seems to care to seek him out. Until he is discovered, I am caretaker of the castle."

"You mean you visit it?" gasped Miguel.

"From time to time."

"But there may be witches about!"

"All the more reason for me to watch the castle and the countryside around it. Seeking out these wretches is our duty, and we cannot expect much help from the people. If Carlos

Diaz told the truth—and I believe he did—there is a cult around us, yet no one has come forward. And someone must have known! They are quick enough to inform on heretics; perhaps they fear some magical revenge from the witches. So we must take this Margarita de Mendoza at once and use her quickly. If she names the others, we shall take them all. If she will not speak, we shall make an example of her and prove to those whose tongues are frozen with fear that the Inquisition is stronger than black magic. Why do you look so pale and stupid, boy?"

"We are stronger, surely?"

"To doubt it would be heresy."

"You spoke of taking them all," said Miguel. "Even the one with the horns? Even a demon, perhaps the Devil himself?"

The Grand Inquisitor reflected on this. "I do not know," he replied evenly. "But you must not be too credulous. Since there are witches, there may be demons among them, yet I have read that such creatures with the heads of goats are often only men in masquerade, deceiving others for the power it brings them. You need not expect to meet Satan face to face."

Miguel's relief was evident. He had been leaning toward the Grand Inquisitor, twisted tensely in his chair, but now he sat back relaxed and a small sigh escaped his dry lips.

"But we will meet Satan," continued Diego de Villanueva. "We meet him every day, for such is our task. He has no need to walk abroad on earth when there are so many men and women filled with his spirit and eager to obey him. This case is no different than any other. . . . And yet it is, for we have found the first witch in Spain. There is glory in it, for the Inquisition and for those who serve her.

"Take the book, Miguel. Go to your cell and read, and think on its authors, two humble Dominican brothers like ourselves, who have fought this evil and won fame and power for their work."

Miguel had almost caught his teacher's fever. Clasping the huge book to his chest, he passed through the door and into the gloomy hall beyond, its length composed of a series of vaulted arches. He was too caught up in his own thoughts to notice the dark figure standing in the shadows.

As the sound of Miguel's sandals flapping on the stone floor faded into the distance, Pedro Rodriguez stepped into the dimly lit room. He was a giant of a man with a seamed, sunburned face and streaks of gray in his heavy black beard. He stood filling the doorway like a soldier awaiting orders.

"Pedro," said the Grand Inquisitor. "You found Carlos Diaz?"

Pedro nodded.

"Good. It may be unorthodox to reward him, but he has done me a great service. You heard what he had to say?"

Pedro inclined his massive head again.

"Then you know how important it is. My chance has come at last, and it could hardly have come at a better time. I will be ready soon. What has been done in Germany can be done in Spain."

"Will you go to the castle?" asked Pedro.

"Yes, I must. Tonight. Saddle a horse for me, Pedro, and leave it in front of the Holy House. I will be ready to leave shortly."

"And the witch?"

"That must wait, if only for a day. There will be time enough after the accusation has been formally submitted. It will only be a few hours. Tomorrow night you will take what men you need to arrest Margarita de Mendoza."

"Men? To arrest one woman? Am I a weakling?"

"It is best to be cautious, Pedro. She may not be alone. Surely you know that I have confidence in you!"

"So be it, then. I will get the horse."

An hour later, the Grand Inquisitor was riding through the foothills. Around him were the silent shapes of trees dimly illuminated by the distant moon. Beyond were the purple slopes of the Pyrenees and the castle of Don Sebastian.

The old mare knew the way as well as her rider did, and he was grateful for her solid strength beneath him. In other lands a monk might have been expected to show his humility by walking to his destination or at best riding a mule, but here in Spain the breeders of horses were so influential that it was considered unpatriotic to travel without the aid of their art.

Diego de Villanueva, well mounted, contemplated the pleasures of patriotism. It had brought him more than a mount; it had brought him a powerful position, and he was sure that greater rewards lay ahead. In Spain, as in no other country in Christendom, the interests of church and state were inextricably bound together. It was no coincidence that Torquemada, the Inquisitor General, had been Queen Isabella's confessor as well. The monarchs whose marriage had united Spain and whose battles had defeated the Moorish interlopers did not tolerate dissent. In 1492 Ferdinand and Isabella, at Torquemada's urging, had signed an edict outlawing the Jewish religion and there were whispers that the Moors would soon be forced to abandon their faith as well, despite promises made to them when they had surrendered Granada. Then they would be New Christians too, liable to persecution for heresy at the first sign of backsliding.

The queen was pious and wanted Spain united under God; the king was a politician and wanted Spain united under the Crown. Both their ambitions were well served by the Inquisition, and neither monarch had any cause to complain when the royal treasury was enriched, as it continually was, by the confiscated property of convicted heretics. Since there was no conflict between spiritual and temporal authority, as there was in so many areas of Europe, a man serving both masters, as Diego de Villanueva did, could rise to great heights.

He planned to become the greatest witch hunter in the world. With the support of the Inquisition, it seemed to him that he could hardly fail. For years he had studied every available source on the subject of witchcraft, not only books like the *Malleus Maleficarum* but forbidden texts that offered instruction in the practice of black magic. Now his own book was almost ready and he was certain that it would become the definitive work on the subject. He had information no other writer had ever used before, and now he had within his grasp the first member of the cult ever discovered in Spain.

The Grand Inquisitor trusted his mare, hardly troubling to watch the path. If Miguel were with him, he reflected, the boy would surely be peering through the trees, searching for witches lying in wait. Diego de Villanueva knew better. They had held their sabbat just the night before; they would hardly be abroad again the next night. He had nothing to fear from them, he thought, and much reason to be grateful.

He rode out from the shadows of the trees and up a bare slope awash in pale moonlight. At the crest of the slope stood the castle.

This black and forbidding edifice was dominated by a huge, square tower looming above the walls and dwarfing the smaller round towers at each corner of the castle. For centuries the great tower had stood alone, guarding a pass through the mountains. It now served as the keep of the castle, which had been built around it generations later from small stones mixed with clay and mortar. The stones that sheathed the ancient keep, however, were massive boulders buffeted by time. The old tower had frightened Diego de Villanueva when he was a boy, and he had never understood his elder brother's love for it.

A drawbridge guarded the only entrance to the courtyard. The Grand Inquisitor drew his horse up at the edge of the moat and stared down into the foul green water. He saw his own reflection and that of the white moon behind him, both obscured by floating scum. The water did not look deep, but a man who got into this moat would find it difficult to get out again. The castle, though small, had been built to withstand a siege; it was surely safe from trespassers. No crazed peasant women held their revels here.

A groan of wrenching wood sounded above the Grand Inquisitor's head and he heard chains rattling. He looked up to see the massive drawbridge dropping down upon him. The mare danced back skittishly as the wooden planks struck with a muddy thud on the bank of the moat.

Diego de Villanueva watched the gate swing ponderously open and he listened to the creak of heavy hinges. He peered into the shadowed blackness of the courtyard.

"Sebastian?" he called. There was no reply. "Sebastian?"

"Yes, brother," said a low voice, echoing from dark depths beyond the rough gray walls. "It is Sebastian. Who else would it be?"

The Grand Inquisitor gave no answer but urged his mount forward, across the drawbridge and into the castle.

3. Six Black Candles

PEDRO cursed quietly at the sight of the sheep. They might as well have been watchdogs. There were dozens of them in the rude pen outside the wretched hut, and they had begun to mill around as soon as the men approached. Pedro realized that he and his two companions would have to wade through the nervous animals to get to the entrance to the hut. It would be noisy.

"Well," he said, "we'd better move quickly if we can't move quietly. She may be asleep now, but she'll be awake before we can get past that herd."

"We should be asleep ourselves," said one of the men. "This is no time of night for a man to be out. It looks like rain, too."

"Be quiet," Pedro said. "You're being paid well enough to stand here and grumble, aren't you?"

"I suppose so. Still, I wouldn't mind having one of those lambs. This Mendoza woman won't have much use for them where she's going."

"We're not thieves. We're here working for the Holy Office, and any confiscated property goes to the Inquisition. I don't want to see any stealing. Of course," Pedro continued a little less sternly, "one or two lambs might get lost after we take the prisoner. I have no orders to leave a guard here."

The second man looked happier, but the third continued to finger the hilt of his sword nervously. "Do we have to stand here talking all night? Let's get it done."

"Ready," said Pedro. "There should be just the woman, but watch out for others."

The three men stepped out from the sheltering trees. As they neared the pen they began to run, a futile burst of speed that only served to alarm the animals. The officers of the august Inquisition had to clamber over the rough-hewn wooden fence, then found themselves confronted by a shifting mass of bleating, woolly flesh. There seemed no room to move.

The beasts must be enchanted, thought Pedro, as he kicked at the sheep and beat them back with the flat of his sword. One of the men tripped over a frightened ewe and sprawled, swearing, in a pile of dung. Pedro, still a few yards from the door, was already bawling, "Open! Open in the name of the Inquisition!"

There was no response.

By the time Pedro reached the hut he was furious. He kicked in the ramshackle door without the now-foolish formality of a knock and stood panting on the threshold. His two companions were close behind him.

It was a warm summer night, but there were low flames in the fireplace of rough stones. Something was cooking in a black iron pot. There was not much else in the room: a table, a three-legged stool, and what looked, in the flickering amber light of the fire, like a pile of rags in the corner.

"Christ, it stinks in here," said the man who had fallen.

"You're no rose yourself," Pedro said, but he had to admit that there was something wrong with the smell of the place. It was not an honest odor like that of cooking or animals or unwashed human bodies.

"It's that witch's brew in the pot," said Pedro.

"Witches!" his two companions echoed in chorus, backing instinctively toward the door, and Pedro thought himself a fool for mentioning the word. They need not have known.

"Don't worry, you heroes," he snarled, hoping to stiffen their backbones. "There's nobody here."

He stepped over to the table. Piled on it was a strange assortment of leaves, roots, berries, and fungus, which he gathered up and carried to the fire for a closer look. From the Grand Inquisitor's instructions he recognized one plant, with black, shiny berries and red flowers shaped like bells.

"Belladonna," he said. He had no idea what it was, except that it was evidence. He peered into the pot at the congealed, sticky-looking liquid and nearly gagged at its sickening stench.

He stumbled away into the corner, then realized that the pile of rags there was alive.

"It's a woman," he said, dropping to his knees beside her.

Curiosity overcame fear as the others hurried to him. "Is she dead?"

"No," answered Pedro. "She's breathing. But she can't be asleep, after all the noise we made. . . . Ugh! She's covered with that stuff in the pot! Get me a light!"

One of the men picked up a stick of wood and thrust one end of it into the fire. A moment later he was holding a torch over Pedro's head.

Pedro saw a young woman whose tanned face was framed by a luxuriant mass of tangled black hair. Her lips were full, her cheekbones high, her closed eyes framed by dark brows and thick lashes. She might have been beautiful, but her face was smeared with the thick black slime from the pot.

Her arms and her long legs were similarly smeared; in fact, every inch of her body seemed covered. She wore only a ragged homespun shift of a drab color and lay on her back in a pile of sheepskins. Her breasts rose and fell with rapid, shallow breaths; there was sweat on her brow.

"Well, this must be Margarita de Mendoza," said Pedro. "Bring her along. Let's get out into the air."

The man covered with dung bent down, thrust his hands roughly under her armpits, and pulled her up. "What ails her?" he asked.

"Who knows?" said Pedro. "At least she won't give us any trouble."

As Margarita was dragged to her feet her eyes shot open, glazed and green as a cat's. She looked in dull surprise at her captors.

Pedro stood at the door, the black pot filled with herbs in one hand. "You are in the hands of the Inquisition," he said.

Her expression did not change, but her right foot flashed out in a well-placed kick that sent the man before her crashing into the table, gasping with shock and pain.

"Bastards!" she screamed, breaking free of the startled man who held her. He fell back heavily into the fire and sat stupidly for a second in the flames. Then he jumped up shouting and cracked his head on the stone fireplace.

"Idiots!" said Pedro. He moved patiently across the floor as Margarita raised her hands above her head and began to chant in some strange tongue.

He knocked her down with a huge fist and hoisted her onto one burly shoulder, still holding the pot in his other hand. "You should have stayed asleep, wench," he said.

At the door he turned for a last look at the two men groaning on the dirt floor. "Go home," he told them. "You've made such fools of yourselves that I doubt you'll talk about this night's work, but if you're tempted, you'll have to deal with me, even before you meet the Grand Inquisitor."

He stepped outside, moved stolidly through the milling sheep, and draped Margarita's limp body over the fence. Once over it himself, he resumed his burden and made for his horse, tethered under nearby trees. He folded the woman across the saddle like a slaughtered sheep and set out for the city.

Diego de Villanueva was waiting at the Holy House for Pedro and his prize. The shepherdess was still unconscious when the Grand Inquisitor's familiar carried her in and dumped her unceremoniously on the floor.

"Here's your witch," said Pedro, "and a pot of stuff she was brewing. She has it all over her. And some of that belladonna. What is it?"

"A foul and dangerous drug," said Diego. He sniffed delicately at the contents of the pot. "She used it in this potion. Too much of it is deadly, but a small amount produces trances and visions. Witches rub themselves with ointments like this to commune with demons."

Pedro held out his great hands in dismay. "I've got some on me! What should I do?"

"Wash it off. And don't worry. A bit like that won't hurt an ox like you. It's most effective when rubbed on parts of the body more sensitive than your rough hands."

Pedro looked at the woman and leered.

"Get that look off your face, Pedro, and get a bucket, too. You should clean some of that poison off her."

Pedro stomped off on yet another errand and the Grand Inquisitor bent over the prisoner lying on the cold stone floor. "Margarita!" He prodded her side delicately with a sandaled foot. "Margarita de Mendoza!" He kicked harder, then sighed and stepped away.

"She sleeps like the dead," he said as Pedro returned with a wooden bucket full of water. "I hoped that the drug might have loosened her tongue, but she seems completely senseless."

"She was lively enough a few minutes ago," said Pedro. "Maybe this will rouse her." He emptied the bucket slowly and methodically over Margarita, drenching her from head to toe. She moaned, arched her back, and then sank back into stillness. The wet rag she wore clung to her slender, full-breasted body. Her long, tanned legs sprawled. Pedro liked what he saw.

"It's no use," said Diego. "Take her to the dungeons. I'll talk to her tomorrow."

Again Pedro picked up the unconscious woman, but this time he carried her in his arms, not draped over his broad shoulders as before. He had begun to think of her as something more than a prisoner. She looked much better to him with her face cleaned, and he was conscious of her weight in his arms as something more than a burden to be borne.

In the dark corridor he considered the possibilities of the situation. She seemed less of a witch than a woman to him now, but it might not be wise to risk his soul for a few minutes of fun. Still . . .

He stopped at a heavy door, knocked, and saw a hooded head peer through a barred opening. The door swung back, and Pedro's lust lessened at the sight of the silent figure before him. Another monk, and there would be two more before he reached the dungeons. The Inquisition did not encourage what he had in mind.

He started down a flight of narrow stone steps, realizing all at once how tired he was. It must be very late.

Another door at the bottom of the stairs, and another monk, with keys in one hand and a torch pulled from a wall bracket in the other.

"A prisoner," said Pedro.

The monk did not bother to answer but led Pedro down a damp, chilly tunnel by the wavering light of the torch. Still another monk waited at the end of the tunnel. His hood was not the cowl worn by most Dominicans but a blank black mask that covered his face and rose to a grotesque peak a foot above his head. His eyes were vaguely visible through two small holes. He opened an iron door. Pedro passed through and heard it clang shut behind him, the key grating in the lock.

A ring of still more keys hung from a hook on the wall. Any one of them would admit him to a dungeon where he could have his way with Margarita, but his enthusiasm had waned.

"That faceless one would cool off anyone," he muttered to Margarita, as if she could hear him. "Not much good anyway, with a woman who won't even know I'm there. Besides, Friar Diego said that perfume you were wearing might be dangerous, and I couldn't wash it all off you while he was watching."

He sighed and shifted her weight so she was supported by one of his strong arms. With his other hand he reached out for the keys and dragged Margarita to an empty cell.

A feeble groan issued from a door nearby, but Pedro ignored it and opened the dungeon he had selected for the new prisoner. He could see nothing inside but blackness, although he heard the scampering of rats frightened by the open door.

"At least you won't be living alone anymore," he told Margarita. "And it won't be much worse than your old home at that, not until they put you to the Question."

He let her down gently just inside the cell; his hands came up foul and muddy from the floor. He wiped them on his doublet and slammed the door behind him.

He was glad to be leaving, to pass through the barriers with their hooded guards, to climb the steep stairs, hurry through the empty corridors, and find himself at last under the open sky, free from confinement, breathing fresh air.

He was more weary from the night's work than he would ever admit. His arms ached. He was growing old.

At least he had not raped the witch, and now he was glad of it. He had done his duty, but no more. This way it would be easier for him to go home and face his daughters. They were not sons, but he loved them both and was proud of their beauty and virtue. They were good girls, Pedro thought, and tonight, at least, he had been a good man. It had not always been easy since his wife had died a dozen years ago.

His house was only a few steps away. It, too, was locked, but that was not to keep the girls imprisoned, only to keep them safe from the dangers lurking outside. He shook his head to clear it of an incongruous image. There was no comparison between his daughters, locked in for their own protection, and Margarita de Mendoza, sealed in a dungeon for unspeakable sins.

He knocked and was answered almost at once by a light voice from within. "Father?"

"Yes, Teresa."

The door was opened by a pale, slight, pretty girl of seventeen. Her eyes were sleepy, but she managed a wan smile.

"You shouldn't be awake, Teresa."

"I'm sorry, father. I can't sleep when you're away at night like this."

32

Pedro took his daughter in his arms and kissed her cheek. "And the little one?"

"Dolores is in bed. She wanted to stay up with me, but I wouldn't let her."

"Let's go to sleep ourselves, daughter. It's very late."

Margarita leaped to her feet as soon as the dungeon door slammed shut. She had been conscious for some time, but it had seemed wise to lie still and hope for the best. If her captors thought her drugged or beaten into insensibility, at least the questioning would not begin at once. Now that she was alone she felt safer, but she backed herself into a corner to avoid the rats. It was too dark to see them, or anything else, but she knew they were there. Fortunately, they seemed as frightened of her as she was of them.

The stone walls she leaned against were cold; the air was foul. Her bare feet were ankle deep in an icy slime that smelled worse than mud. Her hair and clothes were drenched and her teeth chattered uncontrollably.

Her whole body was shaking—from the aftereffect of the drugs, from a numbing fear, but most of all from hatred. She nursed the small flame of fury within her, for it was the only warmth she had. Margarita watched the flame grow until it enveloped her. It filled the cell with an unearthly light, but she knew that the light was a lie. The flame was a belladonna dream, like the vast head of the goat that floated above her.

The goat was a lie and the goat was her lover, the Prince of Lies. It was he who instructed her, who presided over the ceremonies in the forest. It was the goat who embraced her, the goat who entered her. He was her slave and her master, and he would enter her again.

She stood rigid against the wall, eyes rolling, teeth clenched. She breathed deeply and felt the spirit pass into her lungs. She breathed again and saw the spirit and the flame and the goat flow into her body like a luminous cloud.

Then it was dark again and she sank down into the corner.

She sat in the mud, her knees drawn up to her breast, her head bent forward, arms embracing her legs.

She knew she was a dead woman, but she knew that the Inquisition would not break her. She would not confess, would not inform. Her hate was stronger than theirs.

The Inquisition had exiled her parents, lost her a husband, and stolen her home. They had left her nothing but witchcraft, and love for the Lord of Flies. That she would not betray.

After a few hours her mouth grew dry. When thirst became intolerable, she twisted a few drops of water from the hem of her garment and licked the moisture from the palm of her hand.

She had no way of knowing if she would ever be given water or food or if she would ever see light again.

Her mind was still fogged by visions and she had no idea how long she had been in the cell. She was grateful for the drug, though, for it gave her strength. Small smiling imps scurried among the rats, and she spoke with them. They sang songs to cheer her, and they spoke of the goat, the goat with the body of a man, whose great eyes glowed with wisdom.

At last the iron door opened and light spilled into the cell. The dreams disappeared and in their place Margarita saw two men dressed in black robes. Their hands held torches whose sudden brilliance nearly blinded her; their faces were shrouded in the darkness of hideously pointed hoods.

They stood on either side of her, each grasping one of her arms, and they led her down long passageways, up slippery stairs, and through an endless succession of locked doors. They were silent and surprisingly gentle; she would almost have preferred curses and brutality to their grim efficiency.

The last door opened. The scene before her had the vividness of hallucination, but she knew that it was real.

The entire room was draped in black velvet. There was a long table also draped in black. On it were a Bible, a crucifix, and six black candles in silver sticks. Seated behind the six flickering flames was a man whose long, clean-shaven face was partly hidden by a black cowl. Still, she had no trouble recognizing him as Diego de Villanueva, the Grand Inquisitor. He did not look up as she entered. He held a sheaf of papers in his hand and seemed totally absorbed in them. She wondered if her name was written there.

No one spoke; no one moved. The masked men beside her were as still as statues.

Next to the table was a low pulpit covered with more papers and an ink horn. A young monk stood there with a quill in his hand. His cowl hung back over his narrow shoulders, which seemed to make him more human than the others. He appeared to be nervous, and he looked a bit foolish with his freshly shaven head. He glanced at Margarita but dropped his eyes at once and attempted to busy himself with his papers.

Finally the Grand Inquisitor broke his silence.

"What is your name, young woman?"

Margarita did not answer.

"Come now, surely you will at least confess to your name! You must realize that we know it already."

There seemed no point in resisting on this matter. "Margarita de Mendoza," she said.

At once the young monk began scribbling with his pen.

"What is your father's name?" asked the Grand Inquisitor.

Margarita's resolve was immediately strengthened by the mention of her father. These questions might be a matter of form, but they might be something more. She avoided the bright, icy eyes of the Inquisitor and shook her head. Her long black hair fell into her face.

"What is your mother's name?"

Margarita stared sullenly at the floor.

"My dear young woman, what are we to think of you if you refuse to answer simple questions such as these? Will you speak?"

There was no sound except the scratching of the pen, and then even that stopped. The Grand Inquisitor stood up.

"I fear that your soul is in the gravest jeopardy. We only wish to guide you back into the light. Do you know why you are here? Have you nothing to confess?

"I must tell you that you stand accused of a terrible heresy. Yet we desire to be just and merciful."

Miguel, transcribing the interrogation, recognized the formula as that laid down in the instructions of Torquemada, the Inquisitor General of the kingdom. He knew what the next question would be and began to write it down before it was asked.

"Have you any enemies who might have reason to bear false witness against you?"

Margarita looked up at the Grand Inquisitor and gritted her teeth.

"You are my enemy," she said.

The Grand Inquisitor stood rigidly for a moment, then sighed and sat again behind the six black candles.

"You are terribly misguided," he said. "I am here only to help you, my child, to save you from eternal torment. Will you not speak?"

Miguel looked at Margarita expectantly, but she remained silent.

"Very well," said the Grand Inquisitor. "We will give you time to contemplate your condition, time to be alone and consider the state of your soul. A few days in darkness may make you long for the light."

The masked men on either side of Margarita were suddenly active again. One turned her around; the other opened the black-draped door.

She realized with a sudden contraction of her stomach that they were taking her back to the dark hole again. They might leave her there forever. Panic rushed over her, with an impulse to run back into the velvet room, to confess, or at least to answer the simple questions, to do anything that would keep her for a few minutes more in the feeble glow of the black candles.

It was too late. She was already out in the hall, and the door had slammed behind her, but not in time to shut out the Grand Inquisitor's final instructions: "Put her in chains."

4. The Tower

WELL, brother, have you captured your witch?" asked Sebastian de Villanueva. It was the first time he had spoken for days.

Diego did not answer at once. He often found his brother's moods disturbing. Tonight Sebastian had met him at the drawbridge as always but had not said a single word. Instead, he had greeted the Grand Inquisitor with an elaborate bow and exaggerated gestures of welcome.

A grotesque parody of a host, tall and gaunt, Sebastian had beckoned his brother across the empty courtyard, always remaining a few paces out of reach. His black velvet clothing made him almost invisible in the night, though the moonlight sometimes flashed from the silver filigree on his doublet or from his bejeweled fingers.

He had led the monk through the dark chambers of the castle, abandoned dusty apartments whose rich furnishings were falling into decay. Here there was no light at all, and Sebastian's presence could be sensed only by the light tread of his Cordova leather boots and the rustle of his red velvet cloak. Diego could not hear even the sound of his brother's breathing, though his own lungs were laboring as he followed Sebastian up the countless narrow steps to the top of the great tower. He kept one hand to the wall, fearing that he might stumble and fall, as he surely would have had he not already known the way.

Gasping for breath at the topmost step, the Grand Inquisitor had been ushered into his brother's study. Here at last was illumination, if only a solitary crimson candle perched atop a yellowed human skull that dripped with red wax. The skull rested on the corner of a small table, its center inlaid with black-and-white squares of onyx and ivory.

Sebastian finally broke his silence as he seated himself behind the table, well out of the light, in a tall and fantastically carved chair that was almost a throne. He spoke again before Diego had a chance to reply.

"I see you are winded, brother. A cup of wine, perhaps?" He reached into the shadows behind his chair and produced a silver goblet studded with rubies. It was already full.

Diego looked at its contents doubtfully. The thought crossed his mind that the wine might be poisoned, but he dismissed the idea almost at once. Sebastian needed him as much as he needed Sebastian. He drank greedily. It was a good vintage.

"No news?" asked Sebastian. "No prisoners? No witches?"

Diego bridled at his older brother's mockery, which he had endured for more than forty years. This was the only man in the world who still made him feel like a fool.

He stared over the rim of the cup at the face of his brother, dead white even in the yellow glow of the lone candle. The expression was sardonic, the eyes lost in shadow. It was a lean face, with a long black mustache that drooped over the emaciated jaw. The hair was long and black, too; parted in the center, it reached to Sebastian's shoulders. An ugly scar, more livid than the ivory skin, ran down the left side of the face, above and below the eye. In the dim light the fine garments were revealed as ragged and worn.

"You look well, brother," said Sebastian. "Of course, there is no need to tell me how I look."

"But who else will tell you, Sebastian? You are not much seen in public of late, and I believe you have no looking glass."

"Yes," Sebastian said. A corner of his mouth turned up slightly. "I am spared at least that one sign of vanity."

"You asked about the witch," said the Grand Inquisitor. "We have her in a cell beneath the Holy House."

"You seemed so excited two nights ago when you told me you were on her trail. Has she been a disappointment?"

"She has not spoken yet. Of course, she has had only the initial interrogation. A few days in the dungeons alone may loosen her tongue. If not, there is always the rack. I was surprised, though. She refused to answer a single question, even to defend herself. A stubborn woman."

"A bitter woman, perhaps. What else but fury and frustration would drive a soul to embrace its own damnation?"

"A moment ago you mentioned pride, Sebastian."

"One of your seven deadly sins, is it not, Friar? Might it make a monk lust for the secrets of Satan and think that he could gain them all without losing his soul?"

"It might make a man publish a book exposing the ways of witches. Only that. None of us is without sin, though, and I confess to a certain sort of pride. But what do you have to be so superior about? Even now, when the world thinks you dead and I know you for a godless parasite, you still sit on a throne at the top of a tower, decked out in velvet and precious stones, for all the world as if you were still a nobleman."

"I confess, too, brother. Will you absolve me, you, the humble monk, sitting on a bench and dressed in sackcloth?"

"Enough, Sebastian! Why should we bicker? We may not love each other as I have heard that brothers do, but we serve each other's needs. I admit that without your help my book would be nothing. But remember that without my protection, you would be in Hell, where you belong."

"Even so, brother. Let us be sociable. We will speak of the book later. A game of chess?" Sebastian waved a long white hand toward the black-and-white squares on the table.

"I think not, Sebastian. You always win. You toy with me, and I don't like the way you play."

39

"Surely you don't object because I give you the white pieces and take the black for myself?"

"I don't like the way you always attack my bishops."

"And you always try to take my castles. I admit, though, that you are less successful. So let us forget chess. Perhaps the cards?"

"The cards?" Diego licked his lips. "Yes, the cards."

"The symbolism bothers you less, does it, when the symbols reveal your own future? Very well, brother, I will read your fortune."

In his right hand Sebastian held a pile of pasteboard cards. "You will insist on using these for vulgar prediction, as the gypsies do? They have a higher purpose. I have told you before that they are not cards, but the pages of a book, a book more full of meaning and mystery than any that you or I will ever write. A book of pictures. But you only listen to what you want to hear."

Sebastian held out the pack to his brother.

"Shall I mix them?" asked Diego.

"Just touch them, brother. No need to trouble yourself."

As Diego reached out and tapped the top card, Sebastian drew the deck back. He opened his right hand and the cards poured from it in a great arc, high above his head. They seemed to float and shimmer in the air for an instant; then they fell, twisting and turning, to form somehow a perfect stack in the center of the table.

As Diego sat staring, the top card detached itself from the pack, flipped gracefully over, and landed face down on the table. The next card did the same, coming to rest beside the first. It happened again and again until there were ten cards dealt out in a neat row. And all the while Sebastian sat quietly with folded hands.

"Tricks with bits of paper," Sebastian said. "Any juggler could do as much."

Diego smiled nervously. "You always were a bit of a mountebank, Sebastian."

"Why do you hesitate, brother? This is your future! Surely

the Grand Inquisitor wishes to have his questions answered! Turn over the first card. It is yourself."

Diego did as he was told, then smiled more complacently. "The Hierophant," he said.

The card showed a seated figure wearing a red robe and an ornate triple crown. His hand was raised in a benediction and crossed keys lay at his feet. Kneeling before him were two men with the shaven heads of monks.

The faded drawing on the worn card had been done years ago in black ink, which was now turning brown. The colors, too, had dulled with the passage of time. Diego believed that his brother had designed the cards, but he had never asked. He was more interested in what they had to say.

"What does it mean?" he asked. "Surely I am not to be pope!"

"I think not. This is you as you are now. Be not too ambitious, Diego. You are already in a seat of power. It may mean no more than what you see. This is only the first of ten."

"Are there no hidden meanings?"

"Many. Here, perhaps alliance, or instruction. Or one who seeks the supernatural."

Diego reached impatiently for the second card.

"The Queen of Swords," he announced.

"She crosses you," said Sebastian.

"The Queen?"

"You must not take my little pictures too literally. It might be any woman. A dark woman, and melancholy. She may be given to visions and fond of dancing."

"If this is who I think it is, then I am the one who crosses her. Let me see the next."

He picked up the third card and looked at it in some surprise. "Five Coins," he said.

"A doubtful card, brother. It may mean poverty, but you are already sworn to that. It might represent some sort of bargain."

"I know what it means," said Diego. He reached for the fourth card.

"The Ten of Swords," he said.

41

"A bad card," said Sebastian. "Cruelty and misfortune. This lies beneath you, however. It is not your future but the foundation on which you stand."

"So be it," said Diego and reached for the next card.

"Behind you," said Sebastian.

Diego started slightly and turned half around, then stopped. "Oh. You mean the card," he said. "It is the Knight of Cups."

"Perhaps he really is behind you, brother. This signifies the approach of a young man. He is a lover of pleasure, and a dreamer. Do you know him?"

"No."

"Beware of him."

"Why?"

"Because he is a good man."

"Spare me your wit, Sebastian. The next, I believe, shows what is before me?"

At the top of the card was an angel, with wings spread and a trumpet at his lips. Below was the sea and three figures—a man, a woman, and a child. They were naked and their skin was gray. The woman's arms were raised toward the sky; the man's, crossed on his chest in the position usually reserved for corpses. Each of the three stood in an open coffin.

"The card of Judgment," said Sebastian.

"What sort of an augury is that? We all face the Last Judgment," said the Grand Inquisitor. Nevertheless, he shivered once, looking at the angel.

"It would be wiser to view it as a smaller judgment," said Sebastian, "a decision of some sort. It might refer, let us say, to the reception the authorities will give to your book on witchcraft and black magic."

"Then let us see the next card," Diego said. He picked it up but kept its back to Sebastian. He studied it skeptically. The drawing showed a hand emerging from a white cloud, holding a long stick.

"The Ace of Wands," Diego said. "What does it mean? No doubt you will try to worry me with it—but I think you have more cause than I to fear a shaft of wood, Sebastian."

Sebastian smiled. The candlelight gleamed on his sharp white teeth. "The Ace of Wands has great power. It signifies strength in an enterprise, a beginning. Yet it can also mean a disaster of some kind. It is a mystery. Consult the next card."

"Two Swords," said Diego.

"The eighth card represents your surroundings. Another bad card. Strife and sorrow."

"Who cares for my surroundings? What does the ninth card portend?"

"It is your hopes, brother."

Diego turned over the ninth card and placed it on the table. It showed a stone tower shattered by a thunderbolt. The three windows were in flames. A man and a woman fell from the structure toward the rocks below.

"The Tower Struck by Lightning," said Sebastian dryly. "I believe the cards have read your mind."

"Enough of your jokes!" said Diego. "What does it signify?"

"I thought the picture alone would surely satisfy you, but no matter. In general it signifies disaster, an unforeseen calamity."

"And you say that this is my hope?"

"I say nothing, brother. The cards speak to you. I am only their interpreter."

"Are there no other meanings?"

"Each card signifies many things. It might also mean ambition. And it represents the planet Mars. Do you wish for Mars, brother? Come. I will show him to you."

Sebastian grasped Diego by the arm and led him to a wall covered by a Moorish tapestry representing a lion hunt. He drew the tapestry aside to reveal a narrow window. There was no glass, and Diego felt a faint breeze. He looked at the range of misty mountains spread out before him and at the dizzying drop to the ground.

"Look!" said Sebastian, pointing into the clear sky. "The faint red star there, the one that does not glitter. There are your hopes, brother."

The Grand Inquisitor craned his neck. There were thousands of stars. He could not follow the direction of Sebastian's finger. He began to feel a touch of vertigo. Sebastian's grip was strong and cold, even through the rough cloth of a monk's robe.

The Grand Inquisitor pulled away and walked to the center of the room. "I see nothing," he said. "Astrology, cartomancy, all these things are wicked foolishness. And I am a fool to listen to you."

"Then you do not wish to see the last card? The one showing what will come?"

Diego stepped to the table and leaned on it heavily with both hands. He looked at the nine cards spread before him and the one still face down. Then he looked up at Sebastian, who lounged mockingly against the tapestry.

Diego's fingers reached out for the piece of pasteboard. Still staring at Sebastian, he turned it over. Slowly his eyes lowered. He saw a red sky and a setting sun. A smiling skeleton walked across a fertile field, a scythe in its bony hands, reaping human heads. Its smile was the same as Sebastian's.

"Death!" said Diego in a whisper. Then he began to shout. "It means nothing! This is only a trick! Pieces of paper! You mixed the cards, Sebastian! And you dealt them! This is not my future! It is yours!"

Sebastian smiled in the shadows.

"Calm yourself, brother," he said. "Death is the last card for every man. For every man but me."

Diego stared in silence at the ten cards. A skeleton, a tower in flames, two kneeling monks, a hand with a wand, an angel with a trumpet, a knight, a queen, coins, and swords. The pictures swam before his eyes.

"The card may mean other things," said Sebastian. "Not death, perhaps, but something similar—a transformation."

"It means nothing," Diego repeated.

"You are right, of course. It is only a game. Let us speak of other things. The book! It is coming splendidly. You will astound the world with it. Even the great Torquemada will be surprised!"

Diego had resumed his inscrutable exterior. "You say it is going well?"

"It should be ready in a few weeks. There are still a number of points that trouble me, but I am working on them. This book will make your fortune!"

"My fortune," said Diego. He looked again at the cards, then shrugged and turned away. "Show me the manuscript," he said.

"Presently," said Sebastian. "I think you are still upset. Have some more wine."

Diego reached for the silver goblet. He would have sworn that he had drained it long before, but when he picked it up he found it was full to the brim.

"And forget the cards," Sebastian said. "You are right: it was a trick; it means nothing."

He gathered up the cards in one pale, cold hand.

And when he opened the hand it was empty.

5. The Question

THE more Miguel learned about witches, the less he liked them.

That dark and sullen woman had been in the dungeons for almost a week. Each day the Grand Inquisitor interrogated her, and each day she refused to answer. Miguel was present during all these fruitless exchanges, the ink at the end of his pen drying up as he waited for the confession that never came. Every time he saw her she was thinner and filthier. Her green eyes stared at him strangely. It seemed that she thought him a contemptible creature, and it was small satisfaction to Miguel that he was inclined to agree with her.

It was worse that she had no respect for the Grand Inquisitor. She broke her silence only to swear and spit at him. Miguel was appalled at her effrontery. Didn't she know who Diego de Villanueva was? How could she resist the harsh and honeyed words with which the Grand Inquisitor sought the secrets of her soul?

Such resistance could have only one result, the Question.

Miguel had never seen the Question administered, but he had no desire to be initiated into its mysteries. He knew that it was not just a question—there had been enough of those already—but that it rarely failed to elicit an answer. The answers came between screams, from a long dark room where men masked in black waited beside their cruel machines. Did Margarita de Mendoza know what was waiting for her? Why would she not confess?

He thought sometimes that he should go to her alone and warn her. It was not that he wished to spare her but that he wished to spare himself from witnessing her torture. He was afraid to see it. Yet he did nothing, for he was more afraid to be alone with her, because she was a witch and he had begun to learn what witches might do.

He had worked and worried his way through half the *Malleus Maleficarum*, which the Grand Inquisitor had ordered him to read, and Miguel found it even more disturbing than he had expected. He had imagined that it would be a catalog of crimes, of the things that witches did. Raising tempests, killing crops, crippling cattle, stealing children, causing enemies to sicken and die—all these he would have been prepared to consider. However, it appeared that the real wickedness of witchcraft lay elsewhere, in activities Miguel found it painful even to contemplate. The details were all too vivid for a young man of his modest nature, but the principle was clear enough. One phrase from the book rang through his mind each time he looked on Margarita: "All witchcraft springs from carnal lust."

Miguel learned that it was the greatest joy for witches to copulate with devils. The demons took male or female forms and visited abandoned men and women in the enchanting guises of incubi and succubi. Countless sources were cited for the truth of these allegations, and the points were argued with what seemed to Miguel like irrefutable logic. No particulars were omitted and more than one reason was offered for the devilish enthusiasm with which such seductions were accomplished. They served not only to corrupt the sinful but to increase their number. Miguel wondered how demons could reproduce mortals, but the *Malleus Maleficarum* had the answer. Devils appeared to men as succubi and drew forth from them the seed of life, which could then be delivered to women by the same devils in their roles as incubi. Or the semen could be entrusted to the care of another demon who had a willing woman in his power. In either case, the offspring of these triangular unions were certain to be among the vilest of mortals.

In Miguel's imagination these ideas conjured up deplorable pictures, which invaded his dreams. Sometimes he saw dim, smoky creatures keeping assignations in the sky and passing things from hand to hand before speeding off upon their rounds. More often, though, came the nightmare of a succubus floating just above his narrow bed, her eyes green, her lips scarlet, her black hair streaming down in cloudy masses to envelop him. The worst of it was that the dreams were exciting. Only his humility kept him from the absolute conviction that some dark power had embarked on a campaign to seduce him. As it was, he tried not to sleep.

While awake, he felt obliged to read further in the book, where he learned that it was the sport of witches to obstruct the act of love for others. There were spells to prevent women from conceiving and, more commonly, to prevent men from performing, thus destroying marriages and luring mortals into adultery.

Even more disturbing was a statement that witches had the power to remove the male organ entirely. There was a separate chapter on this topic, which Miguel encountered with a sinking stomach, even though there were arguments to assure him that the spell was only an illusion, however much it might appear to the victim that he had been utterly emasculated. Miguel read with mounting horror, yet told himself that this sort of curse should not mean much to a monk who had already taken a vow of chastity. Did Miguel need fear that a devil would take away his manhood, when he had already surrendered it to God?

He realized that his left hand was clutching and crumpling the page, which was beginning to tear free of the binding, and he spent the rest of the night trying to smooth it out so that the Grand Inquisitor would not notice. After that night, Miguel's fear of witches began to develop into a positive hatred. He

48

hurried through the book to the third part, where methods were described for detecting witchcraft, capturing it, torturing it, punishing it, and destroying it in flames. Yet still the dreams came.

The six black candles were lit again and the Grand Inquisitor sat behind them. Miguel stood ready with his pen and papers, but his eyes were on the door.

"Will she speak this time?" he asked.

"There is no reason to expect it, but we will take the trouble to inquire once more. If her attitude has not improved, then we will be obliged to try another method."

"The Question?"

The Grand Inquisitor merely nodded.

"At once?" asked Miguel.

"I imagine it will be no more than a few minutes, unless she has unexpectedly seen the light."

"And will it make her speak?"

"I have never known it to fail. Yet this is no ordinary heretic. Some of those are fanatical enough, but there is nothing like a witch for clinging stubbornly to sin. Some of them seem half-possessed and have a strength that will bear almost anything. Others, especially the old women, are reported to collapse at the very sight of the instruments. We can only wait and see. I know this will be your first sight of the Question, Miguel, but bear up and remember that this is also my first witch."

Miguel smiled weakly at the little joke, which he knew was an attempt to reassure him. As such, it was a failure. He could see no grounds for comparing Miguel Carillo to Diego de Villanueva. Still, he tried to respond in the proper spirit.

"It will not be your last witch, I venture," said Miguel. "You will root them all out of the hills, for a certainty you will! And you will become the first witch hunter of Spain and the greatest in Christendom! And your book will be . . ."

"Who spoke of a book?" interrupted the Grand Inquisitor sharply. "Have I mentioned a book?"

"Well, no, that is, not really, but I thought from what you have said that you were working on something . . ."

"All right, Miguel. I had not meant to tell you yet, but it seems I speak too freely. There will be a book. There is much to be learned about witches and their ways, and I hope to cast some light into these dark corners. Perhaps you can help me."

"I? How?"

"With your eyes, and your ears, and your pen. Continue to take down every word the witch utters, and it may be that your transcript will find a place in my work. Stay calm, and do not let the Question disturb you. I know it may seem unnecessary to you, since we have testimony and evidence enough to convict Margarita de Mendoza already. But we may persuade her to name her confederates. And there is another reason: her immortal soul is in the gravest danger. If she confesses and repents she will be saved, but if we condemn her without this final effort, she will be left to an eternity of tortures worse than anything that we can bring to bear upon her corrupted flesh. Do you understand?"

"I do, and I will try not to fail you. I have read about the witches, and I have no pity for her now, though I hope to see her saved."

"Silence! They are coming. Look to your work."

The door opened slowly on well-oiled hinges.

Miguel raised his eyes in spite of his firm resolve to be indifferent. The witch was becoming a horror. Her tanned face had turned pale, except for the purple circles under her sunken eyes. There seemed to be no flesh to smooth the strong line of her jaw, and her sharp cheekbones looked as if they might break through the skin. This face that haunted Miguel's dreams looked to him like a beautiful skull. The emerald eyes turned toward him and one corner of the red mouth lifted. He looked away.

Silence filled the black velvet room. The black candles burned steadily in the stale air and the black-robed jailers stood silently beside their prisoner. Miguel stared at his white paper and nothing happened for a long time.

At last the Grand Inquisitor spoke.

"Margarita de Mendoza," he said. "You know why you are here. You know your crimes, and we know them. We have witnesses and evidence. Yet you have not confessed. If you admit your guilt and name your confederates, then God will forgive you. If you do not, there is no hope for you, in this world or the next. We are weary of waiting for your answers, but I ask you once again to speak.

"And let me tell you this. If you refuse, you will not return to your cell. You will go to another chamber, and there we will persuade you to confess. Believe me when I tell you that you will wish you were back in the dungeons. Consider carefully and accept God's mercy now."

Margarita's heart gave one tremendous thump. She felt suddenly light-headed and there was a ringing in her ears.

"The Devil has more mercy than your God," she heard someone saying far away, then realized that the voice was her own.

"Take her," said the Grand Inquisitor.

Miguel's pulse raced with a kind of sick excitement. He tried to calm himself by remembering the system for administering the Question. There were five parts to the procedure, as outlined in Torquemada's instructions, and the first stage, the threat of torture, had elicited only blasphemy. The woman could burn for that alone, but the point of the Inquisition, he reminded himself, was not to punish her but save her.

Miguel saw her lips moving silently as the guards turned her toward the door, and he wondered if she might be casting a spell. He determined to keep his distance. He had read of a German witch who had breathed into the face of her executioner, and the man had died in three days.

Miguel looked at the Grand Inquisitor, who rose from his seat and gestured for his vicar to follow.

Miguel had never visited the torture chamber and had never

even seen the dungeons. As the small procession made its way down dark stairs and through dank passageways, he was amazed at the extent of the Holy House. The rooms above were nothing compared with the secret chambers underground. The walls were wet. The air was cold, but the torches made it smoky, like some icy hell.

A door opened and Miguel knew that it would be the last, for there was no way out of the vaulted stone chamber into which he followed the Grand Inquisitor. The room was unmistakable in any case.

Miguel looked and tried to calm himself with the knowledge that what he saw was the second stage of the Question. Miguel himself found it more than a little unpleasant, and he thought with resentment that he, like the prisoner, was to be subjected to each stage of the torture; all but the last.

The room was half-illuminated by the ruddy glow from braziers heaped with burning coals, and fitfully brightened by the white flames of candles flickering in the fresher air from the door. The hooded jailers entered with their torches, revealing figures crudely painted on the gray stone walls: gigantic black beasts with horns and claws. Such murals were far from reassuring, but they were only a background for the machines and their attendants. Miguel saw four more men masked by the black, pointed hoods, and he heard the door close behind him with a groan and a thud.

He wished to be gone, but reluctantly he took his seat behind a small table. Behind this was a thronelike chair obviously intended for the Grand Inquisitor, but Diego, not ready for it, instead turned to face the prisoner.

"You see what we have prepared for you, Margarita de Mendoza. Will you speak?"

Margarita did not answer, but Miguel saw that her lips were still moving. Could she be praying? To whom? Her eyes were glassy and seemed to be looking at something not in the room.

"Do you know what these machines are?" asked the Grand Inquisitor. "Let me show you. This is the hoist," he said, and the guards turned Margarita to face it. "You see that it is only a rope, hanging from that pulley in the ceiling. But if your arms were tied behind your back by one end of that rope and some-one pulled the other end, you might find it painful. It might dislocate your shoulders. If not, you could be lowered, then raised again. Eventually something would come of it. Or you could be left hanging, with weights on your feet to pull you down. And while you hung, you might be whipped. I am sure you need not be shown the whip to know its uses."

Nevertheless, one of the hooded men stepped forward, bran-dishing a whip, lest there be any doubt in Margarita's mind.

"The hoist might stretch your arms a bit," said the Grand In-quisitor, "but we have a better instrument for that. This is the rack." He passed to the next machine with the air of a mer-chant displaying his wares.

"This is a bed of sorts, but you will not find it very comfort-able. It is too hard; but that is not the half of it. If you lie here, these iron bands will be clamped to your wrists and ankles, which look sore enough already. The bands are attached to chains like those in your cell, but these chains are wrapped around wheels. When the wheels are turned, the chains draw tight and something between them must be stretched. The metal is stronger than your flesh. You would not enjoy a rest on the rack. You are already tall for a woman."

This is the third part of the Question, Miguel thought; any-one who was not mad would confess now. Yet he felt that he was more dismayed than Margarita de Mendoza, who glanced at the devices of her destruction as if they were of only passing interest.

"This is the chair," said the Grand Inquisitor, his voice rising as he warmed to his work. He leaned over a mass of glowing coals that threw his features into red relief. Smoky sweat broke out on his brow. "A woman could be locked in that chair with the stocks below it holding her feet. These coals are here to cook those feet. It is not a comfortable chair. . . . Will you speak?"

Miguel shuffled his blank papers but found the sound so loud that he stopped suddenly.

"Let me show you the ladder," the Grand Inquisitor continued quietly. A ladder studded with iron braces slanted slightly toward the ceiling. "You might find yourself locked on this ladder, with your feet above your head and your head held in place by a metal band. This is merely in preparation for the water. Some call this treatment the water, but I prefer to think of it as the ladder, since I have seen so many squirm up it to salvation. There is a clamp here to keep your mouth open, and there are gallons of water in these jugs. There is also a long strip of linen. When we give you the water, this cloth seems to flow down the throat behind it. The result is a choking sensation something like strangling, though we will try not to kill you. But none of this will be necessary if you will speak now."

The tour of the establishment seemed to be over, and Margarita apparently sensed as much. She looked at the Grand Inquisitor as though seeing him for the first time, then shook her head.

"No? Very well," he said. "Prepare her."

This is the fourth stage, thought Miguel, but his mind was no longer on Torquemada's instructions. Instead, his eyes were on the prisoner.

The guard on Margarita's right reached toward her, his white hand reaching out of a black sleeve to grasp the neckline of her bedraggled dress. He pulled at the cloth and yanked her head down with it. The dress tore away, and when Margarita pulled herself up she was naked.

Miguel had never seen a naked woman before. He looked away toward the wall and was confronted by the black silhouette of a painted monster. He turned again toward Margarita and could not look away.

She was gaunt. He could have counted her ribs, but his eyes were drawn almost hypnotically to the full fleshy breasts that seemed incongruous with her haggard frame. He saw the nipples grow hard in the cool air, and the lustrous swirl of black hair curling above her thighs. He stared less in lust than in amazement. She is beautiful, he thought. And then he heard her laughter.

He saw her eyes, staring back at him full of mockery. With her hands on her hips she threw back her head and laughed at him. His face grew hot and he felt naked himself. He wanted to run but could not move.

He saw the hand of the Grand Inquisitor fly toward the woman's face and heard the sharp sound of a slap. The laughter stopped.

"Evil has many disguises," said the Grand Inquisitor, "but none more treacherous than this." He was addressing the ceiling, but Miguel knew that the words were meant for him.

"There is no need for further delay," said the Grand Inquisitor.

"We know what you are," he said to Margarita, "and soon you will be glad to admit it. But how shall we persuade you? The ladder, I think."

Four hooded figures converged on Margarita, each clutching at an arm or a leg. She went limp, her lips still working soundlessly, and was hoisted onto the ladder, her feet above her head. The clamps closed on her ankles, wrists, and forehead.

"I understand that your keepers have been reluctant to provide you with water, Margarita de Mendoza. I promise you that this will be remedied at once. Perhaps when you have had enough water you will be willing to tell me what you know about witchcraft. I see only one problem. You cannot move your hands or feet and will not be able to speak, with the metal in your mouth and linen in your throat. But try to make some sign when you are ready to speak. We wish to be merciful."

This is the fifth stage, thought Miguel, and closed his eyes.

"Begin," said the Grand Inquisitor.

6. The Dream

NO, damn her, she won't talk! The ladder, the rack, the chair, the hoist—all useless! Oh, she screams well enough, but nothing more. She must be enchanted. And all the while, that stupid boy Miguel gapes at me, waiting to write down her confession, wondering why his hero is failing. She burns on Sunday, Sebastian—I've had my fill of her!"

Don Sebastian de Villanueva sat in the shadows and said nothing. The Grand Inquisitor saw that his brother had grown thinner, like the witch, that his long black hair fell across his face like hers.

"You are very like her, Sebastian. Must you be silent too? You are both monsters! A wicked woman and a walking corpse. Must my future depend on such as these?"

"I fear that it must, brother. Even monsters have their uses. Without her witchcraft and my wisdom, you will never fulfill your ambition."

"Your wisdom! What has it brought you? You may think that you have cheated death, but you are still a prisoner. You spend your nights in this castle and your days in a coffin. Where is the wisdom in such an empty existence?"

"You may think me a prisoner, brother, but I am not always here."

"What? You leave the castle without me? Would you ruin both of us?"

"Calm yourself, Diego. You misunderstand me. I remain within these walls, but when I lie sleeping in the crypt, I find that part of me is elsewhere."

"Where? In Hell?"

"Not exactly, though I know you are disappointed to hear it. There is no name for such a place. It is not in your theology."

"Tell me of it, Sebastian," said the Grand Inquisitor, leaning forward across the ivory-and-onyx chessboard.

"It may be no more than a dream, Diego. But sometimes I think that it is real, and that this is the dream."

"Tell me your dream, Sebastian."

Sebastian smiled, showing his long teeth. He sprawled in his carved chair and gazed up at the ceiling as if he could see the stars beyond it. "Very well, brother," he said. "I dream that I am in the topmost tower of a castle. It is night. I am surrounded by ancient volumes filled with evil incantations. And there I sit, through all eternity, answering the endless questions of my brother the Grand Inquisitor. And it is Hell for a certainty."

Diego's shoulders slumped. He started to speak again, then clamped his thin lips together and stood up, shaking his head. "I will not play these games with you, Sebastian, and it is not wise for you to toy with me this way. You should be more careful. You are growing old and thin. You are dying. And you need me to quench your thirst."

"You cannot frighten me with death," answered Sebastian. "I have died before, and I will again. I die daily, as one of your saints said. It is especially foolish of you to threaten me, though, when I know that you are here to offer me a feast."

Diego sat again. "True," he said. "We should not argue. This witch, Margarita de Mendoza, must be made to serve us both. You will visit her tomorrow night, the night before she is to die. Take some of her blood. And if you cannot make her speak, the fire may have her."

"I will do my best for you, brother. My visits to the dungeons have helped you before, and not only by giving me the strength to keep to this cursed castle and write your book. I have frightened a few confessions out of your prisoners, but I wonder about this one. If she is really a witch, I may not impress her much. The innocent ones are easier to shock."

Sebastian sat up suddenly. "Tell me, brother," he said, "is it true that in Toledo the monks disguise themselves as demons and creep into the dungeons to terrify the prisoners and force confessions from them?"

"I believe it may be true," the Grand Inquisitor answered judicially.

"Well," said Sebastian, "in the great cities they have more money for such extravagances. But here in the outlying districts you cannot afford to buy expensive costumes, so you are forced to employ real demons. Poor Diego. How can you expect success from such a shoddy substitute as I?"

"You must succeed, Sebastian! It is something to have caught a witch, and I have enough evidence already to convict her, but I want that confession. It would make a splendid chapter for my book on witchcraft, and if she names the other members of her coven, I will have more than a chapter. I will have the greatest *auto-da-fé* in the annals of the Inquisition and even Torquemada will be forced to take notice."

Sebastian sighed and slouched still lower in his chair. He seemed to be boneless. "You amaze me, brother," he said. "Do you really think you can impress that crazed old hypocrite Torquemada? Do you think he will be anxious to promote you? He wants no rivals."

"Torquemada is a great man, Sebastian. He created the Inquisition. But it will outlive him, and I believe he knows it. Someone must succeed him, and I plan to be the one."

"What a day for Spain that will be!"

"I might be more moderate. I understand that our Inquisition is the horror of Europe and that even the pope thinks Torquemada is too zealous. It may be unwise to pursue these petty heretics. But witches! They are hunted everywhere but here. Why should that be? And why should I not be the one to take advantage of the situation?"

"I wish you well, brother," said Sebastian languidly. "And what will become of me when you are Inquisitor General?"

The room in the tower was very still for a moment.

"You are very valuable to me, Sebastian."

"But shall I be when I have finished your book for you?"

"I am sure I will have further uses for you. I believe there is no man in Europe with your knowledge of sorcery and demonology. Trust me, Sebastian. I will never betray you."

"I trust you as you trust me, Diego. For nine years your prisoners have provided me with the blood I need and I have no complaints. But what I see of the future is cold and cloudy. Let it pass, though. Let us take one night at a time."

"I am more concerned about tomorrow night. Will you be able to make her confess?"

"You are asking me if I am more frightening than you are, brother, and I confess I am more afraid of you than I am of myself. Perhaps the witch will look on a creature like me as a friend. Were all your tortures useless?"

"All. We have worked on her for days."

"You must have enjoyed yourself, even if she did not confess. The torture was suspended, of course?"

"Of course. We would not disobey Torquemada's instructions."

"The man's mind amazes me. It might seem unduly cruel to some if monks were to torture their victims more than once, so he declares that the Question is never really stopped but merely suspended. And this gives him a clear conscience."

The Grand Inquisitor was smiling in spite of himself. "I admit that some of the technicalities are preposterous, but they all have their uses. When we condemn a prisoner to death, we do not execute him ourselves but just abandon him to the secular authorities, who do not have such spiritual natures. Our hands are always clean."

"Wonderful," said Sebastian. "And your tortures are such that it can never be said that the Inquisition has spilled a drop of blood. Yet you send a vampire to feed on the condemned."

The Grand Inquisitor laughed. "I see no discrepancy, Sebastian. We are pledged to spill no blood, but I trust you not to spill a drop."

"Indeed," said Sebastian. "And I promise not to waste any of this woman's blood. I will savor it. She must be strong, and courageous. I wish I could have it all."

"Not all, Sebastian. I must have her alive to be burned at the stake."

"Even so," agreed Sebastian, "though it makes me feel a failure. I have been a vampire for nine years, and I have yet to take a life."

"There is safety in moderation, Sebastian. I provide you with all the blood you need, and you have never left behind a corpse that might betray you."

"It might be a joy to drain her dry," said Sebastian. "Is she beautiful?"

"She was. But her stay in the Holy House has not improved her appearance."

Sebastian frowned.

"Courage," said the Grand Inquisitor. "You will surely find her preferable to the old Jews you have taken before. Yet she herself is half Jewish. I am amazed by your taste. How can you, a high-born nobleman, stand to drink their tainted blood?"

"It is very good blood, I assure you."

"I believe you would drink the blood of a Moor."

"As soon as you are ready to provide it, brother. I imagine it will not be long before Ferdinand and Isabella forget their promise to the Moors and outlaw their religion as well as that of the Jews."

The Grand Inquisitor was disgusted. "I suppose it is possible for a godless monster like you to tolerate the Jews," he said, "but I should think that even you would draw the line at blacks.

You died fighting them, Sebastian, and have the scar to prove it."

"The Moors did not kill me. It was that cursed cannon," Sebastian said, fingering the white scar running down the left side of his face. "And it hurt like hell. You will not enjoy dying, Diego. But it was a Spanish cannon, cast by some incompetent workman, and I did not love my country when I found half my face falling off. War is a sure cure for patriotism."

"You should be thankful the cannon exploded. A clean blow from a Moorish lance might have slain you at once and left no time for the rituals that made you one of the living dead."

Sebastian stood up slowly and drew back the tapestry that covered the tower's lone window. A light rain dribbled over the black mountains. "You may be right, brother, but I hate those guns. They will change things. A battery of cannon could crush the walls of this tower in an hour, though it has stood for centuries. Soon there will be no castles. There will be a new world, stranger than the one discovered by that Italian navigator. This is the end of an age, and we are its relics."

"Not I, Sebastian. I am part of the new world you fear."

"Perhaps, Diego. Yet you are my brother, and we are both haunted by the same mysteries, which will have no place in the world to come. You think your Inquisition is the birth of a new light, but I believe it is the death rattle of the old darkness that has nurtured both of us. The persecutions will cease, for no one will care what others believe. And most of them will believe in nothing."

He dropped the tapestry wearily and the window disappeared behind a lion's head. "Yet in one sense I agree with you. Your Torquemada has found something, though it stinks in my nostrils—and I have smelled my own grave. What will survive from your work is the idea of the organization. It is a new sort of evil; beside it witchcraft is nothing."

"What are you talking about, Sebastian?"

"You don't know, do you? That is the beauty of it. A civilization can wreak more havoc than any single man or woman, yet no one is really to blame. It is evil without a sense of sin. Each man will do his duty, Diego, even as you do, and thousands may die for it, but no one will have blood on his hands. I would rather sell my soul outright."

"Sit down, Sebastian, and calm yourself. Sometimes I think that cannon cracked your very brain."

"Just enough to let in the light, brother."

"You fought for Spain yourself, Sebastian," observed the Grand Inquisitor.

"Did I not. A few years ago there was no Spain, only an unruly flock of rival kingdoms. Since my death she has grown into a unified and awesome power, slaughtering her subjects at home and reaching out across the sea to conquer continents we never dreamed of. She is more of a monster than that poor witch in your dungeons, yet every crime committed in the name of Spain is transformed into a virtue. I know not where it will end, but I have no wish to see it. I wish it were morning, so I could sleep."

"You will sleep soon enough, Sebastian, but the sun will not rise for hours. I want to talk with you about the book, and I want to know more about your dreams. You want that woman's blood, but you must work for it."

"Why ask me?" Sebastian sneered. "Doesn't your religion teach you about life after death? Are you still unsatisfied? Have you more questions, Grand Inquisitor? This castle, not the church you swore to serve, provides your catechism."

Diego said nothing but rubbed his hand reflectively across his mouth. "I see you do not deny it," Sebastian continued. "I shall never forget that first night after my death, when you came here thinking you would be alone. How you cried and cursed yourself, standing outside the walls, because you had abandoned your claims to the estate and could never be lord of the castle. And the idiot look on your long face when I came to greet you!"

The Grand Inquisitor bridled. "Of course I was surprised. A

man does not expect to meet his brother's ghost. And don't tell me you came to greet me. You came out of the darkness to kill me and you would have, if I had not been wearing a cross."

"Do not depend too much upon the cross, brother. I admit it startled me a bit at first. I don't like the look of the thing, somehow. But I could bear it if I had to."

"Perhaps. And perhaps not. The cross is strong, Sebastian, even in my hands. At least it stopped you long enough so we could talk. The pact we made that night has kept you alive. Without me and the blood I provide you would never have lasted as long as you have."

"True, brother, much as it pains me to admit it. Vampires are fragile creatures. Most that I have heard of were peasants who stumbled from their graves and attacked their own families. They were found out at once, then destroyed. We are so helpless during the daylight that I sometimes think I may be the last of the breed. But at night, Diego—at night! Even now, weakened as I am, I could turn into a beast before your eyes. I could become a glowing mist and pass through a crack in that door. I could sprout great leathery wings and fly out of this window. And you would be left here alone."

"Enough, Sebastian," said the Grand Inquisitor nervously. "I have no wish to see your tricks tonight. Is that all you have learned from your devils? Tricks to frighten children?"

"They might frighten more than children, brother."

Sebastian sat erect, his white hands clutching the arms of the chair. His face went slack and his dead eyes rolled until only the whites were visible.

"Stop it, Sebastian!"

The eyes were gone and the empty sockets filled with smoke that poured over the pale face. Sebastian held up his hands, as though to watch them melting into mist, but he had no eyes, had no face, and then no hands. He was a cloud of smoke, faintly green and pulsing with luminescence as it floated over the empty chair.

"Sebastian! Stop!" The Grand Inquisitor crossed himself and

turned away from his brother. He was looking at the door and at the gigantic shadow of himself cast by the candlelight. Smoky shadows rose to envelop it and the flame flickered out. The room was black.

"Sebastian?" whispered the Grand Inquisitor.

Only silence answered him. Even the green glow was gone. He sat very still, afraid to move, and listened to the sound of his heart pounding.

A spark flew from somewhere and the red candle sputtered back to life. Don Sebastian de Villanueva stood in the farthest corner of the room, bent over a shelf of crumbling books. His long black hair streamed over the collar of his crimson cloak. He reached for a dark and dusty tome and turned slowly toward the center of the room.

"What? Still here, brother?" he asked. "I hoped to be rid of you."

"Damn you, Sebastian. I could kill you tomorrow."

"If I thought you dared, then you would die tonight. But you need me to finish the book and to scare your witch into a confession. I was only demonstrating one of my techniques—do you think it might work on her?"

"Well, you are quite a magician, Sebastian," said the Grand Inquisitor with uneasy geniality. "And I know you are capable of more than performances like that one. You practiced sorcery for years, of course, and you should have some skill. I wonder why I never suspected you when you were alive, especially after . . ."

He tried to make the words fade away inconspicuously, but they hung heavily in the air.

"After what, Diego? After the Inquisition took my wife and killed her?"

"Nobody meant her to die," said the Grand Inquisitor hurriedly. "A paltry penance would have been enough. But she wouldn't admit anything. Who would have thought she was so weak? She died before the torture was well begun . . . or so I heard."

"You heard," Sebastian repeated coldly. "You speak as if you were hundreds of miles away, as I was. If I had been there, it would never have happened. But you were there, Diego!"

"Not I, Sebastian! I knew nothing of it. I was a mere novice, little more than a boy like my vicar, Miguel Carillo. How can you suspect me? Do you think I was consulted? And how could I have stopped them, even if I had known? Her beliefs were strange and she did not keep them to herself. And she spoke against the Inquisition!"

"If more had spoken then, your Inquisition might have died aborning. She could not believe that Christians could be so cruel, and she died for it."

"Nobody meant her to die," the Grand Inquisitor said again. "She should have confessed at once. What was she clinging to?"

"Who knows? But I am sure it was harmless. Gracia believed in a sweet world of saints and spirits. She had visions, but they were not like yours or mine. Apparently, she preferred them to life in your dungeons. I think it might have been very easy for her to die."

"But it was not easy for you, Sebastian?"

"I was not like her. I had no faith. I was not ready to die."

"Will you ever be? What is it like, Sebastian, to be dead? What lies beyond this life? What do you dream?"

"So many questions, Diego! Don't you believe the teachings of your own church? It is very simple, really, what we learned as children. The good boys go to Heaven and the bad boys go to Hell."

"Must you mock me, Sebastian? I believe you know nothing. Anyone can create an air of mystery by keeping silent. What is the color of your wonderful dreams?"

"The color?" Sebastian sank into his chair. "My dreams are silver."

The Grand Inquisitor rose in fury, but his words were cold and calm. "Beware, Sebastian," he said. "Do not depend too much upon my patience. I have not protected you for years because I love your mockery. We have made a bargain, you and I, but it is worthless if you do no more than dream. I want that book. I have waited long enough for it. The time is ripe, and I will not be denied. Deliver it soon and you will find me a grateful man. Delay too long and you will learn what it means to cross the Grand Inquisitor."

7. The Knight of Cups

ANTONIO wore a new suit of clothes dyed brilliant blue. Together with the horse he rode his outfit had cost him nearly all the money he had, but he was a stranger here and it was necessary to make a good impression. His purse was almost empty, but that hardly mattered now that he had reached his destination. He had not traveled all this way to spend but to be paid. Besides, he reflected, it was unwise for a wayfarer to carry large sums of money. There were thieves everywhere. He had worn ragged garments throughout his long journey but had put them in his saddlebag this morning and donned his new suit, stiff but splendid. He would make a proper entrance.

Antonio was unimpressed with the city. There was not much to it, once past the public square with its cathedral and courts. It was not so much a city as a town, he thought. Compared with Rome or Florence it was nothing. There were a few fine houses, several stories high and built of good stone, but these were all clustered around the plaza. A few moments away there was nothing splendid, only narrow streets that seemed to be made of dust, lined with squat buildings of mud. Some were built of bricks, but they were mud bricks. The homes and shops were equally ugly.

The city was as bad as the country around it, he thought. For days he had ridden through ragged mountains, bare hills, and plains that were nothing but red sand dotted with scrubby bushes. At least there was a river here and a forest leading up into the mountains beyond the city. It was better, but it was not much; this land was bleak. He had heard that the soil of Spain was richer toward the south, but he had no business there. He would have to find his fortune here, in the mud and dust.

He knew that he would have to ask for directions, but he was content to wait a while, to ride aimlessly through the back streets looking for some sign. He had no wish to talk to strangers, since this meant admitting his ignorance of their region and its barbaric tongue. He had studied it for months, but still it stuck uncomfortably to his tongue, as the people he met on the road had been quick to notice. There would be time enough for talk.

His eye caught two girls walking some distance ahead of him. Their backs were to him but he could see that one was little more than a child. The other looked more promising. She was tall and slim, and the hair beneath her red cap was blond. Her coloring was unusual enough to attract his interest; most women he had seen here had black hair and black eyes. Red was common enough, though; it seemed to be the only color these people had ever seen. Everything not red was white or gray or black. Her dress was black.

Antonio urged his horse forward. As he approached the girls, he began to whistle loudly. The tune was nothing special, but it served its purpose. The smaller of the two turned her head at once. She was a pretty little thing, he thought, but his song was not for her. Finally the taller one looked behind her and he saw at once that they were sisters. He was delighted with their appearance and continued to whistle with the diligence of a master musician. Both members of his audience were smiling.

It must be rare, he thought, for them to see such a well-dressed and handsome fellow on these streets. No doubt they would be even more impressed if they knew who he was. He stopped his serenade and grinned at them. The little one laughed and her sister, blushing, turned her around and hurried her forward. Before Antonio could catch up to them, they disappeared into a doorway.

He stopped his horse before the building and looked it over. It was taller than its neighbors, which only made it more of an eyesore, but it looked beautiful to Antonio as soon as he saw the faded wooden sign over the door. Whoever had painted the sign had not been an artist, but its message was clear enough. A hand, inexplicably blue, grasping a lopsided yellow goblet could only be the sign of an inn. Anyone was welcome here, he thought. There was nothing to prevent him from following the girls, and even if he couldn't find them, at least he would be able to wash the dust from his throat. Besides, someone might give him directions. He dismounted rapidly and tied his reins to an iron ring in the wall.

The inn was so much darker than the sun-drenched street that Antonio was blind for a minute. His first impressions of the place were the sour stench of spilled wine and the harsh voice of a man shouting. The words were coming so rapidly that he could understand only a few of them, but he did hear the names "Teresa" and "Dolores." He needed no interpreter to know that the speaker was angry. A low voice answered gently, and Antonio thought he knew its owner.

His eyes adjusted to the dim light and he saw a great bull of a man whose black beard was touched with gray. He sat at a small table in the corner of the whitewashed room with the two girls standing before him. Antonio disliked the man at once, even if only because he was berating the girls, but decided to keep his distance for the moment.

He sat down alone at the only other table in the room, a long slab of oak with two benches and room for twenty men. The other nineteen must know of a better inn, thought Antonio. He stared at the bare wall in front of him as if there were a splendid mural on it, and listened.

"What will people think," roared the man with the black beard, "if the daughters of Pedro Rodriguez walk the streets without a proper chaperone? You are not peasant women! Would you disgrace yourselves? And what are you doing in a low place like this?"

"We came to find our father," said the taller girl quietly. She sat beside the brute and put her arm around him, soothing him as a rider would a troubled horse. "We have not come far, and our reputations are safe. Dolores is too young to have a reputation anyway, and she is my chaperone." She smiled up at her frowning father and continued rapidly, "We had to come. It might have been something important. The Grand Inquisitor wants you. A monk came to the house asking for you. I could have told him where you were, but I thought you might not want them to know where a familiar of the Inquisition was spending the morning."

"All right, Teresa," muttered the man, half-placated. He took a deep drink from a metal cup. "But you must be careful. You are almost old enough to marry now, and you must behave properly. Nothing is more important than honor!"

"Don't worry," said little Dolores. "I was watching her. Anyway, why do we have to stay locked up at home all the time? It's boring! You'd think a touch of the sun would kill us. We're safe enough, father, and you can escort us home. Nobody even saw us."

Antonio smiled at the lie and risked a glance at the little girl. She winked at him. He looked hurriedly down at the tabletop.

"So nobody saw you," repeated Pedro, in a voice just loud enough to be heard. "Not even that bluebird who followed you in?"

Antonio tried not to move. He wanted to jump up and answer this insult with a challenge, but the man was Teresa's father and it would be a shame to kill him. Furthermore, the man was an officer of the Inquisition, and even a foreigner knew enough to beware of men with that sort of friends. So Antonio pretended he had heard nothing, but his hand under the table was on the hilt of his sword.

A man came through the dark doorway in the wall farthest from the entrance to the inn. He was short and fat and bald and his shirt was as filthy as the smoke-stained walls. He leered at Antonio and began to babble inarticulate pleasantries. Half his teeth were missing. He looked to Antonio like a figure from a morality play exemplifying the evils of wine. If he did not discourage his customers, it could only be because his appearance was enough to drive them to drink.

"Wine," said Antonio.

"At once, sir," said the innkeeper. He backed away bowing, casting alternate glances at Antonio and the small table in the corner where Pedro Rodriguez sat with his two daughters. They had lowered their voices at the arrival of their host and their conversation was no longer audible.

The innkeeper shuffled back to Antonio's table with a battered metal cup and set it down with a clumsy flourish. Antonio sipped the wine and grimaced. It tasted like leather. It amazed him that these Spaniards could brag of their wines, yet insisted on storing them in skins that spoiled the flavor. Judging from the look of this place, though, it seemed unlikely that the taste of the skin had done the wine much harm. At least it was wet. He drank again.

The little man hovered over the table. "You are a stranger here?"

"Yes," said Antonio.

"I am Carlos Diaz," said his host. "And this is the Inn of the Golden Cup." Raising his arm in an expansive gesture, he looked around the room as though seeing it for the first time. Something in the sight of it seemed to strike him and he dropped his arm suddenly. "I bid you welcome," he added inconclusively.

Antonio offered up a silent prayer for the swift departure of Carlos Diaz and addressed himself to his drink. He looked warily at Teresa.

She seemed oblivious to him, but Dolores was smiling at him and her father was scowling.

"Begging your pardon, sir," said the persistent proprietor of the Golden Cup, "but might I ask the young gentleman where he has come from? Travelers are so rare in these parts."

Antonio had trouble deciding whether the fellow wanted information or merely wished to be congenial. In either case, Antonio's origin was no secret and could hardly fail to make an impression. He glanced at Teresa again.

"I come from Florence," he said loudly.

Carlos Diaz looked puzzled and his brow furrowed with concentration. "Florence?" he said. "I have never heard of the place. It must be in the south. Am I right?"

Antonio nearly choked on his wine. "What? Never heard of Florence? The finest city in the world! Are you a barbarian? Never heard of Florence! There is no city greater, unless it is Rome!"

"Ah! Rome!" said Carlos. "I have heard of Rome. The pope lives there. You must be an Italian. I know! Florence! Is that the home of our great Spanish navigator Columbus?"

"Spanish?" shouted Antonio. "Columbus is Italian! And he comes from Genoa!"

"Really?" asked the innkeeper. He seemed genuinely fascinated. "Genoa! Then what is Florence?"

"Florence is in Italy too," said Antonio disgustedly. "To the north of Rome." He heard light laughter coming from the corner. "Leave me alone, will you? Go away!"

"Yes, sir," said Carlos. "Sorry, sir. I am not an educated man like you, sir. . . . Florence!" He retreated apologetically.

"Wait," said Antonio.

"Sir?"

"You may be able to help me. I am looking for someone."

"Ah! Then I am your man. I may not know much about the world, but I do know this city. Carlos Diaz knows everyone. Just give me the name!"

"The man I want," said Antonio, "is Diego de Villanueva."

The innkeeper's gap-toothed mouth fell open. "Diego? The Grand . . . You can't want him! People don't look for him; he looks for them!"

Antonio had had enough of this inn. He got to his feet and turned to go but found his way blocked by the massive bulk of Pedro Rodriguez, who pushed him back down to the bench and said, "What do you want with Diego de Villanueva?"

Antonio was on his feet again in an instant, his sword half-drawn. "What is it to you?" he shouted. "Stand aside, fellow, or you die!"

"What is it to me?" said Pedro, stepping back. "Well, I am his familiar. And you, I take it, are an assassin!"

Carlos Diaz ran unashamedly for the far corner, where Pedro's daughters stood terrified. Pedro and Antonio drew their swords together and the naked blades shone in the dim light.

Something is wrong, Antonio thought. His own sword, a fine weapon, was the blade of a gentleman, suitable for duels and other affairs of honor. But this familiar was no gentleman—with both hands he brandished a war sword more than three feet long, with a heavy, triangular blade. It looked big enough to break Antonio's sword in two.

Still, there was no way out for Antonio. If he could strike the first blow, he might have a chance.

Pedro's huge sword swept back to gain momentum for a killing blow, and Antonio dropped to one knee. If he could get one quick thrust in under Pedro's guard, he might save his life.

Antonio jabbed upward, but the old soldier was too quick for him. His massive wedge of steel swept down with incredible force, shattering Antonio's blade in his hand. His arm vibrated with the impact, but at least the broken sword had deflected Pedro's first swing.

The war sword reared up again.

Antonio tossed his useless hilt away, fell flat on the dirty floor, and rolled under the table. He cracked a shin on the legs of the bench, but the thick oak above his head stopped Pedro's blade.

For just a moment the sword was caught in the wood. Pedro pulled and Antonio slapped both hands against the underside of the table. He braced his feet and thrust up with desperate strength.

The table flew end-upward and crashed into Pedro, sending him sprawling back against the wall. But Pedro's sword was free, and Antonio's oaken shield was gone.

Antonio scampered back across the floor and stumbled over the metal cup that had held his wine. On his knees, he clutched at it, cursing.

Pedro advanced with his sword and a smile.

Teresa screamed.

"Thank you, lady," said Antonio. And he threw the cup.

Its heavy base caught Pedro above the right eye and he dropped without a groan.

Antonio leaned over his fallen adversary. The man was unconscious but still breathing. A trickle of blood ran into his eye.

"Thank God he's alive," whispered Antonio. He had never killed a man, much less in front of his daughters. He picked up Pedro's sword and, just for luck, the cup. His knees were shaking and the sword was almost too heavy for him to lift.

Breathing hard, he walked to the corner where Carlos Diaz stood with Pedro's daughters.

"He'll live," he told Teresa, and then he turned to Carlos.

"You," said Antonio. "Diego de Villanueva. Tell me. Where is he?"

Carlos looked at the sword and the blood-stained cup and tried to get behind Dolores.

"Ask for him at the Holy House. Two streets down. You'll find it with no trouble. The only great building that's not on the plaza. The Holy House."

"What sort of a place is that? Who is he?"

"You don't know him? He is the Grand Inquisitor!"

"Christ!" said Antonio. "The Inquisition? What sort of kinsman do I have here?"

"Kinsman?" echoed Carlos, but Antonio ignored him and turned toward the door. Teresa and Dolores rushed to their father's side.

Kneeling beside Pedro, Dolores shook him and called on him to wake up. Teresa only stood and stared at the young stranger dressed in a suit the color of the sky, who walked out of the inn with her father's sword in his hand.

Carlos Diaz could not have cared less about the sword, but this foreigner was leaving the Inn of the Golden Cup with some of the furnishings.

It took a moment for Carlos to swallow his fear, but then he rushed for the door. "Wait!" he cried. "If you please! The cup! You're taking my cup!"

Diego de Villanueva made his way toward the inn in a state of cold fury. Tomorrow was the day of the *auto-da-fé* and Pedro Rodriguez, who was indispensable, was missing. Diego had sent his vicar, Miguel, to look for Pedro, but the young idiot would never think to look in the obvious place, and it was not the role of the Grand Inquisitor to disillusion his underlings by informing them that a familiar of his august institution might spend his mornings drinking in a low tavern.

And so, to preserve decorum, the Grand Inquisitor must play errand boy. It was a curse to have such colleagues. His temper was not improved by the knowledge that the witch in the dungeons had yet to confess. His only hope lay with his brother Sebastian, a godless monster. Still, Sebastian might make Margarita talk tonight, and at least he would finish the book soon. But it was enough to make a man nervous.

As the Grand Inquisitor turned the corner he heard someone shouting, "The cup! The cup!"

It made no sense, but something in the word chilled him. He was reminded of something that Sebastian had told him but he could not quite remember it.

There was the inn, and in the doorway Carlos Diaz; the voice was his.

What caught Diego's attention, though, was the sight of a young man with dark curly hair and a neatly trimmed beard running along the edge of his jaw like a shadow. He sat astride a gray stallion and in his right hand held a sword. In his left hand was a cup dripping blood.

The Grand Inquisitor turned in his tracks. He had seen this man before. His picture was on one of the cards he had seen in the castle. Sebastian had warned him. The card was the Knight of Cups.

This was no time to stop at the inn. Diego knew it was nonsense, but something in the sight of this man had rattled him. He would return to the Holy House. Pedro would show up eventually.

The Grand Inquisitor hurried back along the dusty street to the Holy House, one hand lifting the hem of his white robe as a woman might lift her skirts. He was suddenly afraid to be alone in the streets, and his head was filled with stories of Inquisitors who had been assassinated. Behind him came the slow steps of a walking horse.

He turned and saw the stranger riding behind him. Torn between dignity and panic, Diego resisted the temptation to break into a run, but he was walking so quickly that he looked as if he were in some sort of grotesque race. He had no idea who the man in blue might be, but he could not forget the cards or Sebastian's mockery. Somehow the image of the rider with the cup was connected with the grinning skeleton and the angel of judgment: it was an omen.

There could be no doubt that the rider was following him. The worst of it was that the fellow moved at such a leisurely pace, for all the world as if he were a casual visitor admiring the sights of the city. Diego lost his nerve and bolted into a side street. He turned again, into an alley, and leaned gasping against the side wall of a small house, his feet resting in slop someone had thrown from a window. A pig, set loose to forage for garbage in the streets, stared up at him quizzically.

The maneuver was successful; at least, the man with the cup did not catch up with him. The Grand Inquisitor hid in the alley until pride overcame his anxiety. Then he peered timidly around the corner of the house. There was nobody to be seen.

He stepped out, assumed the pompous air suitable to a man in his position, and made his way to the Holy House.

Once inside, he was immediately accosted by Miguel, who was visibly agitated. The Grand Inquisitor attempted to brush him aside, but the young monk would not be denied.

"There is someone here to see you," said Miguel. "A stranger, a foreigner. His name is Antonio Manetti. I told him how busy we are, but he says he has come halfway across Europe to see you, and he has waited long enough. He seems to be a young man of breeding and says he is your kinsman. It hardly seems possible, but he says he is here to claim the estate of your brother Don Sebastian!"

Diego was too stunned to betray his emotions. He blinked once, but his face retained its customary bland expression. Inwardly he was reeling. An heir to Sebastian's castle! It was impossible! In a month or two it would not have mattered, for by then the book would be finished and Sebastian destroyed forever. But now! Nobody could be allowed near the castle until Sebastian's usefulness was at an end. Something would have to be done to keep this heir from his inheritance. It would be a pleasure to kill him, but it might not be prudent.

The Grand Inquisitor steeled himself. He would have to invent a story and devise delays to keep this interfering foreigner busy. Meanwhile, he would have to interview the fellow. Tomorrow's *auto-da-fé* would provide enough of an excuse to buy a little time.

It was not really a surprise, but it was no less of a shock for Diego de Villanueva when he entered his chambers. There, seated beneath a crucifix, was a dark young man dressed in blue, his hand still absent-mindedly clutching a battered metal cup.

8. The Goat

WE should arrest him at once!" said Pedro, pacing the floor of the Grand Inquisitor's chamber as if imprisoned himself.

"No," said the Grand Inquisitor.

"But how can we let him run free? He has attacked an officer of the Inquisition, your own familiar! What will the people think?" Pedro's weathered face was flushed with shame and anger. The purple bruise on his forehead was still clotted with dried blood. His huge hands gripped the edge of the table as he leaned heavily over the seated monk.

"There is nothing we can do, Pedro. His claim seems to be good. He may be only a distant cousin, but he is my kinsman. We cannot touch him."

"Well enough for you, Diego de Villanueva! He is part of your family, and you will not have your honor besmirched. But what of my honor?"

"You are right that family matters enter into this business, Pedro, but you must understand. He is related not only to me but to Sebastian—in fact, he is Sebastian's heir. If this young fellow becomes our prisoner, what will happen to his property?"

"His property?"

"Exactly, Pedro. We have seen often enough how wealthy men are condemned to enrich the royal coffers. If Antonio Manetti is taken prisoner, his inheritance will go to the Crown. And his inheritance is Sebastian's castle."

"The castle?"

"If we arrest Antonio, then the king's officers will be at the castle in a matter of days, and that must not happen, not yet. We will have to wait."

"I don't like it," said Pedro sullenly.

"Do you think I like it? Now, of all times! I don't know how we'll delay the transfer of property, but nothing must happen until the book has been completed and accepted by the authorities. Then there will be time enough to take care of this upstart and of Sebastian as well. But we must wait!"

"We could murder the rogue," Pedro suggested diplomatically.

"We dare not risk it," answered the Grand Inquisitor. "No one wants him dead more than I do, Pedro. He will be a terrible thorn in my side. But we must be patient and we must protect Sebastian. You will have to swallow your pride for a few weeks."

Pedro acquiesced. "He is stopping at the Inn of the Golden Cup," he said.

"I know," said the Grand Inquisitor. "I suggested that he should. At least there we will have Carlos Diaz to watch him and we may get some evidence that will be useful when we are ready to prosecute. Besides, there was no other place he could afford to stay. This lord of the castle has hardly a ducat to his name. But enough of Antonio Manetti. Tonight we must deal with the present lord of the castle."

"Don Sebastian?"

"He is coming. In fact, he should be here shortly. Sebastian will question the prisoner Margarita de Mendoza. She will be abandoned to the flames tomorrow, and Sebastian is our last chance to get a confession from her. You may leave now, Pedro, but first prepare the way for him."

Pedro turned silently and left the room, but he returned in a moment with an armful of the wooden crosses that decorated the halls of the Holy House. These he placed in an ornate chest, along with the crucifix Diego had removed from his own wall.

"Very well, Pedro," said the Grand Inquisitor. "Sleep well. We will have a busy day tomorrow."

Pedro stopped at the door. "You should be sleeping too," he said.

"Not tonight. There is too much to do. I will sleep tomorrow."

Pedro walked slowly through the dark, bare hallways and let himself out of the Holy House, leaving the door open behind him. The night was clear, but as he looked up he saw a shadow pass across the stars. He crossed himself. Something was soaring through the sky. He shuddered, shrugged, then trudged stolidly toward home.

A moment later Diego de Villanueva came to the darkened doorway and stood there waiting for his brother. If he was an eager host it was only because he was cautious. Visitors in the hours after midnight were best admitted quietly; a knock on the door of the Holy House might rouse a drowsy monk, and a corpse discovered standing on the threshold would be something of an embarrassment.

So the Grand Inquisitor kept his post like a common gatekeeper, peering eagerly into the darkness. His anxiety was half fear of Sebastian and half eagerness to see him. Diego's pulse raced but the minutes dragged; he was not fond of waiting. He gnawed nervously at his thumb, and his teeth caught a jagged bit of the nail. He pulled at it and ripped the piece away in a narrow strip that tore into the cuticle. He sucked in his breath at the sudden pain and stared at the bright drop of blood welling up in the self-inflicted wound.

As if in answer to a signal, Sebastian appeared in the doorway.

Diego started, and wiped his thumb surreptitiously on the

rough folds of his white robe. "You come quietly enough," he said. "Don't just stand there. You might be seen. Why don't you come in?"

"You know," said Sebastian.

"Ah, yes. Well, then, enter, Don Sebastian de Villanueva, and welcome to you."

Sebastian, wrapped in his red cloak, crossed the threshold.

"Follow me," said Diego, turning toward the gloomy shadows of the hall. "I can never understand that," he continued. "Is it really true that you cannot enter a building without an invitation?"

"You have seen," Sebastian replied, "but it need not be such a burden. Many mortals seem strangely eager for a visit from a vampire. We have ways of making ourselves welcome."

Diego turned at the door to his chambers. "But you really need to hear the words before you can take that single step? It seems impossible. Are you such a courteous creature?"

"There are only a few hours until dawn," said Sebastian, following his brother into the room where black candles burned. "Shall we spend them discussing my powers, or shall I question your witch?"

"You are right, of course," said Diego, "but I wonder at your sudden eagerness to see her as soon as I mention your weaknesses. You were in no such hurry when it came to getting here."

"I was writing, brother. I became so engrossed in a passage of your book that I forgot your invitation to dine. Whatever I do, though, it seems that I am working for you. I am more like a serf than the master of a castle."

"The castle. I have something to tell you about that," said Diego. "No, it will wait. We must hurry. Put this on, Sebastian." He handed his brother a Dominican white robe and black cowl.

"This disguise is more terrifying than anything I might hide beneath it," said Sebastian. "But I suppose it may serve to calm any wakeful monks abroad tonight in the Holy House."

"They should be asleep, Sebastian, and the guards have been dismissed. Yet the night before an *auto-da-fé* is a restless one, and there is nothing to be gained by taking a chance. No one must see you. Are you ready? Shall I go with you?"

"Stay here," said the voice from the black hood. "I will not have you spying on me. And I will know if you follow."

"So be it," said the Grand Inquisitor sullenly. He turned his back to the door and when he looked around a moment later saw he was alone. He dropped into his chair with a sigh and opened a book, but it rested unread in his lap. He sat quite still, his chin supported by his left hand, eyes fixed on the spot on the wall where the crucifix should have hung. And he waited.

Margarita waited too. She sat in the cold slime that covered the floor of her cell and stared into darkness as black as the robes of her jailers. Her wrists and ankles were bound together by short lengths of chain, with the shackles clamped to lacerations left by the rack. The torn muscles and tendons in her arms and legs ached intolerably. Her shoulders, wrenched by the hoist, were so painful that she could not lean back against the stone wall, and the soles of her feet were covered with burns and blisters.

The Grand Inquisitor waited for dawn, but Margarita waited for death. She had been told repeatedly that an *auto-da-fé* was approaching and that her continued silence would leave her tormentors no choice but to burn her alive. Just a few hours ago, as nearly as she could reckon, the Grand Inquisitor's vicar, Miguel Carillo, had slipped into her cell to warn her that she had only one night left to live.

She had almost been touched by his pleading, which seemed more compassionate than his master's august ultimatum. The young monk acted as if he might really be concerned with the state of her soul, not just with her secrets. He had actually gone down on his knees in the filth at her feet and begged her to confess and be reconciled. She had begun to believe he was sincere, but then she remembered how calmly he had sat beside her, transcribing every scream and curse evoked by the turning of the rack, and the thought had made her scream again, this time in fury.

At that he had hurried from the dungeons, leaving her alone with the knowledge that the next voice she heard would summon her to die. She almost longed for it. She certainly would not betray the others in the coven to spare herself, but she dreaded the coming day. Her cell was always dark, so there was no way to tell if it was night or morning. Her heart staggered at any sound, for it might be summoning her to the flames, but the only noises were the scurrying of rats. There would be another sound soon, though, and her ears strained for it.

"Margarita!"

It was no more than a whisper, but she jumped when she heard it, and the links of her chains rattled. Her eyes searched through the darkness for the source of the voice, but it was impossible to see anything. There was nothing more to hear. Her suddenly tensed limbs began to relax again as she decided that the voice must have come from her own mind, but then it spoke again.

"Margarita!"

She was tempted to answer, but she reasoned that this must be another device of the Inquisition, so she kept her peace and only peered anxiously into the impenetrable gloom.

There was something in her cell—a faint glow, a spot of dull red that floated above her head. It grew brighter as she watched, then burst into flame. The sudden light blinded her and she threw an arm up to shield her eyes. When she lowered it a moment later she could see a burning torch and then the man holding it. His face was hidden by the folds of a black cowl, the top of which touched the dripping ceiling.

It was only reasonable to assume that he had come to guide her to her death, but his manner of entering made her wonder. She had never seen anything like it before, at least not in the Holy House. It was almost like magic.

"Do you know me?" he asked, thrusting the torch into a bracket on the wall.

His voice was deep, and cold enough to belong to an Inquisitor, but it did not sound like anyone who had questioned her before. Yet there was something vaguely familiar about it; even as she shook her head in reply to his question, she realized she had heard him speak before. But where? She tried to see his face, but it was hidden in shadows and folds of black cloth.

"If you do not know me, do you know at least that you are to die tomorrow?"

Margarita nodded. It was easier not to speak; her throat was still sore from the strips of linen she had been forced to swallow during the water torture. She was surprised to find herself answering the stranger at all.

"Would you bring more suffering upon yourself? Can you imagine the agony of the flames? Will you not accept the mercy of the Inquisition?" His questions rang hollowly in the confines of the narrow cell. "Your confession could buy you much, Margarita: more days of questions, more nights in the dungeons, and finally a rope to strangle you at the stake before your clothes catch fire. Will you refuse such blessings? And why? To prove your hatred for the men who hold you captive? To protect the naked wretches who danced beside you in the moonlight? To keep your promise to the Prince of Lies?"

Margarita's bewildered green eyes stared upward at the face she could not see. Something was wrong with these questions. They reflected her own thoughts too well, and that worried her more than the threats and arguments of the Grand Inquisitor.

"Who are you?" The words choked in her swollen throat. "What do you want of me?"

"I wanted to see you again, Margarita. You are foolish to be so brave, but it is bravery nonetheless."

"What else could I do?" she replied. "You have said it all yourself. I know your voice."

"And you know my face," said Sebastian. "This face, at least."

He pulled back the black cowl.

Whatever Margarita had expected to see, it was not what Sebastian showed her: flaring nostrils in a long gray muzzle, sorrowful brown eyes, and two long, sharp horns—the head of a goat.

She gasped, and her quick painful intake of breath turned to hysterical laughter. She crawled on twisted limbs toward the thing in monk's robes and embraced its legs. "The master," she whispered, and began to weep.

Fingers cold and hard as iron clutched at her shoulders and pulled Margarita to her feet. She fell against Sebastian and felt his arms engulf her. The rough goat's hair brushed against her face as her head rested on his shoulder, and she inhaled the rich animal smell of him gratefully.

"You have come to save me," she said. It was not a question.

Then he held her at arm's length, and her mind reeled to see that his face had changed. He now had the head of a man and a gaunt pale face with sunken eyes. Black hair draped it, and a long mustache hung below the bony chin. It was the face of a corpse.

"Who are you?" Margarita asked again, panic in her voice. "Are you the master?"

"I am Don Sebastian de Villanueva."

"Don Sebastian? The brother of the Grand Inquisitor?"

"Even so, Margarita. And I am not here to rescue you. Rather you are here to rescue me. A witch should recognize the signs, my brave and beautiful Margarita. I am one of the undead and I have come for your blood."

Margarita stumbled backward out of his arms. "Satan!" she cried. "Am I betrayed again?" Her voice rose to a scream and her body was convulsed by sobs. "Then take my blood and welcome to it, for after this night I have no need of it!"

She threw back her head, exposing her long white throat like a sacrificial victim eager to be slaughtered. Sebastian's sluggish heartbeat quickened at the sight. He cast aside the monk's robe that disguised him and moved forward. As he glided toward her, his lips drew back in a bestial snarl, exposing his long ivory teeth, the canines sharp as swords.

Margarita's outspread arms reached to clasp him as he touched her, and she drew him closer as his cold lips sought her jugular. His teeth cut the warm flesh, and he felt the hot, salty blood rush into his mouth. She gave a little cry, half pain and half ecstasy. He felt her throat move under his lips. She grew limp beneath him and began to slide down the rough stone wall to the floor. Sebastian followed her, his arms supporting her weight, his eager mouth still fixed to the flowing wound, until they were on their knees together, almost like children at play. His white fingers tangled her long black hair; hers clutched and twisted his crimson cloak.

The torch above them sputtered; its flame sank into a ruddy glow, and then went out. There were small soft sounds in the darkness; they might have been kisses.

The Grand Inquisitor dozed in his chair. He had slipped into a nervous sleep in spite of himself. He had worked hard and he was tired. His dreams were vague but not pleasant; something in them startled him so that he suddenly sat bolt upright. His brother stood before him.

"Sebastian," he said. It took a moment for him to remember where he was. The first thing he realized was how much his brother had changed. Sebastian looked years younger, more like the soldier who had fought the Moors than the wizard who brooded alone in the tallest tower of an empty castle. He seemed taller and stronger. His face was flushed and the hollows around his dark eyes had disappeared, but the pale scar of the wound that had killed him was as vivid as ever. Diego had seen this transformation before, but something about it never failed to sicken him. He fought off his nausea and drowsiness.

"Well, Sebastian?" he said. "Well? I see you have supped—what else have you done?"

"Nothing, brother. I have failed you. She would not speak. I fear she will never speak."

"What? You haven't killed her?"

"No. She sleeps below. I leave her killing to you."

Diego sighed and rubbed his hand across his eyes. "I knew you would disappoint me. She is a stubborn wench. There is no way of understanding how she could resist everything."

"If you believe in witchcraft, brother, you must believe that witches have powers. Perhaps she has some trick that renders her insensible to pain. A simple trance would suffice. Surely she employed some power to defy you, Diego, for you have used her cruelly."

The Grand Inquisitor rose from his chair. "Do you dare reproach me, Sebastian? You, who still have her blood on your lips?"

Sebastian scowled. "I do what I must to survive, brother. But your work is past all understanding." His mouth twisted. "Keep away from the castle."

"But Sebastian! The book!"

"The work will continue. But for now, I have no wish to look upon your face."

"As you will, Sebastian." The Grand Inquisitor edged toward the door. "The sun will rise soon. You must leave at once."

Sebastian did not move. "There is one thing more," he said. "Margarita gave me a message for you."

"A message!" gasped the Grand Inquisitor. "What is it? Have you been fooling me? Is it a confession?"

"No, brother. Not a confession, only this."

Sebastian's hand lashed out with stunning speed and the back of it struck his brother full in the face.

Diego staggered from the blow, but he stayed on his feet. His hand flew up to his cheek. He stood in shocked silence as Sebastian vanished into the shadows of the hallway. Blood trickled from the corner of the Grand Inquisitor's mouth.

On the floor beside Diego's chair was a black-and-white Dominican habit. Someone had ripped it into shreds, and the pieces were spattered with fresh blood.

9. The Yellow Robe

THE bells woke Miguel at dawn. He sat up slowly and perched on the edge of his hard wooden cot, his bare feet dangling in the dried rushes that covered the cold stone floor. Hunched over with his head in his hands, he regarded the blank wall of his narrow room with bleary eyes and no affection.

"Too many bells," he muttered. They rang four times a day to summon the monks to services: at dawn, noon, dusk, and even at midnight, when everyone was asleep, so that he was awakened twice every twenty-four hours by their insistent pealing. Their sound, which had once seemed a hymn of praise, was now oppressive.

He steeled himself for another day of cruel monotony, then remembered with a queasy thrill that this morning would bring something different—the *auto-da-fé*. This day would be filled with pomp, processions, and preaching. It would be a spectacle and a celebration and would end with flaming death.

One of those to die would be Margarita de Mendoza. Perhaps then his dreams would stop. A few good nights of sleep might make his life more tolerable.

Miguel stood up to pull his rough robe over his head. As he tied the length of hemp around his waist he felt his stomach growl ominously, and he cursed under his breath at the thought that there was no breakfast in store for him, since the monks never ate until after High Mass at noon. What was worse, Miguel suddenly realized that today's special ceremonies would make even that meal impossible, so that he would have to go hungry until nightfall.

Still, there was nothing to be done about it. He stepped through the small, doorless archway and into the corridor beyond. At once he saw the Grand Inquisitor striding down the hall toward him, with Pedro close behind. Pedro was already dressed in the ceremonial garments the *auto-da-fé* demanded: a black suit with a white cross emblazoned on the chest to signify that he was a familiar of the Holy Inquisition. Pedro's face was clean and his beard combed, but his eyes were bloodshot and there was a purple bruise with a brown scab on the right side of his forehead.

Miguel bowed his head and tried to hurry by, but the Grand Inquisitor stopped him with a gesture. "Wait," he said. "We will dispense with your presence at the morning Mass, Miguel. There is too much to be done. Go with Pedro. He needs your help with the preparations. Here are your records." Miguel had time only for a glance at his superior, but he noticed that he seemed to have cut his lip. Then the Grand Inquisitor turned away, leaving Miguel alone with the grim giant in black.

"Come on," said Pedro, and led Miguel to a chamber where half a dozen monks and familiars stood silently waiting for instructions. In this storeroom were the trappings that made the *auto-da-fé* such a spectacle.

Above everything loomed the green cross, the emblem of the Inquisition. It was propped in a corner of the ceiling, held in place by a pole some ten feet long so it would rise above the heads of men and horses when carried in the procession that was to come. The cross itself looked rough and unfinished. It had not been smoothed and planed but seemed rather to have been fashioned from two rudely hewn logs of fresh wood symbolizing the living faith. In truth, though, it was dead wood painted green. One of the monks pulled it down and began to drape it in black velvet.

Another opened a chest and drew forth the banner of the Inquisition. It displayed an oblong field upon a black background, with the green cross in the center growing between an olive branch and a sword aimed toward Heaven. Inscribed around the oval was the legend "Exurge Domine et Judica Causam Tuam, Psalm 73." The monk attached the banner to a pole while one familiar took from another chest what looked like a pile of yellow cloth. Miguel knew it was dozens of sanbenitos, the garments of shame that heretics wore to meet their punishment.

What drew his eye, though, was something more grotesque than any of these ceremonial objects—a group of ugly half-human figures huddled together in a dark corner. They were brittle and brown, their eyes black blots in empty faces. These were straw men, the effigies of those who had escaped the Inquisition, to be draped in yellow robes, carried through the jeering throngs, and finally burned at the stake along with the living bodies of those who had not fled in time.

But there was something worse, something Miguel had hoped he would not see. Stacked beside the sinners built of straw were three wooden boxes, each long and wide enough to hold a human body. Each box, covered with dirt and mold, had a name scrawled on its side in charcoal. These were coffins ripped from graves so that the corpses could be borne aloft to the flames. Not even death brought an end to the judgments of the Inquisition, and those whose heresies were discovered too late still merited posthumous punishment. Miguel knew this but had hoped to be spared the sight of those grinning, yellow-clad skeletons during the first *auto-da-fé* at which he was to officiate. He prayed that at least these newly uncovered heretics were long dead, so they would be no more than skeletons.

Miguel stared blankly into the dark corner and from far away heard the faint sound of hammering. "What is that noise?" he asked suddenly.

"The carpenters," answered Pedro, "putting up the scaffolds and benches for the *auto*."

"What? Are they still at work? They should have been done long ago. And nothing is ready here, either. We shall be late!"

"Calm yourself," said Pedro. "This is not Madrid, where there are so many heretics that the ceremonies take up the whole day. We have plenty of time."

"But we must be finished by dark," Miguel protested. "The people are always so excited by the end of the ceremonies, and we must not have an act of faith turned into an occasion for a night of revelry."

"They are excited by the flames, you mean," said Pedro. "Never fear, though; we should be done by dusk, with time enough to send them home before darkness falls. Anyway, the Grand Inquisitor has ordered a late start today."

"Why should he do that?" asked Miguel. The idea of a break with tradition worried him. In Madrid, the *auto-da-fé* always began at dawn.

"Politics," said Pedro. "Or something like it. You know that the parish priest always delivers the sermon at the *auto*? Well, today he will not. The Grand Inquisitor has reserved that honor for himself. Something to do with the witch, I think. He wants to speak to the people about witches. So the good priest has had his feathers ruffled, and he complained. Of course, he could hardly defy the Inquisition—he is only a priest—but the Grand Inquisitor decided on a compromise. Since it is a Sunday anyway, he declared that a High Mass be held as usual, where the priest may speak to his heart's content. When he dismisses his congregation, the *auto* will begin."

"I see," said Miguel, but he was not pleased by these irregularities.

"No matter whether you see or not," said Pedro sharply. "All this talk wastes the same time you're so worried about. Where are your records? How many have we today?"

Miguel fumbled with papers. "Thirty-seven in all," he said.

"Three of them dead already," said Pedro. "You there!" he

shouted to a pair of the familiars. "Break open those boxes, and dress the dead ones in their golden gowns." He smiled at his pleasantry.

Miguel turned his head away as the black-clad familiars attacked the coffins with crowbars, but he could not block out the sound of tearing wood, or the sudden musty odor that filled the room. He heard the clatter of bones as they spilled onto the stone floor.

"Careful with those!" Pedro shouted.

"Three dead," said Miguel. He was almost shouting himself, as if trying to drown out noises he had no wish to hear. "Three dead. Seven fled, that is, seven contumaciously absent, to be burned in effigy. Twenty-seven living, of which four are impenitent and one relapsed. These five will be abandoned to the secular authorities."

"Five to be burned alive!" shouted Pedro to the familiar who held the yellow robes. He began to sort through them for those bearing the markings that indicated that the prisoner was condemned to death.

"No! Wait!" said Miguel. "The relapsed heretic has repented."

"Oh, yes," muttered Pedro, "the old woman." He turned again to the man with the sanbenitos. "Four to be burned alive and one to be strangled before burning!"

Miguel winced. He hated to hear the judgments of the Inquisition bawled out as if they were orders for goods in the marketplace. He watched the man in black lay out the yellow robes, covered with crude drawings in red paint of dancing devils and bursts of fire. On four of the robes the flames pointed upward, but on the fifth they pointed down, a sign for the executioner that he should use his strangling cord before applying the torch.

"Of the twenty-two remaining . . ." began Miguel, as he heard the nails ripping from the half-rotten wood of the third coffin. In spite of himself he turned to look. The two familiars, white crosses emblazoned on their black doublets, dragged two withered arms from the shattered wood. A stench of decay seeped into the room.

"Christ!" said one of the familiars. "This one is too fresh!"

"Not fresh enough!" said his companion, his face set in a grimace of disgust. He pulled again and a face emerged from the splintered box. Withered and brown and eyeless, it looked like one of the effigies, but it had been a man.

"Of the twenty-two remaining!" shouted Miguel. His stomach lurched.

"What a stink!"

"Get that thing on him before he falls apart!"

Miguel turned away from the sight of three men attempting to dress the rotting corpse. "Of the twenty-two remaining," he repeated, "six are lightly suspected, seven are gravely suspected, and nine . . ."

"Hold on a minute! Which is the one for the gravely suspected?"

"Fools!" bellowed Pedro. "The plain yellow for the lightly, the ones with half a cross on them for the gravely, and the whole cross for the violently suspected!"

"Six are lightly suspected!" screamed Miguel. "Seven are gravely suspected! And nine are violently suspected!"

He was grateful now that there had been no breakfast.

"The roll of those to be abandoned!" he continued, keeping his eyes on the paper. "One Margarita de Mendoza, shepherdess, of this parish, impenitent, guilty of witchcraft and sorcery . . ."

By the time the monks came to take her away, Margarita was past caring. Her mind was cloudy and she could hardly think. She saw clearly enough what was happening to her, but she did not seem to be a part of it. The voices around her were dim and distant, the men who dragged her to her feet only moving shadows. They were almost carrying her, since her twisted legs and blistered feet could hardly bear her weight.

"I will never walk again," she thought, and a voice in the

back of her brain laughed at the idea. Of course she would never walk again—she would be dead by sunset. What did it matter if she had been crippled?

Nothing mattered but the throbbing where Sebastian had kissed her throat. Had he betrayed her? Why had he come? He had whispered to her in the darkness, but the memory of the words drifted away. Something about the sunset, but she would be dead by then. She could not remember, but she had been drugged by his kiss and would not suffer. For that at least she was grateful. His voice still rang in her ears, but all he seemed to be saying was her name: "Margarita. Margarita. Margarita."

It was only a whisper, perhaps only the memory of a whisper, and yet was more. He was somehow still with her and she with him, in a place that was small and cold and dark, yet somehow vast and radiant with silver.

"Margarita," he said. Then a voice spoke again. "You did not betray me."

But was it his voice or hers?

All at once the dimness of the dungeons vanished and the world turned bright as day. The yellow light was almost blinding, but she saw devils dancing in it.

Miguel sighed and lowered the yellow robe. The woman must have gone completely mad. Even when he held the sanbenito before her eyes, she did not respond. Everyone in Spain knew the emblem of infamy, and surely the demons and the flames emblazoned upon the robe were plain enough, but Margarita only looked at them and smiled.

"Cover her," said Miguel to one of the familiars. Her shift was so torn and frayed that she might as well have been naked, but the sanbenito would remedy that. Miguel turned to the next prisoner.

When the devils dropped away from her eyes, Margarita had a brief glimpse of a sunny courtyard full of people. Then something dropped over her head and she was plunged back into darkness.

"Margarita," said the voice.

Hands pulled at her and she squirmed, then her head popped through an opening and she could see again. She realized that someone was dressing her, which had not happened to her since she was a child in her father's house.

There was a man beside her who looked like her father. She tried to focus her eyes.

"Is it you?" she asked him. "Are you here too?"

The man turned to face her but did not answer. There was no need to; it was another old man. But he had the same white hair and flowing beard, same strong nose and sad brown eyes. He tried to smile at her, but his thin lips only twitched.

The devils were all over him, all over the long yellow robe pulled over his head like a poncho. Margarita looked down and saw the same red demons dancing on her breast. She realized all at once that she was wearing the sanbenito, as was the man beside her. She glanced around and saw dozens of the yellow robes, some like hers, some marked with crosses, some with no insignia at all. Scurrying among the robes were others, dressed in black suits with white crosses on the front. There were Dominicans, too, with their white cassocks and black hoods and black cloaks trailing behind them. She recognized one of them, the frail young monk who was always writing. There were others she had seen in the dungeons, but the Grand Inquisitor was not among them.

The men in black and white bustled about like characters in a play, but the people in the yellow robes were strangely still. None of it seemed real. Seeking out others like herself, Margarita found four whose sanbenitos bore the same markings: the old man who looked like her father, two younger men who might have been brothers, and an old woman who stood in a corner crying and looked very odd. She was certainly plump, almost fat, but her face was drawn and thin as if she had been starved. She has no trouble standing, thought Margarita; she must have given in almost at once.

So we are the five who will burn, said Margarita to herself. She closed her eyes against the morning sun and listened for the darkness. Someone whispered her name.

Someone grabbed her by the throat. She opened her eyes and recognized the giant who had arrested her. She had not seen him since that night, but she remembered him. As he tied a rope around her neck its rough surface scraped against the small wounds in her throat. The other end of the rope bound her hands together in front of her. As he tied the last knot tightly, the man with the gray beard and black suit grinned at her. "More fuel for the fires. What a waste." Then he was gone.

A monk came by and thrust a huge green candle into her hands. She tried to drop it, but he laced her hands together with a piece of cord.

Monks stood on either side of her, urging her to repent while there was still a chance, but she hardly heard them. She was listening for another voice.

A man in black led a string of mules into the courtyard and someone lit the green candle.

10. The Green Cross

ANTONIO stepped out of the dim shadows of the cathedral and down the marble steps to the sunny plaza below. The crowd flowed around him, moving with what he took to be unseemly haste, though he had to admit that the service had been all but endless. Indeed, he might have been tempted to forego the Mass if he had known just how interminable it would prove to be; but he was a pious man, up to a point, and would have been a madman to act anything less than devout while a stranger in Spain.

But how the priest had raved! He had shouted and whispered, threatened and cajoled, smiled and wept, and his sermon alone had lasted well over an hour. Antonio had distracted himself by admiring the rich interior of the cathedral, the first halfway-impressive building he had seen since entering Spain, though it was nothing compared with the glories of Rome or even Florence. In all fairness he acknowledged that this was not one of Spain's great cities, but it was the city where he was forced to stay, a fact that had begun to disturb him.

He hoped that the castle of Don Sebastian de Villanueva was worth his journey and certainly wished that somebody would help him find out. So far he had discovered almost nothing except that this was a city where a man could end up fighting for his life in the very hour of his arrival, an intelligence that had been anything but reassuring. Antonio's kinsman, Diego de Villanueva, had taken great pains to assure him that the quarrel with Pedro Rodriguez had been based on a misunderstanding and would not be repeated, but beyond that the tall, grim-faced monk had been irritatingly incommunicative. He had lapsed into Latin, which Antonio understood little better than Spanish, and had conveyed nothing more than the advice to be patient, along with some half-intelligible remarks about some imminent event that rendered further discussion impossible. No doubt it was a monkish sort of failing to speak dead languages, but Antonio had found it a most unsatisfactory interview.

At least he was happy to be free of Pedro Rodriguez. Antonio had seen Pedro's daughters at the Mass sitting almost directly below the pulpit, but they had not acknowledged his presence, and indeed he had no reason to think they were aware of it. He doubted that it mattered much, after the incident at the inn yesterday, and cursed his bad luck. Teresa was the prettiest girl he had seen yet in the city and he had taken a strange fancy to her, even though they had not exchanged a word. And now they probably never would. Why did women have to have fathers?

Antonio had descended the steps of the cathedral lost in thought, but when he raised his eyes to look at the plaza he was astounded. During the few hours he had spent at Mass, the public square had been transformed into some sort of amphitheater, although no one but Antonio seemed surprised to see it. A gigantic wooden platform had been erected forming three sides of a square, and tiers of benches rose from it. Pulpits, altars, and lecterns stood in the center of the square, along with a small structure that looked unpleasantly like an empty cage. Dominican monks were hurriedly draping everything in black cloth.

Something in the appearance of these friars disturbed Antonio. Monks were common enough; in fact, the man who had told Antonio about his inheritance had been a Dominican in Florence, who had seemed perfectly friendly, even genuinely pleased to be the bearer of good tidings. But these men were different. Perhaps there was nothing more to his feeling about them than the discomfort he had experienced in the presence of his kinsman the Grand Inquisitor, but after all, the Dominicans here were the officers of the Inquisition, and their reputation had cast a chill over all of Europe.

He realized now what sort of pageant was being prepared here. He had heard talk of it last night and this morning, but everyone spoke Spanish, and so rapidly that he had hardly known what they were saying. Now he understood without being told. He was about to witness an *auto-da-fé*.

Reluctantly he admitted to himself that his curiosity was stronger than his indignation; he would stay and watch. At least it would be something to tell his friends about when he was home again, he thought, then realized with a chill that this city was to be his new home. If all went well, he might be here for years, or never see Florence again. He looked at the busy friars so eagerly covering their world with black crepe. What was he doing here in this bleak country?

He wandered off the plaza for a moment; there was nothing happening yet to keep him there. He was thinking of food and believed he was going in the direction of his inn, but realized his mistake almost at once. He had turned into the wrong street and was about to retrace his steps when he smelled something that stopped him. There was a little stall built on to one of the houses here. A scrawny old woman stood behind a counter on which were several small, steaming pies. Antonio watched a ragged man purchase two and walk away munching one with every evidence of enthusiasm. He decided to follow suit. The transaction was quickly accomplished, but he was startled and a bit disturbed when the old woman slammed the shutters in his face and closed up shop a second after serving him. She must be off to see the show, thought Antonio, as he wandered back toward the square.

The pie was too hot to eat, too hot even to hold, and he was forced to toss it back and forth between his hands to avoid burning his fingers, even though he felt a bit of a buffoon.

"Are you going to eat that thing?"

Antonio looked up from his cooling dinner and saw Dolores Rodriguez, Teresa's little sister. "What?" he said.

"The empanadilla!" she said. "Are you going to eat it?"

"What did you call it?" asked Antonio. "Of course I am. What else would I do with it?" Matching the word to the deed, he bit into the tough crust, which was yellow in the center and burned on the edges. A spicy sauce that dribbled down his chin was so hot that tears sprang into his eyes. At least there seemed to be some sort of meat in it, but the seasonings masked the flavor completely. "It's very good," he said.

"It's terrible," said Dolores. "Nobody but a fool would eat one. They say the public executioner provides the meat for those things."

Antonio's mouth dropped open and the pie fell out of his hand into the dust. "What?" he said again.

"It's only a joke," said Dolores. "At least I think it is. But they're made from bad meat, covered with spices so you can't taste it. Everyone knows it. You're lucky you dropped it."

Antonio kicked at the dusty pie.

"You're funny," said Dolores. "Why are you here?"

"Why, to see the *auto-da-fé,* like everyone else."

"That's not what I mean, stupid. Why are you here at all?"

"Oh, well, I am an heir. I have come to take possession of my castle."

"You? A castle?"

"Me," said Antonio, but he couldn't help smiling. The idea struck him as unlikely, too. "It was the castle of Don Sebastian de Villanueva, but now it will be mine."

Dolores looked up at him quizzically. "It hardly seems possible," she said. "You, a relative of the Grand Inquisitor!"

"Only a distant cousin of some kind," said Antonio, not sure whether to be proud or ashamed.

"You should have seen his brother, Don Sebastian," said Dolores. "He was a hero. I think I saw him once when I was a little girl."

"And what are you now?"

"I'm thirteen, stupid! I'm not a little girl anymore."

Antonio, who was twenty-two, allowed himself a condescending smile.

They were just on the edge of the plaza, but it was filling with people: not just the congregation of the cathedral on the square, but the parishioners from two other churches in different parts of the city. Dolores turned to look at the crowd. "Here comes my sister," she said. "I've been hiding from her. She's stupid, too. I think she likes you."

"What?" said Antonio, wishing fervently for something else to say. "Even after what happened yesterday?"

"You mean because you hit our father? That doesn't matter. He hits us all the time. He deserves it. But nobody ever hit him before."

Teresa broke through the mob and put both her arms around Dolores. "Where have you been, Dolores?" she said. "Father would kill both of us if you were running loose, today of all days."

"Good day, señorita," said Antonio, doffing his hat and bowing low. "Your sister has been safe here with me."

Dolores squirmed indignantly in her older sister's grasp. "Come on, you," said Teresa. She took her little sister firmly by the hand and led her into the throng. Just before she was gone, though, she turned to Antonio and smiled. "Thank you, sir, for looking after the little one."

She vanished into the crowd while Antonio stood and grinned, looking at the summer sky. "I think she likes you," he quoted. In his exhilaration he kicked the pie so hard that it stuck to the nearest wall.

From somewhere in the distance he heard a drum beating. He craned his neck, but it was impossible to see anything from where he stood, so he began to press his way into the mob that stood between him and the center of the plaza.

He found that his knees and elbows were more effective than

apologies, but he did not make any real progress until the people around him began, one by one, to drop to their knees. Trumpets sounded a melancholy fanfare.

With everyone kneeling, Antonio had a clear view of the plaza. It was still empty; in fact, even the monks who had worked there were gone. The platforms and benches stood starkly in the brilliant sun of a summer noon, waiting like the setting of a play that was about to begin. Several of those nearest at hand were glaring indignantly at Antonio, who suddenly realized how conspicuous he was as the only standing man among hundreds—or was it thousands? Everywhere around the platforms were multitudes of men, women, and children on their knees. Antonio hurriedly joined their number. By now he was close enough for a good look at the grotesque procession that marched ponderously into the public square.

First came the drummer, beating a slow dirge on the taut skin of the low-sounding instrument that hung from his stooped shoulders. Behind him were three trumpeters blowing minor chords. These, merely heralds, dispersed into the crowd as the procession proper came into view.

A Dominican strode into the square, bearing on a long pole above his head the green cross of the Inquisition. Sable drapings fluttered from its branches, moved not by the breeze but by the exertions of the laboring monk who sweated in the still summer air.

Following the friar was a platoon of familiars, grim men who marched with military pride, each with a white cross on his suit of shining black. At their head walked Pedro Rodriguez, eyes gleaming, his battered face thrust out and upward toward the yellow sun.

Behind the familiars came a monk ringing a bell. The people murmured at the sight of him and many crossed themselves. His bell signaled the arrival of the parish priest, who entered the plaza on a mule. Four acolytes surrounded him; above his head they bore a canopy of red and gold. The priest might not deliver the sermon at this particular *auto-da-fé*, but he had no intention of relinquishing his ceremonial position in the parade. Another company of familiars, lesser men than the first, perhaps, but no less conscious of their own dignity, followed him.

Then came the prisoners, who moved in ranks according to their depth of infamy. The twenty-two who were spared at least the ultimate punishment stumbled along, tripping over their long yellow robes, all marked to indicate the degree of their disgrace. Some wore the plain sanbenito; others were marked with half a cross, and still others wore the cross complete. But all hung their heads in shame, and on each head was the final mark of shame, the pointed yellow cap called a coroza. In each pair of hands, tied together, was a flaming green candle. The ropes that held the candles in place ran back to encircle the necks of the heretics.

At the sight of the prisoners a shout went up from the mob. People leaped to their feet to shout insults and curses. A barrage of fruit, vegetables, and even stones rained down upon the helpless heretics.

Antonio looked on in horror lessened only by the relief he felt as his knees came up off the hard flagstones. It was good at least to be standing again, and in any case there was nothing he could do about what was happening, so he determined to be philosophical.

A second group of prisoners entered the plaza. Their robes, covered with demons and flames, showed that they were bound for a fiery death. Antonio did not recognize the meaning of the insignia, but even he could tell that these were special cases. They each rode on mules between two monks, if only because they could not walk after their stay in the Holy House. These monks, starkly black and white beside the red and yellow of their charges, spoke continually to the prisoners, with fervent gestures that might have been for the benefit of their audience. Everyone but Antonio knew that they were urging the heretics to repent even now and exchange the agony of the flames for the mercy of the strangler's noose.

Surrounding the monks and their prisoners were a number of armed guards who bore on their shoulders long, lethal halberds, weapons that combined the deadliest features of spear and battle-ax. They were well designed to discourage any vain attempt to escape the justice of the Inquisition. Some that had been polished gleamed in the sun.

There were only five condemned to death in this small city on this one Sunday, out of the thousands who died for the glory of the Inquisition and in the name of Christ. The crowd was more subdued in the presence of these heretics, not perhaps because of pity but because it was impossible to throw anything without the risk of hitting a monk or a soldier. The citizens might have even been worried about the danger of striking an innocent mule.

Antonio's gaze was drawn to one in particular among these five prisoners. This was a young woman distinguished not only by her haggard beauty but by the way her lips twisted in a vague, vacant smile. He could hardly bear to look upon her but could not bring himself to look away. Her face was pale, her downcast eyes green, and her tangled hair black as a raven's wing. There were white streaks in it, though, flowing down from her forehead like lightning in a stormy sky. She was almost as pretty as Teresa, Antonio thought, but in a very different way. And she was doomed to die.

She was the last of the heretics, or so it seemed, for after her came a collection of friars bearing more long poles. From these seven poles dangled hideous effigies of straw, their painted eyes staring blankly at the multitude, their withered bodies encased in yellow robes. Upon these the mob vented its greatest fury and the air was black with missiles. A large rock broke the neck of one of the straw men. Its head sagged and its pointed cap dropped to the ground.

The three monks who followed bore a more ghastly burden. Suspended above their heads was a trio of yellow-clad corpses. Antonio could hardly believe his eyes. He strained to see in hopes he had imagined the sight, then wished he had not looked. Two of the three were skeletons, but the last was unspeakable.

Behind it rode his kinsman, Diego de Villanueva, the Grand Inquisitor. Before him was a banner bearing the arms of the Inquisition, with the arms of Ferdinand and Isabella on its other side. The Grand Inquisitor, mounted on a handsome mare, stared sternly ahead at the banner, looking to neither right nor left. His aristocratic features were composed and he seemed lost in some profound meditation, utterly oblivious to the grim relics that swayed above his shaven head. At his entrance the crowd grew still. His appearance climaxed the procession, but a few monks, the most prominent officers of the local Inquisition, rode behind him.

Among them Antonio recognized the young friar, Miguel Carillo, who had admitted him into the Holy House. Antonio was aghast at the thought that Miguel, certainly no older than he was, appeared to have such an important position in the councils of the terrible Inquisition. What sort of young man could he be?

The parade concluded with a group of civilians, the secular authorities to whom the Grand Inquisitor would abandon the condemned with pleas that the law be merciful. Lest there be any doubt about the sincerity of these beseechings, the last man in the procession was the public executioner.

There was a moment of confusion as all these people and animals were massed into the open-ended square formed by the three platforms, but order came quickly out of chaos. The prisoners were hurried into the benches in the platform on the right, and city officials and some prominent citizens took their places in the benches on the left. The Grand Inquisitor, along with his entourage of monks and familiars, took his seat on the central platform. The green cross and the banner of the Inquisition were planted in small stands before him, with the effigies and dead heretics placed beside the benches where the prisoners huddled between monks still urging them to repent. Those who were to die sat on the topmost bench where everyone could have a good view of them.

Finally all were seated and the little parish priest hurried out from a corner and began to celebrate the Mass. Bells rang, incense rose, and sorrowful chanting filled the square. The people stood or kneeled together as the occasion demanded, and when they crossed themselves in unison a great rustling echoed through the plaza. Antonio followed suit, bristling a little at the idea of two Masses in as many hours but hardly being rash enough to ignore the ceremony. His sidelong glances showed him that the crowd was taking only a perfunctory interest in this phase of the *auto-da-fé* and that they, too, were waiting for its conclusion. At last it was over and the priest left the altar, where six black candles burned.

The mob stirred. Antonio looked around for Teresa and Dolores, who were nowhere to be seen, though he felt sure they must be among the spectators. Their father was visible enough; seated high on the central benches near the Grand Inquisitor he seemed to stare straight at Antonio, who felt uncomfortably conspicuous in his sky blue suit. As the people in the crowd began to mill around nervously, Antonio took the opportunity to step back a few paces.

He felt a bit safer now that he was no longer in the front ranks of the spectators but began to regret his position almost at once, when the murmurs of the crowd and his own partially obscured view informed him that the Grand Inquisitor was approaching the pulpit.

Antonio hardly knew what to think. He was a little proud, perhaps, that his relative should be such a great and powerful man, but at the same time he was sickened and ashamed to see his kinsman presiding over such a spectacle. At least there would be a chance to hear him at his best.

The Grand Inquisitor waited with stoical patience until the plaza was completely silent. The afternoon sun blazed down on his shining head as he glanced down at the papers placed before him. He looked to right and left, then raised both arms above his head and began to speak.

Diego de Villanueva looked on the sea of faces rolling around him and was pleased. There was a substantial crowd, which was good, but then again the crowd was always good. Few indeed were bold enough to stay away from an *auto*, whatever the excuse. The whole city was there, and the Grand Inquisitor knew that somewhere in their number were a dozen witches. He had to find them.

He began his sermon mechanically, reciting the formulas that began every *auto-da-fé* while his eyes scanned the upturned faces. It infuriated him that he could not detect the witches, that their unholy features were not marked with some visible sign, like horns or black and bloody halos. But all he could see were blank, stupid countenances waiting for his words. They were like cattle, he thought, but it would be wiser to think of them as sheep and of himself as their shepherd.

The image of the silent Margarita rose before him; he thought of her and of her sheep and grew furious. The anger was useful, however, and he fed on it. His voice grew louder and more strident, but he modulated it almost at once. He felt the power rising within him but he had to save his strength, because this would be a long speech, and it was his chance to smoke out the rest of Margarita's coven. If he could frighten just one of them into confessing, or at least scare some information out of one of the innocent fools who knew them, then he would take them all and his fortune would be assured.

The sun was merciless, but the Grand Inquisitor did not care. Let the people sweat, let them burn, and he would burn with them. The heat drove him slowly into a frenzy.

He began calmly enough, preaching the glories of the faith and promising eternal bliss to all who adhered to it. Then he grew stern, warning against temptation and threatening endless torture to all who yielded to it. He described Hell much more vividly than Heaven.

He began to speak about heresy, railing against it. He defined it carefully for his audience as the sin of sins. All men were sinners, he said, and all women, too; especially women, for they were weak. But sin was inevitable and was forgivable. Why, even the Grand Inquisitor himself—but enough of that. What distinguished heresy from sin was that heresy was the sin of believing there was no sin in sinning, and for that and that alone there could be no forgiveness. It was pride, arrogance, and placing oneself above the laws of God and his ministers on earth. It would be punished, in this life and the next.

The people were with him now. He saw fear in some faces and a sort of glee in others. Pressing his advantage at once, he began to speak of the Jews.

The crowd loved it. The Grand Inquisitor condemned the Marranos, the Judaizers, the backsliders—all who had been given the truth but would have none of it. They had crucified the Son of God, he said, and each of them would be punished for it. Here in Spain they had been offered the inestimable blessing of Christianity; indeed, they had been ordered to embrace it, but many had fled from this honor, and many of those who remained were Christians in name only. All these New Christians were suspect, said the Grand Inquisitor, and should be watched. There might be a woman who never ate pork or a man who changed his linen too often. And there were other signs by which they could be known. All the backsliders and heretics must be taken and punished. A first mistake might be treated with a light penance, such as confiscation of property and a year of the Shame, but a further relapse could be punished only by death.

Antonio, standing in the ranks of the enthusiastic onlookers, was appalled. Could these people really believe this? Could Diego de Villanueva, a man of God and Antonio's own kinsman? Where did such ideas come from? Didn't they know anything? Didn't they know what the pope himself had said and what he had done?

Antonio had been in Rome four years ago, in 1492, and had

seen the thousands of Jewish refugees pouring into the city from Spain in the wake of the edict by Ferdinand and Isabella and Torquemada. He had heard what everyone in Rome had, the pronouncements of Pope Alexander VI, who had welcomed the Jews into the Eternal City, offering them refuge and tolerance, at least, if not complete acceptance.

Antonio wanted to speak out, to tell them all that they were mad. But he saw the yellow robes, the soldiers with their halberds, and the executioner. He held his tongue. He was hot and tired, and the sermon was already longer than the one he had heard this morning. Worse yet, there was nothing to indicate that it was coming to an end.

The Grand Inquisitor spoke next of the Moors, which was ill-advised, since the Moors still had dispensation to practice their religion, but no one here would object. It was also unnecessary, because all the Moors were in southern Spain, but the Grand Inquisitor knew they were hated, if anything, more than the Jews. For centuries, he said, these heathens had occupied Spanish soil and their last stronghold had fallen only four years ago. He spoke in veiled terms of the future, when their hateful religion would surely be outlawed. All the people knew what he meant and were glad to hear it. Until then, said the Grand Inquisitor, there were the Moriscos, who had embraced Christianity and were thus liable to prosecution as heretics. They should be watched as well.

There was not a Morisco within a hundred leagues of the city, but the mob in the plaza would have been happy to see one burn.

At last the Grand Inquisitor tore into his principal topic. The most damnable heresy of all, he said, had now invaded the city. "Witchcraft!" he shouted, and the people cried and moaned and screamed.

He mentioned astrologers, card readers, and other fortune tellers and diviners. All these, he said, and others like them, were damned, but they were nothing to what lay behind them: the worship of the Devil himself.

He likened witchcraft to a plague spreading across Europe. The spawn of Satan had been discovered everywhere, he said, especially in Germany, and in France, a mere mountain range away. It had seemed for a time that Spain might be immune, perhaps because it was such a pious nation, but now he, Diego de Villanueva, had found a witch in this very city!

The people gasped in horror and crossed themselves in unison.

They craned their necks to look for the witch, but none seemed to know who it was.

The Grand Inquisitor spoke of the paths of light and darkness and of those who embraced evil not from ignorance but from a passion for wickedness. He spoke of the powers of witchcraft, and the people shuddered.

Panic ran through the crowd as he swore in ringing tones that there were a dozen more witches in their midst. The people stirred, turned to look around, and each saw friends and neighbors as if for the first time.

The effect was splendid.

The Grand Inquisitor warned the people and the witches. There was still time for the evil ones to repent and confess, to receive the penance that would save their souls. Those who were innocent should be wary, for the tools of witchcraft were curses, poison, and death.

"But where are the witches?" bellowed the Grand Inquisitor. "I will show you one!" His bony forefinger stabbed through the air. Sweat poured from his contorted features and stained his white robe. "There!" he shouted, pointing at a dark young woman staring vacantly into the sun.

"There!" Hundreds of heads twisted toward the monster on the highest bench.

"There!"

11. The Field of Fire

PEDRO Rodriguez shifted uncomfortably on the wooden bench and squinted at the sky. It was late. He could tell by the position of the sun that the sermon had gone on far too long. Nevertheless, Diego de Villanueva had done a good job; the crowd was half-mad, and very likely there would soon be more witches in the dungeons of the Holy House. So perhaps the delay had been worthwhile, but there was no possibility now of finishing the *auto-da-fé* before sunset.

There was still the oath of allegiance to come and the individual sentencing of each of the thirty-seven prisoners, then the formality of abandoning them to the secular authorities and the procession out of the city to the *quemadero,* the field of fire. It would surely be dark before the last of the five impenitents was aflame.

Pedro had no serious objection to this state of affairs; it would be exciting to see the lurid scarlet of burning heretics against the night sky. And if the people ran wild in the darkness he would be among them and might even find a willing wench somewhere in the shadows. First, of course, he would see to it that his own daughters were safely at home. Other fathers would have to look out for theirs as best they could.

Still, something in Pedro's administrative soul was piqued by the thought that the ceremony was not proceeding with the utmost efficiency, and he determined to make an effort to speed things up, even if only as a matter of form. Turning slightly toward Miguel, he whispered out of the corner of his mouth, "We're running behind. Read your sentences quickly, or we'll never be done by dark."

"I know," answered Miguel. "I will do what I can, but there may not be time anyway. Quiet! The oath!"

The Grand Inquisitor, who had waited with his head bowed for a moment at the end of his sermon, slowly raised his arms above his head and administered to the multitude the oath of allegiance. This was to be the last act of his performance, which he rightly considered the greatest of his career.

"Swear!" he shouted, as all assembled in the plaza fell to their knees. "I will defend the Holy Inquisition against all enemies," he said, pausing while the great voice of the crowd repeated his words. "I will be faithful in life and in death," he continued, and the response roared back upon him like a gigantic echo. "I will yield whatever is asked of me. . . . I will pluck out my eye. . . . I will cut off my hand. . . . I will sacrifice my family . . . my fortune . . . my life . . . in the service of the Holy Inquisition . . . and this I swear . . . before God . . . at the peril of my immortal soul."

He turned with a flourish, his black cloak fluttering behind him as he moved with stately steps toward the platform where Pedro and Miguel sat waiting.

Miguel stood at once, the roll of prisoners clutched in his nervous fingers, but even as he opened his mouth to speak, a shout rang out from somewhere in the crowd: "The Grand Inquisitor!" And then another: "Diego de Villanueva!" Pandemonium broke loose as the mob took up the cry, and the name of the monk who ruled the city roared through the plaza until it rang from the buildings around the public square: the courts, the houses of the rich, the cathedral itself. The stained-glass windows seemed to rattle in their frames.

Miguel stood bewildered. Such a demonstration was most unseemly, but there was no chance to stop it, even had he dared try. The tumult continued unabated for a minute, then the Grand Inquisitor turned to lift one hand and with the smallest of gestures silenced the throng. His features were cold and composed, but his eyes glowed.

There was a brief flurry of activity in the stands as the Grand Inquisitor resumed his seat. At his curt order, Miguel, who still stood indecisively waiting, made his way down to his proper place at the lectern. Pedro took the opportunity to escort the nervous young vicar, stopped for a moment to confer with one of the armed guards, then pushed his way unceremoniously through the surrounding crowd. Miguel had begun to read the first sentence, his high, thin, unsteady voice fading into silence behind Pedro as he reached the solitude of a side street.

Pedro sighed with satisfaction and scratched himself vigorously. It was a blessing to be away from the ceremony, from the obligation to sit still and look solemn. Of course, he had left on the Inquisition's business, but there was no great hurry about it. He estimated that the sentencing would run close to two hours, which left him plenty of time to inspect the preparations at the field of fire. Alone in the street, he relieved himself luxuriously against a whitewashed wall, thinking himself luckier than any man who sat in squirming ceremony upon the benches of the Inquisition.

He had a horse waiting at the Holy House. A few minutes of riding past dwellings of diminishing dignity brought him to an open field on the outskirts of the city.

The ground was barren and scarred with black patches where fires had burned before. Here and there scraggly weeds were forcing their way up through the charred earth, but it was a desolate landscape. Fifteen wooden structures stood upon it in a neatly spaced row. Pedro surveyed them from horseback and found the symmetry pleasing. And the number was correct: there were seven effigies, three corpses, and five living human beings to be burned today.

Workmen were arranging logs at one end of the field. Their

job was nearly done, and there was no need for Pedro to urge them on. Instead he stopped to admire their handiwork. The funeral pyres were neatly made, each constructed around a wooden box about half the height of a man. Three steps rose to the top of the box, which served as the base for a stout wooden shaft six feet in height. The firewood was no careless pile of logs and kindling. It was laid in front of the box with geometrical precision, each row of bound logs piled atop the last, with wide planks in between. The fires would burn well and slowly so that the prisoners would have ample opportunity to repent before they were hopelessly aflame. Heretics were less likely to be burned quickly than carefully cooked into oblivion.

A huge white cross was planted in the field opposite the row of stakes so that the Inquisition's victims would have ample opportunity to contemplate it through the smoke. Pedro stopped his horse under one arm of the giant cross; he surveyed the field of fire and recognized someone among the workmen who had no business there. He kicked his mount into a walk and approached the group preparing the last of the fires.

"You! Carlos Diaz! What are you doing there? Come here at once!"

A bald, bedraggled figure shuffled reluctantly toward Pedro. The innkeeper was decked out in a kind of wretched finery that looked shoddier than more humble garments would have. His black suit seemed to be a relic of his forgotten slender youth, a great expanse of dirty shirt showed between the fastenings of the coat, and the hose were torn, apparently by the sheer bulk of the short, heavy legs that bulged unattractively through each rip.

He was also stinking drunk, which would have been apparent even if he had not approached Pedro proffering a wineskin.

"What am I doing here?" muttered Carlos. "Doing my duty. Citizen. Want a drink? All these fellows here—working all day. No food. Brought them bread and wine. No one else cares. Duty. Wanted to come anyway, wanted to see. Want some wine?"

"You are a fool," said Pedro, but he took some wine. "How do you think it looks," he continued, wiping his wet mouth with the back of his hand, "for you to be hanging around here like some sort of ghoul? You're making yourself conspicuous and someone may suspect you. You should be at the *auto* like everyone else. What will people think? Do you expect the Grand Inquisitor to tell everyone that you have special privileges because you're a valuable informer? And how long would you live if he did?"

"You're right," said Carlos, hanging his head in an alcoholic parody of repentance.

"Then get back where you belong. Now! You'll be back here in plenty of time, along with the rest of the people. You won't miss a thing."

Carlos trudged off toward the city but turned back after a few steps and cried plaintively, "What about my wine?"

"I'll keep it," Pedro said sternly. "You don't need any more, and you can't bring it to the *auto* anyway. It's a sacred ceremony, not a drunken revel."

Carlos shrugged acquiescently and shuffled away while Pedro watched the work in progress with the fascination that comes only to those who have nothing to do themselves. He tipped back his head and poured a thin stream of sour wine into his gaping mouth.

Miguel found reading the sentences a terrible strain. It was his duty, since he was the Grand Inquisitor's notary as well as his vicar, and no doubt it was an honor as well. Yet Miguel felt almost embarrassed to be condemning these people, not because he doubted their guilt but because he knew he lacked the authority to pass judgment impressively. He felt small and alone in the arena bounded by the tiers of benches, and he sensed that his voice was weak. The people grew restless; he could hear them stirring. They were as anxious as he to adjourn to the field of fire.

At least the worst was over. The twenty-two minor heretics

had been no problem, except that it had taken so long to sentence them all. Each had been escorted down to stand in the cage and hear a catalog of crimes, but it had not bothered Miguel to see them sweating in their grotesque sanbenitos, especially since most of them seemed so grateful for their punishments. Some would suffer the Shame and some imprisonment; all would have property confiscated, but at least none would die.

The effigies were different. They too were propped up in the cage at the center of the plaza, and they too had to be sentenced. Sometimes the flat straw faces fell against the bars, and Miguel stared at them uneasily as he read the charges. Of course it was only a matter of form, but he disliked addressing these ugly objects as if they were living men.

Still, the effigies were better than the corpses, which were pulled down from the poles on which they had been carried to the plaza and carried one by one into the cage for the condemned. There they lolled, their heads adorned with pointed caps, withered limbs draped in yellow robes, empty eye sockets gazing up reproachfully at Miguel as he condemned their bones to the field of fire and their souls to the flames of Hell. As he looked over his records, Miguel discovered to his disgust that one of the skeletons had been a woman. Her fleshless skull seemed to grin at him as he called out her name.

After that it was comparatively easy for him to deal with the last five, those sentenced to death. The old woman had cried a little, but the two brothers had betrayed no emotion and neither had the old man. All four were Judaizers.

The fifth and last heretic of the day was Margarita de Mendoza. Miguel was almost startled to see her name. He had been reading for so long that he had begun to feel doomed to read forever. Yet the last came none too soon. The sun was sinking, it was almost dusk in the plaza, and the long shadow of the gray cathedral fell across the cage where Margarita stood.

Miguel thought to look upon her face for one last time, but it was obscured by the growing darkness. Already torches had appeared, to light the square. They would be needed soon for the field of fire. As he called out the sentence, Miguel heard a murmur run through the crowd. This was the witch. Miguel cringed inwardly, anticipating some sort of demonstration, but nothing happened. It was too dark, perhaps, or too late. The people were strangely solemn and subdued; perhaps they were afraid.

Miguel condemned Margarita to death in his most ringing tones, hoping the Inquisitor would be pleased with his enthusiasm. As she was led away, Miguel concluded his services by reciting the formula abandoning the prisoners to the secular authorities. The Inquisition was not responsible for their punishment; indeed, it beseeched the civil law to deal leniently with these enemies of Spain and of God.

Even as Miguel mouthed the ritual phrases, the prisoners were hoisted onto the mules that would carry them to the field of fire.

In a daze, Margarita rode in the twilight through the narrow streets, where she was pressed on both sides by somber friars earnestly beseeching her to repent. She hardly heard them; she was listening to another voice.

For hours she had sat in the sun, half in a trance, drugged by the kiss of a vampire. The blessings, prayers, speeches, sentences had all flowed past her like a dream. But with the coming night, she had drifted back into consciousness. She was stronger now and her perceptions keener, but that only served to bring the terror of her position home. She was being carried away to be burned alive. She would have screamed, but she was too busy listening. The voice within her had grown stronger, too.

All day it had whispered and shown her strange, cloudy pictures in black and silver. Now the voice was louder and the pictures clearer. A bright night, a shining darkness, flashed and fluttered against that other vision of yellow robes and scarlet skies. The voice echoed unintelligibly down vast caverns with silver sides; it sounded a note of triumph. The note sang of death and of something beyond it, yet only one word rang clear—the sound of her own name.

She closed her eyes to hear it better and saw hardly anything of what happened at the field of fire.

But Miguel saw it all.

More than half the mob streamed behind the procession, eager for the climax to the solemn ceremony. Attendance at the *auto* itself was virtually compulsory, but those who ventured out into the field of fire did so for their own amusement. Among the many who turned away toward their homes were Teresa and Dolores Rodriguez. Miguel watched them go, wishing he might go with them. He had no stomach for executions. He did see someone accompany them, however, a sight that startled him, for their escort was none other than Antonio Manetti, the young man who had announced himself the day before as heir to the castle of Don Sebastian de Villanueva.

Miguel had no time to consider the meaning of this singular occurrence, however, for he was swept along in the procession. The people behind him were more raucous now, their shouts and cries clashing with the doleful chanting of the Dominicans marching before them. Miguel rode with the Grand Inquisitor at the head of the grim parade, followed by the five prisoners, mounted on mules and surrounded by monks and soldiers.

The mob in the rear dispersed into gesticulating groups as the procession reached the black and blighted field. Here, beyond the shadows of the city, a lurid sunset flamed against the mountains. Miguel shuddered at the sight of the crimson clouds; they would have reddened soon enough from the fires of the *auto-da-fé*. He reined in his mount and waited with the Grand Inquisitor beneath the great white cross at the edge of the field, watching soldiers, friars, and familiars as they rushed their charges to execution.

In a matter of minutes the effigies and corpses were aflame. There was no need for ceremony with these, no chance that they might confess or repent before the fire caught them in its cruel embrace. Smoke poured into the sky as the straw men, bathed in glowing orange, turned black, glowed for an instant as vivid embers, then sank into nothingness. A breeze from the west sent the smoke drifting across the field toward the white cross and Miguel's eyes began to water. When the corpses were set aflame, a darker cloud rushed toward him and started him coughing.

"A bad wind," he said.

"But a good day," said the Grand Inquisitor.

The old woman was first. The monks around her had no special interest in her, for she had already confessed. Two of them led her up the steps of the platform to the stake, then one monk helped the executioner bind her while the other offered her a cross to kiss. As they descended, one gave a laconic signal to the executioner. His black hood nodded and he stepped up behind the old woman with a cord in his hands. He wrapped it once around her withered neck and yanked at the ends. A roar went up from the crowd as she kicked and twitched, but the spectacle was short-lived.

Miguel wanted to look away, but some fascination kept him watching. When the torch was applied he saw to his relief that the dead woman burned no differently from the effigies. Perhaps he would be able to stand this after all.

The deaths of the two black-bearded brothers were more dramatic and afforded the spectators some real amusement. The first one refused the cord and the cross and stared stoically at the monks, who retreated, shaking their heads at his stubbornness. The fire was lit and for some moments he regarded it with apparent indifference, though he began to choke on the smoke. But the flames grew higher and all at once he was seen to be screaming. He could not be heard, for at his first cry he had been drowned out by the cheers and laughter of the mob.

By this time the second man had been bound to the stake. The sight of his brother's agony undid him. It appeared that these two had resolved together to defy the Inquisition, but the second brother suddenly shouted out his repentance. A monk rushed forward to absolve him and the executioner reached for his cord. The spectators were delighted at this development, but their glee knew no bounds when the first brother, already blackened and blistered, saw the pact betrayed and cried out his own confession. The executioner hesitated between the two men, and by the time he decided to deal with the first the roaring flames were too high. There was no way he could approach without being burned himself, so the first brother expired in writhing anguish while the crowd cheered.

Miguel could think only of Hell as he gazed aghast at the roasting bodies and frenzied onlookers. The air was thick with smoke and the shifting light made the scene bend and quiver before his smarting eyes. An odor assailed his nostrils and his empty stomach lurched as he realized that his mouth had begun to water. He had not eaten all day and he smelled meat cooking. But the meat was human flesh.

He almost fell from his horse in his hurry to reach the ground, and he rushed off toward the city, choking and retching dryly.

Thus employed, Friar Miguel Carillo missed the final act of the drama played out that night upon the field of fire. In his extremity he had forgotten about Margarita de Mendoza, but the executioner had not.

The fourth prisoner, the old man, was already aflame by the time Margarita was seized and forced up the three steps to the stake. As she was tied to it, she opened her eyes and saw death staring at her. The whole field was alive with fire. In its garish light shone a multitude of eager, upturned faces bathed in sweat and soot. The yellow robe had been torn from her body so that it could be perpetually displayed in the cathedral to keep her infamy alive, and the people jeered and pointed at the nearly naked flesh beneath her pitiful rags. She looked past them and beheld a white cross planted at the top of a slope. A dark horseman lurked beneath it. She recognized him as the Grand Inquisitor.

At the sight of him a fury rose within her. She screamed and snarled curses, promising him a fate worse than her own. Diego de Villanueva could not hear a word of this, but the monks who still pleaded for her repentance were staggered and stepped back from the force of her invective. The executioner himself turned pale beneath his black hood. He had never burned a witch before, and he feared her powers as much as any man. The torch dangled uselessly in his limp hand.

A big man in black pushed the monks aside. "Fools!" he shouted. "She will die as easily as the others! What are you waiting for?" As he snatched the torch from the executioner, Margarita recognized him as the one who had arrested her.

She spoke to him calmly as he approached. "You will die," she promised him, "and your master there will die, and then your torments will begin."

"You cannot frighten me," said Pedro, and thrust the torch into the pitch-soaked logs.

Flames sprang up with amazing speed. Margarita closed her eyes against them. The people waited open-mouthed for her cries to begin, but they were disappointed. She stood quite still, her lips moving slowly as if in prayer. A blast of heat rushed over her, but a triumphant voice rang in her ears: "Margarita! Now, Margarita! The night! The night!"

From his distant vantage point the Grand Inquisitor saw it first. The people looked only at the witch, but he saw the sky and the vast black shape that hovered there.

"Sebastian!" he shouted, but no one heard him, for the crowd was in a panic. Something huge swept down out of the darkness toward Margarita. Its leathery wings wrapped around the silent woman, and its sharp claws slashed at her bonds. Some of the people screamed and ran; others sank to their knees in prayer and were trampled in the rush from the field of fire. Only a few had the courage for more than a glimpse of the gigantic bat, whose red eyes gleamed brighter than the fire as it snatched up the Grand Inquisitor's greatest prize. Like a demon from the pit the thing writhed through the rising flames. When it soared above them again, Margarita de Mendoza was clutched in its massive talons.

Diego de Villanueva sat frozen beneath the white cross as the mob raced screaming past him. He gazed upward in amazement as the great wings flapped through the purple sky, until the black beast and its pale burden were lost in darkness and distance.

His rearing horse recalled him to his senses, and he turned to address the fleeing populace.

"Behold!" he shouted, in a voice so strong that many stopped to hear him. "Behold and tremble, for such is the fate of witches! Satan himself has claimed her for his own, and she burns in Hell tonight! Behold and repent, you sinners, for only I can save you from such a doom! Behold and despair, you witches, for you have seen your destiny!"

His voice turned to a maniacal wail until the onlookers fled from him as if he were another monster. His arms were raised to Heaven and his fingers clutched at the empty air.

12. The Crimson Cloak

MARGARITA awoke the next afternoon in a room she had never seen before. It was furnished in the Moorish style, and for a moment she thought she had been transported into another land, but the exotic embellishments could not completely disguise the fact that the cold stone walls were those of a fortress.

She lay on her back groggily, looking up at the high gray ceiling and trying to understand how she had come to be here. She remembered the field of fire, the jeering crowd, and the shadowy figure of the Grand Inquisitor. And there was something more: a monstrous creature that was at once a source of horror and delight. There was a memory of the earth dropping away beneath her, as in a belladonna dream, then nothing.

She propped herself up on one elbow and felt a silken sheet slide down her shoulder. She was lying naked on a pile of velvet cushions and was covered with silks and furs. Rich carpets in intricate patterns overlapped upon every inch of the floor. The walls were hung with tapestries showing almond-eyed men and women dressed in strange clothing and posed with amorous delicacy. The furnishings were few. There were cushions in profusion, especially around a low table inlaid with arabesques, and a large chest of the same design stood in the corner. Otherwise the chamber was empty.

Margarita sat up slowly, gathering the silk around her like a robe. She looked toward the wooden door and tried to rise. Her head swam as she stood erect, and sharp pains ran through her feet and legs. She threw one hand toward the wall to support herself and leaned against it, gasping—not so much from the pain as from the knowledge it brought. Tears filled her green eyes as she realized again what the Inquisition had done to her.

She might be free, but the torture chamber had left marks upon her body that not even time could heal.

Shaking her head fiercely to counteract her anguish, Margarita made her way slowly along the wall until she reached the door. It was locked. She leaned against it in an anxiety of bewilderment. Then her gaze fell upon a low table across the room.

On it she saw a silver bowl piled high with fruit, two silver jugs, and a silver goblet. At the sight of these she realized that she was weak with hunger. She stumbled gracelessly over the carpets and dropped on a cushion before the table, snatching at a pear as she sprawled upon the floor. Its sweet juices dribbled into her mouth and down her chin. She had tasted nothing so good for weeks. One jug held wine, the other water. She filled the cup with wine and poured it down her grateful throat in great sensual gulps.

A set of silver combs lay beside the basin, with a single sheet of parchment beneath them. On it were only two words: "Wait," it said, and was signed "Sebastian."

She picked up the note and stared at it intensely, as though expecting a further message to appear, but nothing happened. The room was silent.

Finally she dropped the parchment and dipped both hands into the silver basin. She splashed water on her face and shook it off in ecstasy; she cast her silken wrapper aside and rubbed her naked flesh with wet hands. Streaks of grime and soot ran in rivulets down her shoulders and breasts, until she impatiently picked up the second jug and poured the water all over her body, unmindful of the cushions and carpets growing damp beneath her. She spilled the basin over her head and gasped with delight, then gathered up the silk sheet and rubbed herself till it was damp and clinging.

This improvised bath refreshed her more than the food or drink. She felt that she had washed the stains of the dungeon away and almost believed it when she kept her gaze from her burned and twisted legs.

Kneeling by the table, she ran a comb through her tangled, dripping hair until it was clean and straight again. She looked for a mirror, but there was none to be found, and the reflection she saw in the silver pitchers was dim and distorted. The room was growing darker.

She thought of the chest and slid across the floor to reach it, another cupful of wine in her hand. Beside the chest she hesitated for a moment; she had no idea what might lurk within and was almost afraid to open it. But curiosity overcame her doubts, and she raised the carved inlaid lid. At first she could see nothing but darkness within; then she realized that it was filled with a woman's clothing. She pulled forth gowns, robes, and dresses in eager handfuls—brocade, velvet, taffeta, silk— each garment more splendid than any she had ever owned, even in the sadly distant days when she had been a young lady of some quality. She held them up before her in the fading light, longing again for a looking glass.

The dim chamber might have been a prison of sorts, but it seemed to Margarita her private preserve, designed and appointed for her pleasure. She had no doubts about the wisdom of putting on these clothes, only wondering which garment she would choose. At length, inspired perhaps by some premonition about the night ahead, she selected a white gown of smooth cool silk, its waist embroidered with silver threads. She slipped it over her head, pleased with the fit, then crept across the floor to the pile of cushions and furs that had served as her bed. There in the growing gloom she waited.

She heard footsteps and watched a dim finger of light slide

under the door. Her heart raced and she held her breath. The door swung slowly open. There in its pointed arch stood Don Sebastian de Villanueva, wrapped in a crimson cloak, a golden candelabrum in his hand.

Margarita wanted to speak but could think of nothing to say. Sebastian was silent too. He placed the candelabrum on the table and stood beside it, staring at her. Margarita watched the dancing lights and the trickling red wax that ran down the side of the candles.

"This was my wife's room," said Sebastian, "before she died. And that is her dress you are wearing."

Margarita started, her hand clutching nervously at the white bodice.

"It becomes you," Sebastian reassured her. "That was a stupid way to start a conversation. I rarely speak to anyone now, and I have lost the habit of conversing politely."

"You speak well enough," Margarita said softly. "And you saved my life." She paused for a moment. "This is your castle, then?"

Sebastian nodded. "If a dead man can be said to own anything."

"And your wife?"

"No, she is not here with me. The Inquisition took her, as they did you, and I was not here to help her." His pale face twisted. "I was fighting for the Crown."

"What was her name?"

"Her name was Gracia. But it is senseless to talk of her. She is gone forever, and we are still here, Margarita."

"Why did you rescue me?"

"You think it was in memory of her. Well, perhaps it was in part, but there was more." He came closer and kneeled beside her in the shadowy glow of the candles. "I have known you for months, though you have not known me. I have seen you dance naked in the forest, the most beautiful of all my witches and the one whose rage and hatred matched my own."

"It may be that you hate the Inquisition as much as I,"

Margarita retorted bitterly, "but you seem to have made your truce with them, and with your brother, the Grand Inquisitor." The last words were spoken with a sneer.

"And for you I have broken that truce," Sebastian said grimly. "I can only guess how Diego will respond. It would be easy enough for him to destroy me, but I think he will not. Not for this. He has need of me."

"To frighten the wretches in his dungeons?"

"There is a better reason. He plans to become an authority on the black arts, and I am his tutor."

"How can you?"

"He is my brother, though that means little enough now. But I have need of him, too. He has kept me safe in this castle for many years. Without him I would be a dead man, if I am not already."

"And is death the worst thing you can imagine?"

"I know that it is not for you, Margarita, and that is why you have been spared it, but I thought you might be more grateful."

"I am grateful," said Margarita in a gentler tone. Silk rustled as she moved to take his hand in hers. She bent to kiss his jeweled fingers. "You taught me what I know of witchery, or the goat did. If I seem surprised, it is only that I thought you a demon, a spirit, and now I find that you are still a man."

"I am more human than I knew," said Sebastian, "and I feel for you something I never thought to feel again." Their right hands were still clasped. With his left he reached out to stroke her damp black hair. Margarita closed her eyes and rubbed her cheek against caressing fingers.

"When you came to my cell," she whispered, "I thought . . . no, I don't know what I thought. When I saw the goat, I was sure you were there to spirit me away, and then when I saw that you were undead . . . I remembered what I was told when I was a little girl, how Lucifer is a seducer who torments even those who serve him. But your kiss was sweet." She touched her throat and slowly drew back from Sebastian.

"What are these powers that govern us? I have seen them work, but what are they?"

Sebastian considered her question. "You might know more," he said at length, "if you were a creature such as I. And I have more to learn as well. What I see now is like a dream. There is no way to tell if what I see is the truth or only my own vision. I wonder if there is a truth at all. Yet the fact that I am here, after suffering a mortal wound on the plains before Malaga, is proof enough that magic can be wrought, even if its source remains a mystery. We are like mariners, Margarita, who cannot see the wind but know full well that it drives their ship toward some distant shore."

"Have you never spoken to Satan?"

"I doubt that he exists; certainly not as my brother would have the people believe. The power that works curses is the same one that works miracles, and the light that mortals seek casts the very shadows that they fear. There is only one source, its manifestations molded by the wills of men and women. Good and evil are not causes but effects, and the same force fills everything."

Margarita said nothing, just stared at the bright points of flame above the candles.

"But this is too high a doctrine," continued Sebastian. "The force can be used; perhaps it can even be known. But still, it does matter how we use it. To have it is not enough, for it may still produce a monster like me or my brother Diego. We both sought wisdom and power, and we have not been utterly denied, but what has it brought us? The universe is a mirror that reflects back upon us all our thoughts and deeds. Perhaps that is why I have become a vampire, to be free of my reflection at last."

Margarita looked at Sebastian intently. "Is it peace, then?" she asked. "Is it peace to be dead?"

"It may be," answered Sebastian, "but if it is, I am not dead enough to know. There is no peace for me now, only an unquenchable thirst."

"A thirst for blood?"

"For blood, for knowledge and power—and for life, which I will never know again. Sometimes it is a thirst for death and for an end to all this thirsting."

Margarita took his hand again and held it against her heart. "Sebastian," she said. "Is there nothing for you?"

"Only when I sleep, in the crypt below the castle. To crawl into a coffin every morning should be a horror, but when the sun rises my dream begins."

"What happens?"

"Almost nothing, except that I am transported. The sensations can hardly be described. I lie as still as the corpse that I am, but somehow I move. It feels something like falling, but without the fear. Is it possible to fall upward? A sensation of flying, or floating down a stream. And a high, clear sound like bells or children singing, almost a melody but never quite. All around me grows a radiance and I flow toward it—into it—until I become one with the light. Then I see the power and am the power, but it matters not at all, for every desire is dissolved in the light."

"And is the light silver?" asked Margarita.

He looked at her in surprise. "How can you know?" he asked.

"I have seen it," she said, smiling at him faintly. "You showed it to me. Show me again."

He touched her forehead gently with his left hand. "Wonderful," he said, "that you should share my dream." He leaned toward her for an instant, then gently took his hands from her head and her heart.

"We must stop this," said Sebastian, "stop and consider, for tonight your fate will be determined. You are not a prisoner, you know. You are free to leave this castle."

"Free?" echoed Margarita. "Free for what?" Surprise showed in her pale green eyes and disappointment tightened her full red lips. "What could I do? Did you take me from the fire only to cast me out into the darkness?"

"I agree that you can hardly stay in Spain," said Sebastian, "and certainly you can never return to your home."

Margarita nodded. "I have no home," she said.

"You might be safe, though, if you fled across the mountains into France. Of course, they do not love witches there, either."

Margarita jammed a fist into a pillow. "How can I go anywhere? Look at my legs, my feet! Your brother has left me a cripple!"

"Yet still you have a choice," said Sebastian, "though I am reluctant to recommend it. I have saved you from one death; now I can only offer you another."

"Death?"

"And what lies beyond it. Stay with me, Margarita, and be one with me. Live as I do and die as I do. Be my bride, and mistress of this empty castle, and one of the living dead."

His head was close to hers. She gazed into his eyes, thinking to find them burning with the fires of Hell, but they were dark and dull and dead.

Sebastian stood abruptly and turned away from her. "Do not look at me," he said. "My power is such that I could bend you to my will, but I have no wish to do so. Choose for yourself, Margarita, but choose carefully."

Margarita looked at his back and at the crimson cloak that covered it. "What could I be to you," she asked, "but a wretched wench with twisted legs?"

"Those are the afflictions of a mortal woman, Margarita, and they can be remedied. Let me bleed you as the surgeons do and you will find me a notable physician."

"Then you can make me whole again?"

"That and more, Margarita. I offer you eternal life."

Sebastian heard the rustle of silk and felt a hand on his arm. Margarita stood beside him, swaying on her tortured legs.

"I accept," she said.

Sebastian drew her to him, holding her up with his strong arms. "There is no safety here," he warned; "no peace."

"There is no safety anywhere," Margarita said. "I choose to stay with you." She pressed her lips against his and pulled him gently down to her bed. She slipped off the dress of white silk and knelt before him naked, her body bathed in light and shadow from the warm glow of the candle.

"You are more beautiful than I remembered," Sebastian said. His cool fingers ran along her bare back and pressed into the aching muscles of her shoulders. Margarita sighed and let her head roll back ecstatically. Tender kisses covered her long white throat, but the sharp sting she awaited did not come. Instead, Sebastian drew away to stare into her glowing green eyes. She saw that by some magic he was naked too, his crimson cloak lost among the silks and furs. His flesh was lean and muscular, but as pale and cold as a distant star.

He lifted Margarita and laid her down again upon the bed of cushions, his velvet cloak spread beneath her. He hovered over her, his black hair streaming down, and his long white fingers tracing patterns on her torso. He bent to kiss her trembling breasts and to caress her slender waist. Margarita's arms reached out to embrace Sebastian, and her pink fingernails sank into his back as she felt his fingers slide into the warm, wet curls between her thighs. She opened the way for him and dragged him down upon her. As she took him into her their eyes met, and she sank dizzily into the depths of his darkness.

Margarita felt a momentary panic as he entered her, awed by the strength of the uncanny chill that filled her warm human body. She froze for an instant, ready to recant, then an icy wave of ecstasy swept through her and she was lost.

Sebastian's head sank onto her shoulder and their bodies throbbed together in cold communion. Margarita felt a passion overwhelm her that was more than human. She gasped acceptance. As she did, the bright teeth of her lover sank into her throat. A spasm shook her to the very soul and she was cast into the void.

Something shimmered before her in the infinite blackness, a vast net of pulsating silver strands. Falling away behind her were a man and a woman in each other's arms; rushing toward her was a vibrant gleam that swelled into a blinding flash. It absorbed her, and she became the light.

13. Two Sisters

PLENDID, Pedro! Three in one day! Even better than I expected!" The enthusiasm of the Grand Inquisitor was so great that he could hardly stay in his chair. His hands waved expansively and his thin lips were pulled back from his yellowing teeth in an expression that on the face of any other man would have been a smile.

"All three of them came to the Holy House willingly and confessed without even a question from me. One of them even volunteered the names of several other witches, Pedro. There will be work for you tonight."

Pedro stood sullenly and looked at the floor of the Grand Inquisitor's chambers. He was not overly impressed by this good news. At yesterday's *auto-da-fé* he had done the work of two men, so he was not anxious to spend the coming night arresting crazed women. He had planned to be drunk in his own bed.

"I had no idea it would work so well!" continued Diego.

"You had no idea it would happen at all," countered Pedro bitterly. "I saw your face when that thing came down out of the sky and you were as amazed as anyone. I admit, though, that you recovered quickly."

"All right, Pedro," sighed the Grand Inquisitor. "Not even

your impudence can anger me today. I suppose I could hardly expect to deceive you who have known me so long and known my brother even longer. I wonder why Sebastian did it. Could he have realized how well he was serving me? Not that it matters now, but I wonder. I almost think he meant to spite me by stealing her away in front of everyone, yet all he did was to frighten more witches into timely repentance. What a story for the book! Hundreds of witnesses saw her carried off by a fiend from the pit. What stronger proof could I wish for?"

"What do you suppose has become of Margarita de Mendoza?" asked Pedro.

"I have no doubt that she lies dead in the castle, her heart's blood drained away to sustain my enterprising brother. We shall not see her again, Pedro. Sebastian did seem to have a taste for her. I can hardly begrudge him for indulging his whim, since I would gladly exchange one silent witch for a whole coven of confessions. We have three already, and there will be more. My fortune is made."

Pedro scratched his nose with his thumb. "You have the names of the ones you want me to visit tonight?"

"Miguel has them. You can pick them up on your way out. The boy is not well today; something disturbed him at the field of fire. Sometimes I doubt whether he will ever have the stomach for this work."

"He's not the boy I'm worried about," Pedro replied. "I want to know what you plan to do with this one who claims to be the heir of Don Sebastian. He was seen yesterday after the *auto* talking to my daughters. I will not tolerate that!" His big fist smashed down on the table like a hammer.

The Grand Inquisitor picked up an overturned candlestick and replaced it with infuriating equanimity. "Surely you can take care of your own daughters," he said.

"I could take care of that boy easily enough, too, but you tell me I must wait."

"And I mean it, Pedro. If you cross me in this before Sebastian's work is done, I promise you not only the fate of an assassin but the hospitality of the Holy House. Be patient, Pedro. Our real problem will be to keep this Antonio patient as well. We can hardly have him inhabiting the castle before the book is completed. Perhaps your older daughter could be of some use to us."

Pedro's face turned purple, but the Grand Inquisitor ignored it. "What is her name? Teresa? There's no need to fume at me like that, Pedro, unless you doubt the girl's virtue. If Antonio likes her, she may be able to help us by giving him something else to think about."

"If he comes near her I'll kill him, in spite of all your threats."

"Stop and consider, Pedro. This young fellow has wonderful prospects. The castle may be an obsolete fortress, but its furnishings alone are worth a modest fortune, and the lands that go with it include most of the farms in this district. A family could live in grand style on the rents alone. Teresa could easily find a worse husband."

"You forget what he did to me at the Golden Cup," insisted Pedro, all the more adamant despite the doubts beginning to show in his eyes. "My honor is at stake!"

"Honor is as others perceive it. Who knows what happened there? Only Antonio and your daughters. Oh, and Carlos Diaz, too, but I am sure you have seen to it that he will keep quiet about the incident. None of them will care, and surely it will add to your honor to have your daughter made a noblewoman. You must think of the future, Pedro. I promise you that there are great things before us. I asked to be named Inquisitor of this little district because I was sure it contained what I wanted, but I shall not be here forever. A few more weeks and I shall be the talk of Spain, the great witch hunter of the kingdom. All the great cities will welcome me as I come to drive out their devils. There will be great honor in it, Pedro, and fame, and no doubt riches too. You will be at my right hand. How much better it will be for you to go with me and leave your daughters in luxury than to throw all this away for the sake of a tavern brawl!"

"You talk well enough," mumbled Pedro, more than a little dazzled in spite of himself. "But I like something I can see. This is only talk, and I'll believe it when it happens. For now, I have only a list of names and the promise that I will spend the night chasing hags."

Antonio waited in the shadows of an alley, watching a house across the narrow street. He had been there since nightfall, dressed in drab traveling clothes he hoped would make him less conspicuous. The summer night was warm enough but he was chilled, both by the danger of being abroad after dark and by the growing conviction that he was making a fool of himself.

The house, only a few streets away from the cathedral, was more substantial than those surrounding the Inn of the Golden Cup. It had two stories and its earthen bricks had been white-washed not too long ago. The massive ironbound door was closed and the windows shuttered, but a faint glow between the shutters held Antonio's attention.

Then the door opened, and Antonio slipped hastily back into the depths of his alley. A gigantic black silhouette of a man stood out against the light for a moment; then he stepped out and shut the door behind him. He waited there for a heartbeat, apparently listening to something behind him—perhaps the sounds of locks and bolts falling into place—then he plodded down the street in the direction of the Holy House.

Antonio continued to wait, but his spirits were higher. Pedro had left home, so there was reason to believe that the waiting had not been in vain. In no time at all the door opened again. A small hand appeared holding a strip of white cloth, then shut the door upon it. Antonio saw the signal and immediately stepped out into the street. He paused for a moment, embarrassed by his own eagerness, then shrugged to himself, hurried up to the house, and knocked.

Dolores answered his knock. "You didn't take long," she said archly as she let him in. Antonio looked around him at the chamber that served the family as kitchen, dining room, and living room. He saw a huge fireplace with no fire in it, a heavy table, and several chairs and stools. A mirror hung on one wall above a brassbound chest; another wall was covered with shelves holding plates, cups, and pitchers. Cooking utensils hung beside the fireplace. A painted screen stood in one corner and in the opposite corner a miniature shrine constructed around an image of the Virgin. Antonio saw everything in the simply furnished room except what he had hoped to see.

"Where is Teresa?" he asked.

"Upstairs," answered Dolores. "Does it matter? I thought you came to visit me."

Antonio smiled. "I am very pleased to see you, but I hope to see your sister, too."

"Sit down," said Dolores, and Antonio obeyed. "She'll be down eventually, though I don't see why you should care. I'm as pretty as she is."

"Indeed you are," agreed Antonio, "but your sister is taller. I have a weakness for tall women."

"Do you like her?" asked Dolores, perching on a high stool across the room from Antonio's chair.

"Of course I do," said Antonio, glancing nervously toward the narrow stairs as if he imagined that Teresa might be listening upstairs. "Why else would I come here? Does she like me?"

"She hardly knows you, you know. She's hardly spoken to you. But she must like you a little, since she arranged for you to come here. We're all being very wicked, and father would be furious. I love it. Want some wine?"

"Well," said Antonio. "Perhaps a little. Did you hear what happened yesterday after you went home? Everyone has been talking about it."

"They burned some people, I suppose. I never get to see it. Father forbids it and Teresa doesn't even want to watch."

"She's right. It's nothing for a young girl to see, nor anyone else, for that matter. But last night they say there was something else. A woman was to be burned for witchcraft, but a devil flew down and carried her off."

"A devil!" said Dolores, filling a cup with sour red wine. "I never get to see anything! I suppose you missed it too. Do you believe it?"

Antonio took the cup from her and sat quietly for a moment, trying to create the impression that he was giving her question profound consideration. "I don't know," he said at last. "I can hardly deny the existence of devils—that would be blasphemy—but I wonder how often they appear to men. Still, there must have been something."

"You're right," said Dolores. "You don't know. I suppose it is hard to know the truth, though. Could you believe a stranger who claimed to be the heir to a fortune?"

Antonio inhaled a mouthful of wine and stared red faced at Dolores while he coughed. "Do you think I'm lying?" he finally gasped.

"I can hardly deny the existence of devils," said Dolores sweetly, "and I have to watch out for my sister. Sometimes she has no sense at all."

"Dolores! Do you think you're a matchmaker?" Teresa stood at the bottom of the stairs, doing her best to look angry with her little sister but at the same time trying to suppress her laughter. "I'm sorry, sir," said Teresa, "that you should be exposed to such an inquisition. My sister is an apprentice shrew, and she belongs in bed."

"No!" cried Dolores. "I'm your chaperone. Would you disgrace yourself? A lady must never entertain a gentleman without a duenna to keep an eye on her."

"Sometimes a duenna can be bribed to look the other way," replied Teresa, moving across the room to stand beside her sister in an attitude of mocking menace.

"And how would you bribe me?" asked Dolores.

"I might be persuaded to let you live," Teresa answered. She took her sister by the arm and pulled her not too gently from the stool.

"You can't make me go! I'm not a child! I'll just listen from upstairs anyway."

Antonio looked into his cup and pretended he was not in the room.

"Please, Dolores," said Teresa, speaking more softly. She bent down to embrace her sister and draw her away from Antonio.

"He wouldn't even be here if it weren't for me," said Dolores sulkily.

"I know," whispered Teresa, kissing Dolores on the cheek. "Please."

Dolores walked slowly toward the stairs, stopping only long enough to wish Antonio a good night, and then was gone.

Antonio smiled nervously. He was suddenly conscious of the bedraggled garments that had seemed such a clever disguise when he had put them on a few hours before. Teresa was equally embarrassed by her own costume, a plain dark dress she had not dared to change for fear of exciting her father's suspicions.

"You shouldn't have come," she said.

"But . . ."

"I know. I asked you, and I arranged the signal—or was it Dolores? It's too dangerous, though. My father might come back for something. He'd kill you."

Antonio would hardly have left under such a threat even if he had been inclined to do so. However, he was beginning to feel decidedly uncomfortable. This was an odd courtship and quite likely inadvisable as well. "Your sister is a clever girl," he said inconsequentially.

"She's an imp," said Teresa, seating herself on the stool Dolores had vacated.

"She's certainly not shy," said Antonio, who had no desire at all to talk about Dolores.

"Isn't my behavior scandalous enough for you?" Teresa asked testily. "Are the women in Florence so bold?"

"I didn't mean anything," Antonio said, inwardly cursing the Spanish language and his inadequate command of it. "You are very good to see me. It is not pleasant to be a stranger in this city."

"I understand that you are soon to be one of its greatest men."

"Will I be any less lonely? You seem more real to me than this castle I am to inherit."

"You will find it as real as the mountains around it."

"I wonder. When I told people in Florence that I was heir to a castle in Spain, they laughed at me. You know, the very words 'a castle in Spain' are a sort of joke there. People say it when they talk about a dream or a wish that will never be granted. I thought to prove them wrong, but now I'm not so sure. I have not felt welcome here, and even Diego de Villanueva doesn't seem to want to see me."

Teresa felt some compassion for him, mingled with a certain surprise at his apparently impractical nature. "You should have no trouble proving to yourself that the castle is no dream," she said. "It stands to the north of the city. Go and look at it."

"I will. Tomorrow. But somehow I thought there would be somebody to show me."

"You will wait a long time for the Grand Inquisitor to give you his attention, I think. There is no one more important here than he is."

Antonio sighed and took another sip of wine. "What was Don Sebastian like?"

"A soldier," Teresa said. "A dark, brooding man. I saw him several times in the city. My father was his lieutenant. He died when I was a little girl."

"I don't really want to talk about him," said Antonio abruptly. "I want to talk about you. Why did you ask me here?"

"Dolores is right. Sometimes I am very stupid. And why did you come?"

"I don't know. Yes, I do. I thought it would be gallant and daring. And you are beautiful. I wanted to see you again. I wanted to know you better."

Teresa smiled. "I am not beautiful," she said.

Antonio smiled too. "Please do not dispute with me about beauty. I am considered a connoisseur. I had planned to be a painter, before I determined to become a nobleman."

Teresa shifted on her stool. "I wanted to see you, too. But now I wish you would go. I'm afraid to have you here."

"I'm not afraid," said Antonio, "and I don't want to go, but I will if you wish it. Soon. Just a few minutes more. How can I meet you again?"

"It seems impossible," Teresa said. "I thought he might be going out tonight, but I can't have you standing outside the house all the time waiting to see a white cloth stuck in the door."

Antonio stood up. "There must be some way, Teresa. Don't you want to? If I didn't have to speak in Spanish, I would make a wonderful speech to you, but now I don't know what to say that won't make me sound like a clown. I want you for a friend, and more."

She looked at him gravely and reached out a hand to him. Antonio took it, then kissed it with more passion than politeness. He looked up into her eyes. Something he saw there encouraged him to kiss her again, this time upon the lips. His first attempt was brief and gentle, as if he expected her to protest. When she did not, he tried again. Her lips were tender, and when she opened them her breath was sweet. For a moment their bodies were pressed together, then Teresa turned away.

"Please go," she said.

Antonio stood behind her with his hands around her waist. "First you must tell me that we will meet again."

"I don't know what to do," she said, while he kissed her hair, her ears, her cheeks. "We're hardly ever allowed to leave the house. Wait. The inn. Perhaps I could leave a message there."

"I don't trust that innkeeper," said Antonio, burying his face in her honey-colored hair.

"I don't mean him. There's a boy, a friend of Dolores. In fact, I think he's in love with her. He will give you a letter when I know where we can meet."

"Bless the boy," whispered Antonio, "and bless Dolores. Love conquers all. Send for me soon, Teresa." He kissed her neck and shoulders and drew her back toward him firmly. Teresa raised one hand to caress his dark, curly head as he bent over her shoulder to kiss her throat. His hands slid up from her waist to clasp her small, high breasts. Her hands covered his, pressing them to her for an instant, then she pulled away from his embrace.

"Please go," she said. "I'll send for you when I can. I promise." She ran to the door, unbolted it, and looked out into the street.

"Come on," she said. She kissed him quickly and pushed him out into the night. The sky was full of stars.

14. The Mountains

MARGARITA'S eyes opened but she saw only darkness. She was lying on her back and sensed rather than felt that she was stretched out upon some cold, unyielding surface. She knew she was awake, but still it seemed she was in a dream and curiously detached from her own body. She tried to move one of her hands, which lay crossed upon her breast. It responded, but it might almost have been someone else's hand, even when it struck something above her and she realized that she was enclosed in some sort of box. Caught up in a cold, remote tranquillity, Margarita was serenely indifferent in the knowledge that she lay in a coffin. She had been transformed.

Sounds of grating and scraping drifted down to her as if from a great height, and a faint light flooded over her. The coffin was open. A pale face floated in the distance, then all at once was close to her own, kissing her cool skin and whispering her name.

Sebastian grasped her shoulders and raised her until she was seated in the long box. Margarita looked around her. She knew instinctively that it was too dark for anyone to see, yet her surroundings were nonetheless visible to her, pulsing with a blue and silver glow that seemed to originate within her own mind. Even Sebastian was luminescent, as was the smile of mild mockery that bared his long white teeth.

"Are you surprised?" he asked. "You are a creature of the night now, and you will see as such creatures do, not like the mortals lost in the darkness. Now the light is your enemy, and the sun a foe who would strike you blind. But you are safe here, Margarita, in the final home of my illustrious family."

The ceiling of the crypt was low and vaulted, its several arches supported by narrow columns of moldering masonry. The floor was thick with dust, the pillars interlaced with the webs of spiders. Stone slabs stretched out in rows each bore a casket, some adorned with the images of those who lay within, portraits in stone dressed in the fashions of generations gone and forgotten.

"I sleep beside you," said Sebastian, "and my brother Diego has a place prepared for him on my other side, when he is ready for it."

"How does it happen that there is a place for me beside you?" Margarita asked.

"It would have been my wife's," Sebastian said, "but the Inquisition burned her body. There has been no one to lie near me for many years."

Margarita thought she should be jealous of this other woman, but in fact she felt nothing. She was too conscious of the changes in herself to worry about anyone else. "I feel very odd," she said. "Will that pass?"

"What you are feeling will not pass," Sebastian answered; "only the sense that it is strange. You have much to learn, Margarita. But tell me how you feel."

"I hardly have the words to express it."

"Never mind. We will have time to talk. The night is ours. Come from the casket." He gathered her up in his arms and let her feet drop down toward the floor.

"No," she cried. "Don't let go of me. My legs will never hold."

"Trust me, Margarita. I promised to cure you. Have you no faith?" He stepped away from her and she found to her amazement that she could stand. She took a few tentative steps forward, then threw herself laughing into his arms.

"You are a wonderful magician."

"The magic is in you, Margarita. You are one of the living dead now, and beyond all human ailments. Even the streak of white in your hair is gone."

Margarita put a hand to her head. "Was my hair white?"

"I forgot that you could not have known, and now there is no way for me to show you. Believe me when I tell you that you are beautiful and your tresses as black as this tomb. From tonight you must put vanity aside. You will never see your face in a looking glass again."

"I have not looked into one for years," she said. "You will be my mirror, Sebastian."

"And you mine," he said. "Come, Margarita."

He led her through the crypt to narrow, crumbling steps that reached upward into the shadows. They climbed the steps and came out into the ruins of a room that might once have been a chapel. There were benches, an altar, and a pulpit, but every sacred image had been removed. Margarita shuddered a little at the sight of it and hurriedly followed Sebastian through another door that led out into the courtyard of the castle.

At once she was enveloped in the radiance of the moonlight, which shone for her as never before. The walls of the castle rose around her in shimmering patterns of silver and icy blue, each stone and crevice alive with its own unnatural luminescence, each of the four round towers a shaft of cold, pale light. Above them all loomed the great square tower, its ancient battlements aglow against a dazzling sea of stars.

Awestruck, Margarita threw back her head to gaze into the shining skies and whatever lay beyond them. She hardly heard Sebastian when he spoke. "What?" she asked in some bewilderment.

"I asked you to tell me your dreams, Margarita. Tell me what you saw when you were asleep in the crypt."

"What did I dream? What could I dream? I was a dead woman."

144

"There are those who would say you are dead even now," Sebastian suggested.

"Then they would be fools, for I have never felt more alive." She spread her arms wide and spun around in a giddy circle.

"Then what is death?" Sebastian asked her.

Margarita was suddenly still. "I have seen death, and it is an emptiness. It is a slaughtered sheep that becomes a piece of meat. The mind is extinguished and the senses stilled. Nothing remains. Death is oblivion. This is not death."

"Have you always believed this?" asked Sebastian sadly.

"What else would I believe? The words of those pious murderers who preach of an afterlife? I believe what I can see, and I have seen that death is an end to everything. When Margarita dies, she will never see the stars again."

"And you saw nothing when you slept in the tomb?"

"Nothing," said Margarita.

Sebastian turned away and stared at the ground.

"What is it?" she asked. "Have I said something wrong?"

"No, Margarita, nothing wrong. You have only told me the truth, but it was not the truth I expected to hear. You have given me something, though: the answer to a question my brother the Grand Inquisitor has often asked. He will want it in the book."

"The book?"

"Something I am writing for him. It is almost finished; now it will be finished that much sooner. I will show it to you. But first I will show you some magic."

"The sabbat?"

"Not that, Margarita. I fear the coven will never meet again, and I suspect that most of the others are in the dungeons of the Holy House. What happened at the *auto-da-fé* must have frightened them, and I have no doubt that my brother has taken advantage of their fear. What they saw was some sort of demon flying away with you, and a sight like that must have sent the weaker ones screaming to confess and be saved."

Margarita looked at Sebastian in amazement. "Did you know this would happen?"

"I thought of it," he said, "but I was determined to save you no matter what the cost. Have you ever played chess?"

Margarita wrinkled her forehead in perplexity. "No, but my father did. What has a game to do with this?"

"I played with my brother until he grew weary of it. He would tell you, if he knew who the master of the coven was, that I sacrificed my pawns to protect the queen."

"I don't understand this game," said Margarita, at once flattered and dismayed. "Was there no other way for you to help me?"

"There might have been, if I had decided on it sooner. As it was, I almost let you die. But I dreamed of you after the night in the dungeons, and when the sunset came . . ."

"Then you do have visions, even when the sun shines and you lie in the tomb! Why should it be different for me, Sebastian?"

"That may change," he said sadly, "with the passing of time. There are so many things I must teach you. You must beware of the second death, from which there can be no awakening. You must be warned against the sun and against fire. They can destroy a vampire, as can a shaft of wood through the heart. Except for these, we are all but invulnerable. There are certain other limitations. You must return to your coffin before the morning comes and sleep in your native soil. You must beware of running water and of several herbs. It is said, too, that there are religious artifacts that are dangerous to such as us."

"Do you believe it?"

"I have never made a sufficient test, but it seems likely that there is some truth to it."

"Nothing from their religion could frighten me," Margarita insisted. "But is our whole existence to be restrictions?"

"There is one more," Sebastian said. "To survive, we must feast on the blood of the living."

"That much, at least, will be a pleasure. I can think of many I would be glad to kill."

"They are the very ones you must spare," Sebastian said. "The greatest weapon of the vampire is secrecy. If we leave a trail of bloodless corpses behind us, we shall surely be discovered and destroyed. Only the pact I made with my brother has kept me safe for so many years."

Margarita's full lips twisted in a grimace. "I feel a strength greater than any I ever imagined," she said, "yet you tell me that we are thwarted at every turn. Why did you choose to become what you are, Sebastian?"

His expression was grave. "Because I did not wish to die," he said. "There are few who do. If every man and woman had the knowledge I possess, the world would be full of vampires. But we do have strengths as well as weaknesses, Margarita. Let me show you."

He stepped toward her, his crimson cloak almost black against the unearthly phosphorescence that Margarita's transfigured vision cast upon the gray walls of the tower. "The power is within you," he said, "but I must call it forth."

He gripped her shoulders in cold hands, and her gaze was drawn to his dark, dead eyes. No fire burned in them, but there was a fathomless depth, an essence not within Sebastian but beyond him. Mesmerized, she sank into its endless vistas. She was losing herself.

Abruptly she broke from his grasp in a spasmodic effort that threw her to her knees upon the ground. She longed to be free of his power, even as she longed to make it her own. Her back heaved from her breathless gasps, and her bare shoulders thrust toward the moon. The power of the spasms shocked her. They seemed to be jolting her to her feet. As she stood erect, a tremendous wrench threw her head back and her arms aloft. The walls of the castle reeled past her startled eyes and she felt her naked feet pulled into the air. She had never felt such strength as surged through her shoulder blades. From the corners of her eyes she could see the tips of the great wings that had sprouted behind her, webbed and leathery, yet smoothed with a soft gray fur like that of a bat.

She soared into the sky.

"Flying!" cried Margarita. "I am flying!" Peals of hysterical laughter echoed against the glowing walls and out across the silent countryside.

She saw Sebastian's figure dwindling below her as she flew in dizzying spirals among the towers. Then he rose to join her, his wings flowering out behind his billowing cloak. The two figures circled in the sky beneath the silver moon and the castle dropped away below them. Margarita watched the effortless surging of Sebastian's wings as he swept toward her. For a moment they hovered together, exchanging cold kisses in the icy air. Then he led her in a downward swoop and they came to rest upon the battlements of the topmost tower.

"Sebastian!" she gasped. "This is wonderful! Why did you stop me?"

"Rest, Margarita. Soon a weakness will come upon you." He sat on the edge of the parapet, wings furled behind him and feet dangling far above the ground. "Beneath us is the chamber where my work goes on," he said. "There is much to see there."

"Why should I grow weak?" asked Margarita, but even as she spoke she swayed against the purple sky. "It is nothing," she said as he caught her in his arms.

"You are drained of life," he told her, "and you will need more. I must find a way to feed you."

"There is a whole city nearby," she said.

"We must avoid it," Sebastian insisted. "Nor can we count upon my brother to provide you with victims. It will be safer if he believes you are gone forever."

"Then what are we to do? You were right, Sebastian. I felt a terrible thirst when you mentioned it, and I feel it now. A thirst for blood."

Her pink tongue darted out over her red lips. Sebastian

smiled to see it. "Perhaps we can find something there," he said, "over the mountains. In France, where they have witches of their own, nobody will think to suspect this castle. Are you too weak to fly?"

"I want to fly again!"

"I might be able to bring something back to you," he suggested.

"No. I want to fly, and with you beside me I will have nothing to fear. If need be, you can carry me. Come on!"

Her wings caught a current of air that carried her over the battlements and into space. Sebastian circled anxiously around her until he saw that she was safe. The exhilaration of flight was so intense that Margarita left any feeling of faintness behind her. She remembered only the powerful thrust of her surging shoulders and the burning hunger that drove her onward.

Like two gigantic bats they soared upward, their great gray wings flapping against the wind or catching breezes that carried them effortlessly aloft. The castle disappeared behind them, and the forest, and the dry sandy plains. Jagged purple peaks rose up to meet them: bare, forbidding mountains capped with snow and dotted with scrubby cypress trees. To an army the Pyrenees were all but impassable, yet Sebastian and Margarita passed over them as easily as the clouds, leaving no more trace than the shadows they cast on the icy summits.

Swiftly and silently they flew, and purposefully, but sometimes one of them swept playfully close to the other for a kiss or a caress. Once Margarita shouted.

"When I have tasted blood, Sebastian, then I will share your dreams!"

His wing brushed hers, but he did not reply.

Hours passed in the flight beneath the shining stars, until at last the mountains sank away into rolling hills and valleys. Sebastian flew lower then and kept his eyes upon the ground.

He circled lower still and suddenly shot out one long arm, his finger pointing toward something below. Margarita saw only a spot on the ground, but as she swept down for a closer look, she realized that something about it was unique. Everything around her had glowed with blue and silver, but the speck moving beneath her pulsed with a faint ruddiness. It was the first living thing she had seen that night.

Margarita dropped out of the sky like a stone. She had time to glimpse the startled, upturned face of a young man with fair curly hair. He looked toward the sky in surprise as a black shadow passed over his head, then Margarita was upon him.

She attacked her victim like a wild beast, and looked like one to the man who fell before her savage onslaught. He saw green eyes like a cat's, a black mane of streaming, wind-blown hair, and a gaping red mouth filled with gleaming fangs. His head struck a rock as he tumbled backward, and he offered no resistance as Margarita crouched over him and tore ravenously at his throat. Blood streamed and spattered from his mangled jugular. Margarita feasted on it eagerly, teeth slashing, lips sucking, and tongue licking at the crimson fountain. Her head reeled and her body quivered with delight until at last her thirst was slaked.

She rolled over and lay on her back beside the dead man. Both of them, covered with blood, stared upward at the distant stars. Margarita's face was a lurid mask of red rivulets trickling down her neck and over her naked shoulders. Her bosom heaved and her fingers ripped at the long blades of grass around her. Her eyes were glazed and almost sightless, so that she hardly noticed Sebastian when he dropped down at her feet.

If she had been looking at Sebastian, she might have noticed the strange expression on his face. He could hardly turn paler than he was, but his dark eyes were wide and his mouth hung half open as he surveyed the gruesome scene.

Finally he knelt beside her, his gray wings sheltering her body. He whispered her name and ran his white fingers through her hair. She stirred then and turned her dazed eyes toward him, a sleepy smile on her gory lips. "What bliss," she murmured. "Better than flying. Better than anything I have ever known." She smiled more broadly. "Except, perhaps, for your embrace."

"You will have more of both," he said, wiping her mouth with a corner of his cloak. "And you will learn to be less savage. These pleasures should be savored."

"And you will learn to be less of a hypocrite," she said, still smiling. "Others taught me savagery, and I will not forget the lesson. When I killed that man, I wished he had been another. I can think of several who owe me a debt that can only be washed away in blood."

"Be careful, Margarita, and remember my warnings." Sebastian's face was grim. "We must stay hidden from the world." He helped her to her feet and kept his arms around her, shielding her from the butchered corpse outstretched on the blood-flecked ground.

"You need not spare me from that sight," she said. "I am no stranger to slaughter. I have killed sheep and seen men burned alive. I was never a weak woman, Sebastian, and now I am stronger. You have given me that gift of power, and I promise you that I will be careful with it. I will not risk my life, now that I can live forever."

"Forever," echoed Sebastian, pressing her close against him. They were briefly lost in each other's arms, then Sebastian stepped back. "We must return to the castle at once," he said. "You will fly faster now, and so you must, for it will be morning soon. These summer nights are short."

15. The Book

NEARLY two weeks passed before the letter appeared at the Holy House.

These were difficult days for Diego de Villanueva, who was forced to maintain his outward composure despite a steadily growing anxiety about the book nearing completion at the castle. More than ever he longed to have the manuscript in his hand and taste the power he believed it would bring him. The wait would have been frustrating enough in itself, but it became almost unbearable when aggravated by the presence of the young man who was Don Sebastian's heir. Antonio visited the Holy House almost every day, each visit bringing new demands for action in the settlement of the estate. The Grand Inquisitor temporized as best he could, but his stratagems were not infinite and he knew that much further delay might bring about the collapse of his ambitions. His only consolation during this trying period was provided by the coven of witches imprisoned in the dungeons of the Holy House, who felt the full force of his impatience.

So when Miguel entered with the letter in his hand and the Grand Inquisitor recognized the writing, he had some difficulty containing his excitement.

"This was found under the door this morning," said Miguel. "It is addressed to you."

Diego restrained an impulse to snatch at the letter. "You may leave it with me," he said.

Miguel put it down on the table, a simple piece of paper, folded and sealed with red wax. Then he stood beside it. "Perhaps it is something important," Miguel suggested. "It might be from a witness who is afraid to show himself but still has important information. Or it might be . . ."

"Speculation is futile," interrupted the Grand Inquisitor, "when the answer is so near at hand." He reached out for the letter, his heart racing. "You may leave me now, Miguel."

And yet, even after his vicar was gone, Diego de Villanueva could hardly bring himself to open the paper. Too much depended on it. He was almost certain that it contained the news he was anticipating, but he could not be absolutely sure. It was difficult to fathom Sebastian's motives at the best of times, but more so now that the Grand Inquisitor had been forbidden to visit his brother. Could Sebastian be such a fool as to finish the book? Did he imagine that he would be allowed to survive once his work was accomplished? Still, the hand that had written the Grand Inquisitor's name and title was certainly that of Don Sebastian de Villanueva. And there was more proof. The red wax sealing the paper bore a cloudy impression. No one else would have recognized the mark, but the brother of the man who had made it read it easily enough. Evidently Sebastian had sealed the letter with his signet ring, then recognized the imprudence of a dead man's continuing the habit of a lifetime and effaced the wax impression.

This was interesting enough, but inconsequential. The Grand Inquisitor drew a deep breath and broke the seal.

For an instant the words swam before his eyes, but he managed to read them, then read them again. There was no signature. The message was simple and direct, only five words: "It is finished. Come tonight."

The Grand Inquisitor sank back in his chair, the paper fluttering in his trembling hand, great waves of relief washing over him. He had hardly slept for days and had not relaxed for a month, but now he sprawled like a drunkard, smiling idiotically at the crucifix on the wall. He had done it. He had won.

"*Vires Malorum,*" Sebastian said.

His brother did not reply and gave no indication that he had even heard. Utterly absorbed, he ran his fingers over the thick sheaf of paper on the ivory-and-onyx chessboard, almost as if he feared that the manuscript might be an illusion. Then he looked up distractedly.

"What? What did you call it? *Vires Malorum?*" He considered the title carefully. "I think not, Sebastian. It reminds me too much of Kramer and Sprenger, with their *Malleus Maleficarum.* We must have something different. Certainly this work is unique, not to be confused with any other. Let me think."

Sebastian sat quietly in his high-backed chair.

"*Vires . . . Vires Tenebrarum,*" said the Grand Inquisitor. "Yes, that will do. What do you think of it?"

"*Vires Tenebrarum. The Powers of Darkness.* Not bad, brother. Use it if you will. It is your book. I still prefer *The Forces of Evil* myself, but let it pass. Your title is less dogmatic, and less insulting, too. I have no cause for complaint."

"So be it," said the Grand Inquisitor. "Well!" He was at a loss for words. This moment, which he had experienced so often in anticipation, now left him somehow dissatisfied and ill at ease. Perhaps it was because he knew that he would never visit his brother in the tower again. He cast his mind back over the years of secret meetings and almost found it within himself to grow sentimental. He would miss the nocturnal duels across the chessboard, the debates on the great mysteries; he would even miss Sebastian and the jealous hatred for him that had driven Diego de Villanueva from boyhood. It saddened the Grand Inquisitor slightly to think that his brother had to die. He wanted to snatch up the book and flee with it but realized it would be unwise.

"So!" he said. "It is really finished! I am quite overcome, Sebastian. There were times when I thought you would never do it. More than once I compared you with Penelope, the wife of the great captain Ulysses, who wove her tapestry by day and undid it by night so that after ten years it was still incomplete."

"This tapestry took only nine years," Sebastian said. "Have you no wish to look upon it, brother?"

"Of course I do. But I can hardly read it here."

"Is the light too dim?"

"No, Sebastian, but it will take me days to read all this. After all, it took you years to write it." The Grand Inquisitor lifted the bulky sheaf of papers in both hands as though to indicate the enormity of his brother's effort.

"No doubt you think me a fool to be done with it," Sebastian suggested. His brother's fingers slipped involuntarily and the uppermost sheet of paper floated gracefully to the floor.

"Let me take that," said Sebastian, rising from his chair. "It is the title page, and I must change it for you." He produced another piece of paper from a shelf above a row of books, and a quill wet with ink. *"Vires Tenebrarum,"* he muttered as he wrote. "I should be writing this in blood, no doubt, but I have none to spare."

"You must have had your fill of Margarita de Mendoza," said the Grand Inquisitor.

"Yes, brother, but that was many days ago."

"And where is she now?"

"She is dead, brother. Where do the dead go?" Sebastian smiled. "You have asked me yourself more than once, and now I have the answer for you. I could not resist the temptation to give this answer to you, and to the world, whatever the cost might be to me, and that is why the book is finished. Even I am surprised at what I have discovered."

"You know?" asked the Grand Inquisitor. "You really know? How did you find it out?"

"Come, brother, leave me a few secrets. Let us say that I found the truth through meditation. I should have seen it sooner." He placed the new title page atop the pile of papers on the black-and-white chessboard. "If I had known, all this could have been finished long ago. But sometimes simple truths are the most difficult to grasp. Even now you have not asked me for the answer but only for the method by which it was discovered. Perhaps you would prefer to know nothing about it." He sank again into his shadow-shrouded chair.

"Tell me, Sebastian. You have written it anyway, and I will know it soon enough whether you speak or not."

"Very well, brother. What I tell you is what I believe, and I am certain of it. But in the book I could do no more than offer it as a belief prevalent among sorcerers and witches. Otherwise, *Vires Tenebrarum* would be condemned as the vilest heresy."

"Yes, yes," urged the Grand Inquisitor. "Tell me what it is."

"Let us suppose that the religion you profess is the true one," Sebastian began. "It teaches that those who believe in its doctrines will be saved and will live on after death in a fashion that preachers love to describe. But those who break the rules and are not reconciled are promised an eternal life of another sort, which the preachers depict even more eloquently. Is it not so?"

"More or less," granted the Grand Inquisitor.

"But even your religion admits that these futures hold true only for those who embrace the faith. For those who remain outside it, another destiny awaits, a sort of vagueness outside your universe, which you call limbo."

"You are making it all too simple, Sebastian."

"I admit it, brother. What I tell you now is not as closely reasoned as the passage in the manuscript. Shall I stop now, and let you read it for yourself?"

"Continue, Sebastian. I will not object again."

"So much, if I may say so, for your orthodoxy. But consider the others, Diego. Every religion teaches something about the life to come. The Jews believe one thing, the Moors another, and who knows how many other beliefs there are in the world? Who knows what the natives of the New World believe? You, of course, dismiss them all as pagans, but consider, brother—suppose that every one of them was right."

"Now you are speaking nonsense, Sebastian. How could every one be right?"

"Bear with me another moment. You know something of what I believe, Diego, and know that these beliefs, called witchcraft, sorcery, alchemy, or magic, are almost universally condemned. Every religion warns its followers to beware the men and women who follow the left-handed path. Might it not be because we know the truth about all of them, or because we could know it?"

"What are you driving at, Sebastian? Where is the answer you promised me?"

"Simply this, brother. Those who practice magic know, if they know anything, the importance of the will. We learn early that the power we seek is already within us and that our task is to express it, nothing more. Through concentration, through faith, we can accomplish anything. Even your religion teaches that faith is the key to everything and the one who believes will be saved. But you claim that the doctrine must be correct. I believe it need not be. In fact, I believe that there is no correct doctrine at all. There is only faith and the power of the will."

"What are you saying, Sebastian?"

"You understand me, brother, though you may pretend you do not. I am saying that the eternity a man imagines for himself is the one he will experience. Those who believe in your Heaven and believe they are worthy of it will find themselves there. Those who have faith in another future will find themselves in it, whatever it may be. The truth is that there is no truth. The world of spirits is infinite. Each man and each woman creates an individual destiny, which neither curses nor blessings can alter. Those who believe in nothing will taste oblivion, and those who wait for Hell will surely find it waiting for them."

Sebastian paused, but his brother did not answer. Instead,

the Grand Inquisitor stared silently at the papers piled before him and at the black and white squares of the chessboard. He looked at the flickering red candle and the yellow skull supporting it. He saw the gray stone walls of the tower, and the Moorish tapestry that blocked the narrow window. And he saw the dark figure of his brother, sitting in shadowed silence like an emperor of evil.

"But how can you be sure, Sebastian? This is only a theory!"

"There is no way for me to prove it to you, brother. Believe it only if you will. But when you die, remember me."

"When I die . . ." said Diego de Villanueva.

"It may not be soon, Diego, if you are careful. And that reminds me. Do you intend to kill me, now that you have the book?"

"Why, Sebastian!" said the Grand Inquisitor nervously. "Do I seem so ungrateful?"

His brother answered him with a smile that looked like the grin of a skeleton. "I am reassured," he said. "I had imagined that you might decide you had no further use for me now that you have the book, and now that your dungeons are filled with witches."

"How could you know about the other witches? I have said nothing."

"When one witch is snatched away by a winged monster, confessions among her colleagues are certain to increase. I knew that what I did at the *auto* would be of some help to you. So you see how useful I can be, brother. Will you let me live a little longer? Perhaps I can help you again."

Something in Sebastian's mocking tone made his brother uneasy. Did he suspect that the Grand Inquisitor planned to destroy him while he slept? No. That was impossible. He would hardly be fool enough to hand over the manuscript if he understood that its last page was his death warrant. But why was he talking about it this way?

"There is still much for me to teach you," Sebastian continued, "and more for me to learn. A mere month ago I could not answer your question about death and its mysteries."

"I am less than certain that you have answered it now."

"But suppose that I have! Might you not need me, if only to teach you how to control your own mind? What do you believe now, brother? What would your fate be if you died tonight?"

The Grand Inquisitor stirred uneasily on his hard wooden bench. "My faith will sustain me," he said.

"Come, Diego. I am your brother, not one of those superstitious souls in the city below us. Do not preach to me. How sure are you of Heaven, you, who have spent your life creating Hell on earth? I believe—and you believe it too—that you have only enough faith in your theology to become one of the damned."

The Grand Inquisitor had no reply to this.

"But do not despair," continued Sebastian. "If I have time enough, perhaps I will be able to enlighten you. There is always hope, and that is the beginning of faith."

Diego de Villanueva made an unsuccessful attempt at a sneer. He was becoming angry as well as agitated.

"No?" asked Sebastian. "There is another reason for you to spare me, brother, at least for a little while. Take your *Vires Tenebrarum* and study it. You may find something in it that you will want to change. I will be waiting to assist you, and even when you have satisfied yourself you may find that you have further need of me. No doubt you will send the manuscript to your mentor, Torquemada, the Inquisitor General. You will need his approval and endorsement, but they may not be easy to obtain. What will you do when he questions you on some obscure argument in the text? What but run to your older and wiser brother for advice? It would be a shame for you to risk everything when you are so close to success."

There was something in this, much as Diego hated to admit it even to himself. The book might bear his name, but it was Sebastian's work, and very likely only he could understand it all. The Grand Inquisitor tried to calculate the amount of time necessary to deliver the book to Torquemada and receive his reply. Miguel would have to be sent with the manuscript and it would take him many days to return, even if he were able to obtain an immediate audience with the Inquisitor General. It might be possible, though, to keep Antonio away from the castle for a few more weeks, and Sebastian was right when he said that it would be wiser to wait.

Suddenly the Grand Inquisitor was very tired. This night, for which he had waited so long, did not mean the end of his worries after all. There would be more delays, more intrigues. He was not yet free.

Sebastian stood up and put a cold hand on his brother's shoulder. The flickering candlelight made him look as if he were laughing, but he made no sound. "You are weary, brother," he said. "You must sleep. Your hours are not like mine and you are busy with your torture chambers. Think on what I have told you and read your book. I will be here when you need me."

He ushered the befuddled Grand Inquisitor through the arched door of the topmost room in the topmost tower and followed him down the dark stone steps. Neither spoke until they reached the courtyard, where a chestnut mare was tethered. Sebastian obsequiously offered to help his brother into the saddle, but the mare shied away from him and the Grand Inquisitor was obliged to mount her unassisted. He did it clumsily, with one hand clutching the bulky manuscript.

Diego de Villanueva rode slowly across the open drawbridge and soon vanished into the darkness. "Good night, brother," Sebastian called after him. "Sleep well."

Sebastian reached for the windlass to raise the bridge, but before he could touch it Margarita stepped from the shadows.

"You should never have given it to him," she said. "It was your protection."

"I hope you are wrong," Sebastian said. "I could hardly keep it from him forever or he would have become dangerous from sheer frustration. As it is, I think I have convinced him not to act too hastily. Even so, you are right; we must be on guard."

"But how can we protect ourselves when we must lie in the crypt?"

"Trust me, Margarita. If all goes well, we shall have nothing to fear. The book is poisoned."

Margarita smiled, and her lover was amazed anew at her ferocious beauty. "You have poisoned the pages?" she asked. "What did you use?"

"Not the pages, Margarita. This is something subtler still. I have poisoned the words. *The Powers of Darkness* will be Diego's undoing."

Margarita seemed to have lost interest in the Grand Inquisitor. She stepped back into the shadows. Her voice spoke to Sebastian quietly from a corner of the courtyard. "I heard what you told him. Was it true, what you said about faith and the future?"

Sebastian looked toward her but saw only a faintly glowing phantom. "I did not mean for you to hear that," he said, "but I believe that it is true. You taught me."

"When I told you that I did not believe in a life after death, and when I told you that the daylight did not bring me dreams like yours?" The voice from the darkness was almost a whisper.

"Yes," said Sebastian.

Margarita ran from the shadows and threw her arms around the tall, silent figure in the crimson cloak. "I don't want to lose you, Sebastian," she cried, "and I don't want to die. You must show me how to believe. You must show me how to have dreams like yours!"

16. The Second Voyage

MIGUEL started out for Madrid, but he never reached it.

Only two days after he began his journey with the manuscript of *Vires Tenebrarum,* he began to hear stories about the king and queen that caused him to change his plans. Rumors said that the sovereigns were no longer in Madrid. For some reason they had decided to hold court at Burgos, or so Miguel was told. Perhaps the move meant nothing more than a desire to be in the north where the weather might be a little cooler. Who could understand the whims of royalty?

For Miguel the reason was unimportant. It was enough for him to know that his goal was so much closer than he had expected and that he would be spared weeks of traveling alone through the provinces. For if Ferdinand and Isabella were at Burgos, then Tomás de Torquemada would surely be there as well, since he was not only Inquisitor General of the whole kingdom but confessor to the queen as well. And it was Torquemada whom Miguel had set out to see, for Diego de Villanueva had given strict instructions that the book should be delivered directly to the one man in Spain whose influence was sufficient to guarantee its success.

Elated by the discovery that his journey would be so short,

Miguel hurried toward Burgos. His timid nature made him uneasy on the road, and he continually imagined himself set upon by thieves, even though he realized there was not much reason for anyone to waylay a monk bound by vows of poverty. Still, it was a great relief to him when he passed through the gates of Burgos with the manuscript still safe in his saddlebag. Almost at once a new source of trepidation occurred to him. Now that he had arrived, he would be obliged to present himself at court, and he realized that he had no idea what to do. Of course, the Grand Inquisitor had given him instruction in deportment, but Miguel forgot everything in his first rush of panic. He was only a humble friar alone in a strange city that was not even the one he had been ordered to visit. He needed help, or at least some idea of where to go.

For a while he rode aimlessly through the streets. He passed any number of people and more than once determined to ask for directions, but he never did. The citizens, no doubt worthy enough, looked suspicious to him, and he could not bring himself to ask anyone the way to the king and queen, if only for fear that anyone he asked might reply with a burst of laughter. Miguel Carillo did not look like a courtier.

As the afternoon turned into evening, the young friar decided it would be wisest to postpone his mission until the following day. Relieved by this decision, he made for the nearest inn. His horse was soon stabled, but Miguel took the saddlebag with him when he entered the common room. A goat was roasting on the open fire and several fellows of various classes were enthusiastically imbibing. It was a rowdy, smoky place, and Miguel wondered if he might be able to find shelter at a monastery instead. Then he saw a Franciscan friar sitting alone at the end of the long table and decided that he would stay at least long enough to get some information.

The Franciscan was a tall man with a long red face. His aquiline nose was freckled, his eyes extraordinarily blue. He seemed no more than middle-aged, yet his hair and beard were white. But the eyes were certainly his most unusual feature.

Their color alone was remarkable, at least in this district, and their expression was more remarkable still. Seamed and weathered and saddened, they nonetheless appeared possessed by a vision. They were not fiery and penetrating like Diego de Villanueva's; instead, they gazed outward dreamily, as if they saw something invisible to others. Miguel concluded that the man was a mystic—no doubt a commendable calling, but not very useful to anyone looking for practical advice.

Miguel had almost decided to look elsewhere for help when the blue-eyed Franciscan spoke to him. "Sit down, young man," he said. Miguel was a little surprised, since he was almost certain that the friar had not even looked in his direction, but he did as he was told.

"Are you lost?" asked the Franciscan. "You look as if you might be."

"I know where I am," answered Miguel, "but I am not quite sure where I am going. I came in here to get directions."

"It is a terrible thing to be lost," said the Franciscan, toying with the empty cup in front of him. "I feel that way myself. It is only when I don't know where I am that I feel really at home, and right now I am only too aware that I am in Burgos."

Miguel was certain now that he was talking to the wrong man. This one made no sense at all. Miguel's expression must have given him away, because the Franciscan reacted to his thoughts. "I am not mad, young man," he said, "or at least I do not think so. I only meant to say that I am a wanderer, an adventurer if you will, so that I am happiest when seeking something new. I have just returned from the Indies."

"The Indies!" said Miguel. "Then you know the great admiral of the ocean sea? Columbus?"

"I know him as well as any man does."

"So the second expedition has returned," said Miguel. "We have heard nothing of it, though I suppose that is not surprising, since our city is a small one on the northern border. Few dispatches come our way."

"You may have your own news, though. There have been

reports of battles with the French in the region of the Pyrenees."

"Battles!" gasped Miguel. "Are we invaded? I knew nothing
of it. Are we at war?"

"Hardly a war, as I understand; not here. But we have been
fighting the French over the succession in Naples, and they lost
with bad grace. Some of their troops have been making forays
across the mountains, but it will not amount to much."

"It may not be much to you," Miguel retorted, "but if you
lived there you would feel different." He imagined hordes of
soldiers rushing into the Holy House and was glad to be far
away in Burgos.

"Of course," said the Franciscan apologetically, "I have been
gone for so long that none of this seems real to me. I have been
in another world. Three years! But even there we lived with
warfare, and treachery too."

"Tell me about the New World," urged Miguel.

"They call it that now, don't they? But it is not a new world.
It is the Orient, which will surely be proved in time, though
even this second voyage did not penetrate far enough to reach
the great cities of the khan. There should be a third expedition
at once, but now there are delays and doubts and politicians.
The people cheered when the *Niña* and the *Pinta* returned
from the first voyage, but they laughed and jeered at the men
who came ashore this June. I admit that the men were a sorry
sight. They had come through war, disease, and starvation, but
by San Fernando! they had come through! The only thing anyone wanted to know was how much gold had been discovered.
May God take them! Is gold everything?"

"Then the second voyage was a failure?" asked Miguel tact-
lessly.

"It was not! By San Fernando it was not! But I fear it will be
considered one," the Franciscan said, lowering his voice. "It was
the crew. On the first voyage there were real seafaring men—
tough, hard-working sailors. But once the stories of that expedition began to spread, a crew of fops and dandies appeared,

eager to seek their fortunes on the second voyage. They should have stayed at home! As soon as they discovered that they could not pick up handfuls of gold on the first beach, they grew surly and rebellious."

"There was a rebellion against the admiral?"

"Worse than that. There was treachery. The trouble began before we sighted land. Men who had been left behind at the colony of La Navidad disobeyed the admiral's instructions. They treated the Indians brutally, raped and looted, and fought among themselves for the spoils. Finally a native tribe rose up against them and the settlement was destroyed to the last man. When we arrived with a fleet of seventeen ships there was no colony, and we had to begin again."

"Were the Indians punished?"

"They were punished and more. Perhaps too much more. The leader of the uprising, a king named Caonabo, was captured by Margarit, one of the most headstrong of the lieutenants—*worse* than headstrong. He was left in charge of the new colony at Saint Thomas while the search went on for other lands, and he treated the natives abominably. These Indians are simple, peaceful people for the most part, and they should be converted, not exterminated. But too many greedy men had come from Spain, and they could not be controlled. The order was finally given that each native should produce a tribute in gold every month, even though the conditions were impossible. There is not much gold there, only farther inland, and the Indians grew desperate. Some tried to fight and were killed. Others fled into the hills and were hunted down with dogs. The worst of all were those who lost all hope and poisoned themselves. I believe close to half of them must have died since the second expedition arrived."

"And did the admiral approve all this?" asked Miguel, more interested than appalled.

"What else could be done? Could a man take the part of these savages in opposition to his own lieutenants? But it hardly mattered. No concession was great enough. These fair-weather sailors became indignant at every turn. They thought themselves too good to cultivate the land, even though it was obvious that the ships could not carry enough supplies to feed them for years. And always there was the cry for more gold. Finally, Margarit took one of the ships—stole it. He headed back to Spain with a crew of malcontents to poison the minds of the sovereigns against the expedition. The result of this treachery was the appearance of another Spanish vessel at Saint Thomas bearing a fellow named Juan Aguado, who was named crown chamberlain, with authority to oversee the whole enterprise, an unacceptable situation. We returned to Spain at once, or would have, but there was a delay when a terrible storm arose. Three ships were sunk. I think it was a judgment of God. Finally, two ships limped back to Cadiz with a cargo of slaves to compensate for the gold that could not be found. King Caonabo, who was among them, died like a dog aboard the *Niña*, though he had been a mighty ruler in his own land. And here we are, awaiting the royal pleasure."

"What did the king and queen have to say?"

"Oh, they were polite and attentive and promised to outfit a third expedition. But what good are promises? Already months have passed. Now there are no men to volunteer for another voyage. Even men in prison prefer confinement to the dangers of the Indies, and they refuse pardons rather than brave the unknown. And ships? There seem to be none, though an armada of one hundred and thirty took the Princess Juana to her marriage in Flanders."

"Then you have been at court?" asked Miguel, suddenly remembering his own mission.

"I have, and it appears that I will be again," answered the Franciscan.

"Then you can help me," said Miguel. "How do I get there? And what should I do to gain admittance?"

"You must not expect much from Ferdinand and Isabella. They have a war to contend with and royal weddings. They have little time for such as you or me, my friend."

"They are not the ones I seek," said Miguel. "My business is with the Inquisitor General."

"The Inquisitor General? Torquemada?"

"Yes. Tomás de Torquemada," said Miguel reverently. "Why do you look so surprised?"

"You will be more surprised, my friend. I am glad you have not traveled far, because you will not find Torquemada at court."

"What? He must be. He is the queen's confessor."

"No longer," said the Franciscan. "He is old and ill and has his troubles with the Holy Office. You will find him at Avila. He has retired to the monastery there that was built on his instructions years ago."

"Retired?" Miguel could hardly have been more bewildered. "Is he still Inquisitor General?"

"I suppose he is. It is said that he is at work on new instructions for the operation of the Inquisition."

"Avila!" Miguel said in despair. "Where is Avila?"

"Almost half a kingdom away," answered the Franciscan. "At least three times as far as you have already traveled. It lies to the west of Madrid."

Miguel looked crestfallen. "Then I am for Avila," he said unhappily.

"Cheer up, my friend. You have an adventure ahead of you. A young fellow should be happy to have a chance to see something of the world."

"This is no adventure," Miguel answered glumly. "It is a duty and one I would gladly be spared. But someone had to deliver the book and I was chosen."

"A book. It must be a wonderful thing to have written a book."

"It is not mine. It is the work of the Grand Inquisitor Diego de Villanueva, who wishes to bring it to the attention of the Holy Office. I am only a messenger."

"Well, you are still young. No doubt you will write your own someday. Learning is a wonderful thing. I am a simple seafaring man myself, but I believe my son Ferdinand will be a scholar."

Dumbfounded, Miguel stared at his companion. What sort of a monk was this who claimed to have no learning and openly acknowledged that he had broken his vow of chastity? It was known, of course, that there were monks who had fathered children, but few of them were intemperate enough to boast about their indiscretions.

Again the bright blue eyes seemed to look into Miguel's mind. "You need not look so startled," said the man in the rough brown robe. "I am quite prepared to acknowledge my ignorance—and my children, too. I had no wish to deceive you, my friend, but I am no Franciscan friar."

"But . . ." said Miguel, completing his sentence with a gesture toward the stranger's costume.

"This?" said the false Franciscan, holding up the hem of his habit. "I wear it for a penance. I fear that I have much to answer for. And it has other uses. I might be recognized if I wore other clothes, and I have troubles enough."

Miguel started to speak but was interrupted.

"You have troubles, too," said the man, "even if they have not turned your hair white. Mine was red not too long ago; but never mind. We must speed you on your journey, my friend. This tavern is no place for you, nor for me either. There is a Franciscan monastery on the road just south of here. If you leave at once, you can reach it before nightfall. They will be glad to shelter you and you will be a little farther along on your journey. I wish you well."

Miguel stood up with his head in a spin. This stranger, whoever he might be, was the oddest man he had ever encountered. Still, that was no reason for Miguel to be discourteous.

"I am Miguel Carillo," he said, "vicar to Diego de Villanueva, Grand Inquisitor. I thank you, both for your help and for your tales of the Indies. May God be with you."

"And I thank you, Miguel Carillo, for your company and for your blessing." The stranger took the young monk by the arm

169

and leaned forward. "My name," he said in a whisper, "is Don Cristóbal de Colón."

Miguel was out of the smoky tavern and in the street before he realized what he had heard. He looked back toward the inn as if it were a vision.

Cristóbal de Colón—Columbus—the admiral of the ocean sea.

17. The Twelve Apostles

THE monastery of Saint Thomas was renowned as the most beautiful in Spain. More than ten years, as well as a considerable portion of the revenue confiscated by the Inquisition, had been consumed in its construction. Building this magnificent edifice was a personal project of great importance to Tomás de Torquemada; it was said that the Inquisitor General had stood humbly beside the common laborers and worked on it with his own hands. He was certainly responsible for the legend engraved upon its walls: *Pestem Fugat Haereticam.* No heretic, no one who was even a descendant of a Jew or a Moor, was ever permitted to enter its sacred precincts. The only exception made was for those who were carried into its dungeons.

The monastery stood outside the town of Avila in the rich green lands along the Adaja River. The countryside was so different from the bleak one beneath the Pyrenees that Miguel began to wish he might never have to return. At the same time, though, he was anxious to be off. He knew all too well that Diego de Villanueva would grow more impatient with every second wasted in unnecessary delay and that only a foolish vicar would use a pleasant landscape as an excuse for a protracted stay. Not even his fear of an impending war along the border could keep Miguel within the tranquil cloisters of Saint Thomas. His mission was too important to be forgotten for reasons of personal safety. He sensed obscurely that his master's future rode with him, and loyalty was Miguel's cardinal virtue. If he waited, it was because he had no choice.

He was waiting for Torquemada.

Miguel had been naive enough to imagine that he would be granted an immediate audience with the Inquisitor General, but he was soon disillusioned. Evidently, the name of Diego de Villanueva, Grand Inquisitor, did not carry as much weight here as it did in his own district. In fact, nobody seemed to have heard the name at all. Miguel was even persuaded, against his better judgment and in contravention of his previous instructions, to surrender the precious manuscript that had never left his side during his entire journey. He had been told to deliver *Vires Tenebrarum* into no other hands than Torquemada's, but the order was impossible to follow. Torquemada was not to be approached so easily. Still, the monk who took the manuscript assured Miguel that it would be placed before the Inquisitor General and that an interview might be arranged soon. Meanwhile, Miguel was left to entertain himself as best he could.

For days he wandered aimlessly across the wide courtyards and down the pillared passages surrounding them. He ate, slept, and read, worshiped, prayed, and meditated. He worried and waited. On the fourth day he was summoned.

Miguel followed another Dominican down long, tiled cloisters supported by marble columns, past paintings of saints and angels. At length they reached a plain plank door. Miguel passed through it and was alone with the Inquisitor General.

The austerity of the room surprised Miguel. The whitewashed walls were bare except for a large silver crucifix, and the furnishings consisted of no more than a pair of chairs and a plain table. Still, Torquemada was renowned for his severity. It was only natural to suppose that his surroundings would be simple. This might have been Diego de Villanueva's chamber in the Holy House, except for two incongruous notes. There was an open window in the far wall, through which Miguel could see a flower garden and hear the distant song of birds. And, even though it was summer, logs burned in the fireplace behind the man seated at the table.

It was this figure that caught Miguel's attention and held it so that he absorbed the appearance of the room without really looking at it. He was not fully aware of anything but Tomás de Torquemada. At first glance, the Inquisitor General was something of a disappointment. Miguel had tried to picture him during the long days and nights on the road but had not been able to imagine anything more impressive than a bigger version of Diego de Villanueva. What he saw instead was a wizened old man, small, frail, and evidently in very poor health. He was dressed, like Miguel, in the black-and-white robes of the Dominican order. The fringe of hair around his shaven head was sparse and grizzled, his grim face a mass of quivering wrinkles. Only the brown eyes, liquid and unusually large, seemed alive.

The Inquisitor General gestured Miguel into a chair with a thin, unsteady hand. The manuscript was on the table between them. Sunlight poured in through the open window, its radiance turning the pale pages yellow. The room was filled with the scent of flowers.

"Miguel Carillo," said Torquemada. The voice was more powerful than the body that produced it. Miguel was disturbed by the discrepancy, and he fancied for a moment that there might be someone else in the room. Then he collected himself.

"Vicar to Diego de Villanueva, Grand Inquisitor," said Miguel.

Torquemada said nothing for a moment, but something like a smile touched his thin lips. "I remember him," he said finally. "He studied with me for some time. When he was ready to become an Inquisitor, he asked to be sent home. It was most unusual, and at the time I wondered why. Now I know. He was an ambitious boy."

Miguel could hardly believe that Diego de Villanueva had ever been a boy. Somehow the thought upset him.

"Have you read this?" asked Torquemada, tapping the

manuscript with a thin forefinger. His voice was suddenly sharp and cold.

"What?" gasped Miguel guiltily. "No! I wanted to, of course, but I did not have permission. I am only a messenger."

"Good. Obedience is a virtue. In your case, virtue will be rewarded."

"Rewarded?" echoed Miguel nervously.

"I meant that you are fortunate not to have read this book," said Torquemada. "What do you know about it?"

"Only that it concerns witches."

"Witches and more. Sorcerers and soothsayers, Miguel Carillo, and devils and demons. Vampires, werewolves, ghouls—every fantastic horror spawned by the Devil is in this book, each abomination described in incredible detail, and with an intimate knowledge of the subject that might frighten any man. You are very lucky not to have read it, my son, and for more than one reason. What do you think of all this, Miguel Carillo? Do you believe this kind of story?"

"It must be true," said Miguel. "We have witches in the Holy House now. I have seen them."

"No doubt you have seen something," replied the Inquisitor General. "But what was it? No doubt you have women in your dungeons, but how do you know they are witches?"

"The Grand Inquisitor said there was a letter for you, sir, describing the case of Margarita de Mendoza, who . . ."

"I have read the letter, with its fabulous tale about a demon from the pit. But let us put that aside for a moment. I want to tell you a story. Perhaps you will learn something from it."

Miguel waited uneasily. Somehow this interview was not proceeding according to plan.

"This is a true story," said Torquemada, "and what I tell you happened not just once but many times. A band of men traveled through the countryside, stopping here and there at lonely inns. There were thirteen of these men, strangely dressed. They appeared at an inn and one of them ordered a meal. He was the only one who ever spoke. The others sat quietly, looking with adoration at one who seemed to be their leader: a tall man with long hair and noble features. The behavior of these men was very strange, almost frightening. When the meal was served, the one who had ordered it announced to the innkeeper that he was playing host to Jesus Christ and His twelve apostles."

Miguel crossed himself. Torquemada watched him with huge eyes, then went on with the story.

"Of course, the landlord was awestruck. Miracles do happen, even to the simplest of men. As certainly as a man may see a witch, so he may see a saint, or even the Lord Himself. The innkeeper washed the feet of the thirteen guests and knelt beside them as they ate. When the meal was over, he was called upon to confess his sins. There is probably not an innkeeper who does not cheat his customers when he can, and he would certainly admit as much to visitors like these, along with whatever else he had on his conscience. After the confession came the penance. The one who spoke instructed the innkeeper to bring forth all his money. The man was too frightened to hold any back, and before long every ducat was on the table where the Last Supper had been reenacted. Then came the judgment. All this money was tainted with sin. Some of it would be returned to the landlord, in payment for the meal. As for the rest of it, nobody would touch it, for it was declared to be the Devil's money. But no sooner were these words spoken than the door of the inn burst open and a horror rushed into the room, its face black and hairy, its head bearing horns. This thing gathered up the money and ran out into the night. Then the thirteen guests departed silently, leaving the innkeeper to give thanks that his life had been spared and his tavern blessed."

Torquemada stopped speaking and stared at Miguel as though passing judgment on him. The wrinkled face of the Inquisitor General was contorted with some indecipherable emotion.

"There are now fourteen men in the dungeons of the Inquisition," said Torquemada. "Fourteen thieves. Twelve played the disciples, one played Christ, one the Devil. They robbed many an inn with their masquerade, and it was only when the reports of miracles became widespread that we were able to capture them. But there was no miracle, Miguel Carillo. Only greed and stupidity."

Bewilderment showed on Miguel's thin face. His eyes goggled and his mouth gaped. He had believed every word of the story and would have been willing to tell anyone that Christ and His twelve apostles were making a tour of Spanish inns. How could he doubt it, considering the source?

Torquemada continued, blandly overlooking his young visitor's evident confusion. "So you see," he said, "how easy it is to deceive people. Most men are fools. And women, too; they may be worse. I wonder. The witches who have been taken in France and Germany are usually women. Whether one believes in witchcraft or not, it is certainly unwise to practice it. Have you ever wondered whether it might be unwise to prosecute them? Consider, Miguel Carillo. There has never been a trial for witchcraft in all the annals of the Inquisition. Do you think this is an accident? A mistake? Have you read the *Reportorium Inquisitorium* of 1496?"

Miguel shook his head.

"Diego de Villanueva should have read it," said Torquemada. "It contains a thorough discussion of this matter of witchcraft and concludes that these witches, these *jorguinas*, are laboring under a delusion. It may be their own delusion, or may be wrought by demons, but for purposes of our discussion it is hardly worthwhile to distinguish between the two. The point is that these wretched creatures have no power to perform magic, whatever they may believe. Witchcraft is folly. Of course, it is still a heresy. The fact that nothing comes of the spells these wretches try to cast is immaterial. They are still guilty of rejecting the true faith and are still liable to prosecution by the Holy Office. But what would be the result of these prosecutions?"

Miguel was dumbfounded but was spared the problem of answering the Inquisitor General's rhetorical question. He looked out the window and saw a fountain among the flowers.

"We have studied the witchcraft trials throughout Europe," continued Torquemada, "and have drawn our own conclusions. It appears that nothing encourages the spread of this cult as much as the attempt to suppress it. Every trial leaves in its wake a new band of witches. The people are weak and stupid, their minds ready to be inflamed by any passing fancy. Let them know that there is such a thing as witchcraft and any number of them will rush to embrace it, heedless of the danger to their bodies and souls. This is human nature, Miguel Carillo. It is not comforting but it is true, and there should be at least a little comfort in it, for when we know the truth we can use it for our own ends. We know that the lives of the poor are empty and futile and that they are ready to follow any illusion that offers them the hope of power and excitement. What does the Inquisition matter to a peasant woman who hears that she can lie with the Devil and then rise up with the power to blight her enemies?"

"Then the book?" asked Miguel, looking at the fire. He would look anywhere but at the Inquisitor General. He was cold and shaking like the old man across the table.

"The book," said Torquemada. "Diego de Villanueva's book. I can imagine what he thought while he was working on it. He asked to be assigned to the district where he was born, on the French border, and he was certain that he would find some evidence of witchcraft there eventually. No doubt he saw this cult flooding down from the mountains over the entire kingdom, with himself riding the crest of the wave. I wonder if he realized that the flood would be of his own making. No doubt he was too busy counting the honors that would be bestowed upon him as the Inquisition's authority on witchcraft. How many men do you suppose there are nursing the same ambition?"

Miguel's face was pale. He had nothing to say.

"There are ambitious men everywhere, Miguel Carillo, and

everywhere there is the struggle for position, even in the Holy Office, even in a sacred order where every effort should be made to maintain the discipline that will sustain the faith. I assume you have heard of my own recent difficulties."

Miguel made a feeble effort to look wise, but had no idea what the Inquisitor General was talking about.

"As you know," said Torquemada, "much of our work has been directed toward rooting out heresy among those in high places. It is much more important to drag down the heretics with wealth and influence than it is to burn some lunatic peasant, but it is also much more difficult. It has been my policy to spare nobody, not even men of the cloth. If I were a politician I might have fared better, but I am only a humble servant of the truth. Some of those who fell under suspicion were men in high places; one of them was the bishop of Segovia, whose grandfather was a Jew. He appealed to Rome and the result was a decree from this new pope, Alexander VI, that the Inquisition could proceed against him only with the consent of the Vatican. Others complained, too, whose positions counted for more than the purity of their faith. It has been two years now since Alexander appointed a pair of men to assist me. Assist me! He made them my equals in authority. The only reason he gave was concern for my health and my advancing years, but that was diplomacy. Now the bishop of Avila and the archbishop of Messina have the support of the pope and are here to implement his policies. They want to force me out; I know it. They might have waited; I have only a little time left before my work on earth is done."

Torquemada sighed theatrically and assumed the air of a martyr. Miguel felt some sympathy for the old man, but it was lost in his bewilderment over the conflicts within the Holy Office. If even the most powerful prelates could not agree, then what was a simple vicar to think?

"But I will tell you something," said Torquemada, his voice growing stronger. "They have not beaten me yet, Miguel Carillo, and as long as there is life in this body I will not see the

Inquisition turned away from its duty to pursue phantoms like those concocted by Diego de Villanueva."

Miguel tried to react. He cast his eyes on the pile of papers sitting in the sunlight and remembered how important they had seemed to him only a few minutes ago.

"But surely there must be more to it," Miguel protested timidly. "What about the evidence?"

Torquemada looked at him grimly. "Even if I believed in the evidence, I would deny it rather than encourage people to accept the idea of witchcraft. We have enough to do with the Jews and the Moors."

"But something came down from the sky," Miguel persisted. "A terrible creature with wings!"

"Did you see this yourself?" asked Torquemada.

"No," admitted Miguel. "But there were dozens of witnesses."

"Men may be deceived. I would not be surprised if this were some trick of Diego de Villanueva's. I will have to question him about it."

Something in Torquemada's last phrase chilled Miguel. He felt his stomach drop, yet still he tried to argue.

"So many saw it," Miguel said weakly. "It will be told. A tale like that will go down in history."

Torquemada shook his head wearily. He was so surprised at this young man's stupidity that he almost forgot to be angry with him.

"History is made not by those who experience it," said Torquemada, "but by those who write it down. There will be no record of this event, I promise you. I will see to it. And in a few years it will be forgotten, Miguel Carillo. No one will believe that it ever happened."

Miguel tried to speak but was dumbfounded. He produced only a sort of inarticulate noise, but Torquemada had the wit to interpret it.

"You would be well advised to stop this futile defense of the book and to consider your own position. This is a very dangerous document."

Miguel looked again at the pile of sun-drenched papers but saw nothing frightening in them. He was afraid not of the book but of Tomás de Torquemada. He realized, however dimly, that his mission had failed and that both he and Diego de Villanueva might be in serious trouble with the Inquisition.

Torquemada's blue-veined hand caressed the pages of the book. "Suppose that everything written here is true," said Torquemada, "even the outrageous blasphemies purporting to describe a sorcerer's beliefs concerning the afterlife. Can you imagine what the effect would be if such a heresy were published?"

Miguel could not imagine. He could only stare stupidly at the Inquisitor General and imagine himself being put to the Question.

"Suppose even that it might be advisable for the Holy Office to engage in a campaign against witchcraft," Torquemada continued. "Not even that could excuse this book. It is so full of information about the spawn of Satan that no one could read it without beginning to wonder about the author. I have wondered myself. How did Diego de Villanueva learn so much about these horrors? It would be easy enough to believe that he had lived among them. Of course, that is not a comforting thought. I hope to ask him about it soon."

Miguel understood these words only too well. He might have tried to defend the Grand Inquisitor, but he was speechless.

"I am glad to see that you have nothing to say," Torquemada remarked in a more soothing tone. "I believe you when you tell me that you had nothing to do with this *Vires Tenebrarum,* and I will respect your innocence. I know that I have been called a bloodthirsty fiend, but you have nothing to fear from me, Miguel Carillo. Go back to your work. Go back to Diego de Villanueva and wait. You will hear from me."

Relief poured over Miguel like sunshine, momentarily washing away his panic at the realization that his master had been found unworthy.

Torquemada stirred in his chair as if impatient to conclude

the interview. He turned to look at the fire behind him. "Perhaps you have wondered about this fire," he said pleasantly. "I find that it soothes me. I am an old man, Miguel Carillo—seventy-six—and I find that my old bones are cold and stiff even in the summer. The fire warms me. And it has other uses."

Miguel stiffened.

Torquemada turned back toward the table and picked up the manuscript. "Six years ago," he said, "in 1490, I had another fire, a larger one. But this one will do. On that day, when I was younger and stronger, I burned six hundred volumes that smacked of heresy. They made a lovely blaze, Miguel Carillo. Yet none of them, I think, was as damnable a book as this."

Tomás de Torquemada shifted his chair so that he faced the fire. He crumpled the first page of *Vires Tenebrarum* and tossed it into the flames. It caught almost at once, burning with a blue-and-yellow flame. In an instant it was gone, leaving only a thin black tissue that writhed and glowed with red as it collapsed into ashes. A second page followed the first. Miguel's head was ringing with the echoes of the screams he had heard weeks ago at the *auto-da-fé*, and he saw blistering faces in the flames as another page caught fire.

Hunched over before the fireplace, Torquemada tired of his game at last. He might have spent an hour burning the manuscript one sheet at a time, but he had other matters to consider. He tossed the entire book into the fire. It landed with a thump and a shower of sparks. For a moment it looked to Miguel as if the weight of the paper might break up the slow-burning blaze, but the pages slithered away from each other and ignited one by one. The bulk of the manuscript began to smoke and smolder.

"You may leave me now," said the Inquisitor General.

Miguel backed away on shaking legs and felt behind him for the door. He took a last look at Torquemada but saw only an old man warming himself before an open fire, his face red and sweating, huge eyes gleaming with reflected light.

18. Judgment

DIEGO DE VILLANUEVA, Grand Inquisitor, stood before his brother's castle and screamed.

He cried out his brother's name and called on saints and demons. He raved and shouted until his horse took fright. When the beast bolted and ran off through the forest to its stable at the Holy House he did not even notice that it was gone. He saw nothing but the castle, its towers black against the cloudy, starless night, and he listened for nothing but an answer to his cries. He cared nothing for his frightened mare or for the city to which it fled. He was a pilgrim seeking sanctuary.

The drawbridge dropped down. The Grand Inquisitor heard its groan and was as grateful for the sound as he would have been for the song of an angel. The entrance gaped before him like a hungry mouth and he rushed headlong into it.

The dark in the courtyard was impenetrable. The Grand Inquisitor glanced nervously around but saw only shadows. The rattle of heavy chains came from a black corner: the sound of the drawbridge closing behind him. Diego de Villanueva was shut up in the castle and was grateful for it. Here he might be safe. The castle had protected Sebastian for years, and they were sons of the same father. Now these towers would have to be his refuge too.

"Sebastian?" whispered Diego. Now that he stood within the walls, there was no longer any need to shout. Yet he was still terribly agitated, as only a man can be who has seen his highest hopes shattered and who finds himself at last a victim of the very tyranny he has inflicted on others. Fear of the unknown is not always the most powerful: the Grand Inquisitor knew only too well what the Inquisition might do to him, and that knowledge made him something less than cautious concerning the reception he might expect to receive from his brother Sebastian.

An icy hand grasped Diego's wrist. He jumped at the touch of it. "Sebastian?" he said again. He could see only a dim form but knew it for his brother and followed willingly as he was pulled across the courtyard toward the keep.

"They burned it, Sebastian," muttered Diego incoherently. "We are lost. Lost in the flames. They burned it. You must save me."

Sebastian kept his silence as he led his brother slowly up the long stone stairway, but Diego could not stop talking.

"They want to kill me," he said. "The old man is jealous of me. That must be it. I know too much. I have surpassed him, and I deserve to be Inquisitor General. They are afraid of me, and they want to kill me. But they will never find me, Sebastian. I will be safe here."

Sebastian stopped at the top of the stairs and pushed open the door to his study. As Diego entered, he felt two hands drop on his shoulders. Sebastian pushed him back against the wall so that his head struck the unyielding rock.

"Speak sense if you must speak at all," said Sebastian harshly. "What do you mean by howling outside the walls like a lost dog? Would you destroy us both? Sit, and calm yourself. Has the world ended?"

Diego dropped down upon his usual bench and sat like a stone. "You are not far wrong, Sebastian," he said. "I think the world has ended, at least for me."

"You are still among the living," said Sebastian as he seated himself in the huge chair across the chessboard from his brother.

Diego's glance dropped to the chessboard and remained frozen there. The onyx and ivory board held only two pieces: a white bishop and a black castle. He looked up at Sebastian in amazement.

"A small problem in strategy," said Sebastian. "How would you play it out, brother? Or do you still prefer the cards?"

"Don't toy with me, Sebastian. You don't realize what has happened."

"Then tell me," said Sebastian. His long white fingers reached over the table and knocked the two chessmen to the floor. "You have my complete attention."

"It is the book. I sent my vicar off with it and he returned today. I saw at once that he was disturbed, and it did not take me long to find out what had happened, or at least the essence of it. The young fool was so frightened that his story made no sense at first."

"It would seem that you have trained him well," said Sebastian.

His brother ignored this gibe. "I suppose I am fortunate that he returned at all, considering what happened to him. I have no way of knowing if he came back to warn me, or only to keep an eye on me until the officers of the Inquisition could arrive. But he finally told me what I had to know. Torquemada read the book and condemned it. After all these years! He said the Holy Office had no interest in witchcraft and that in any case the book was heresy. Miguel thought he meant to prosecute me, and I have no reason to doubt it. Torquemada burned our book, Sebastian! And I am a fugitive from the Inquisition!"

Sebastian's dead eyes stared at the inlaid squares of black and white. "So much for *The Powers of Darkness,*" he said.

"You did your work too well, Sebastian. There was more in that book than any man could have learned in a lifetime. You have ruined me!"

"And perhaps myself as well, brother. What do you intend to do?"

"Do?" shouted the Grand Inquisitor. "What is there for me to do? I came to you because there was nowhere else to go! You must protect me, Sebastian."

Sebastian ran a pale hand through his long black hair. "It might be better if you fled across the mountains," he said. "The Inquisition has no power in France."

"You would like that, wouldn't you? I would be dead before I crossed the border! Miguel had more news for me, Sebastian. We are at war with the French, and already they are making raids from the mountains. There is no safety for me there, Sebastian."

Sebastian sat slumped in his chair, his head bent, the heel of his hand supporting his brow. "You are a messenger of ill omen," he said. "This is something I had not anticipated. How safe do you think you will be here if there is a battle for this fortress?"

"It may not come to that. They say there will be only a little war and we may survive it. Miguel had his information from the mouth of Columbus himself."

"Columbus," said Sebastian. "I remember when you told me of him. We should be in his New World now, for this world has little room in it for you and me."

"The French may spare us, Sebastian, and then we will be safe enough."

Sebastian raised a sardonic face to his brother. "Your plight has made you forgetful," he said. "Let me remind you about Pedro Rodriguez."

"Pedro?"

"He has been my lieutenant, and he has been your familiar. But what master will he serve now that you are a fugitive? There will be a new order in the city with you gone, and he will be quick to curry favor. Pedro knows all our secrets, brother. What better way for him to prove his worth than to betray us? He will surely guess that you are here."

"Then you must kill him, Sebastian. Tonight!"

"I might be better advised to kill you," said Sebastian.

The Grand Inquisitor tried to smile. "You cannot mean that," he said.

"It would certainly be easier than killing Pedro," said Sebastian thoughtfully. "For one thing, you are here where I can reach you, whereas Pedro is doubtless locked up safe at home. You know that I cannot enter a house without an invitation, and I can hardly expect Pedro to offer me one. Even if all this had not befallen us, he would be too concerned for his daughters. No, Diego, the murder of Pedro is impossible for me.

"But it might be possible for you," Sebastian continued. "He would very likely let you in, and perhaps you would have a chance to take him by surprise. I am more than willing to risk it. In fact, brother, I will lend you my sword. Of course you will have to kill his daughters, too."

"You must be joking, Sebastian! I dare not go back to the city. It would be suicide!"

"I see," said Sebastian. He leaned back in his chair and pressed his palms together judicially, his steepled fingers brushing his long mustache. "Then we must consider my other suggestion."

Diego's eyes widened.

"Your death would have many advantages," Sebastian said. "If your body were found in the streets it would at least create a diversion, and no one would come looking for you here."

"Sebastian!"

"Please, Diego. I am thinking. I might be able to come to terms with Pedro; most men will do anything for money. And he would gain nothing by betraying me once you were out of the way."

Diego de Villanueva leaped from his seat and stood weak-kneed and trembling in the glow of the solitary candle. The skull beneath it seemed to be staring at him.

"You would not kill me, Sebastian? I came to you for help. I am your brother!"

"I know you are," said Sebastian quietly, "and I have frequently had cause to regret it. Tonight, for example. You could have stayed at the Holy House and accepted your fate, but instead you ran to this castle, even though you must have realized that your presence here would place me in jeopardy. You have less concern for me than you expect me to have for you."

"You could not do it, Sebastian!"

"Why not, brother? You would have done as much to me, if the book had been successful."

"Never!" Diego spread his hands on the chessboard and leaned across it to emphasize his words. "I promised you!"

"Spare me your promises, brother. I am not blind. I know what you planned."

"But you must have believed me! Why else did you give me the book?"

"I wonder. Part of it was pride, I suppose. I was pleased with what I had done, and I wanted someone else to see it—even you or Torquemada. And regardless, I was obliged to finish the manuscript sooner or later. You had been waiting for years and were growing more and more impatient."

"But Sebastian! All those reasons would have been worthless if you really believed I intended to destroy you." The Grand Inquisitor paced back and forth. He suspected that argument was futile, but it was still his only hope. He thought of running but realized he would not get far, and there was nowhere else to go.

"And there is something else, brother," Sebastian said. "You forget that I wrote *The Powers of Darkness* and that I knew what was in it better than any man alive or dead. It is no surprise to me that the book was condemned. I planned it."

"You planned it?" gasped Diego. His knees buckled and he sat down heavily. His face turned pale and drops of sweat appeared on his upper lip. "You planned to ruin me?"

"It seemed only fair, considering what you had in mind for me." Sebastian still sat quietly and spoke as if all these matters were of no more than passing interest. His apparent indifference infuriated Diego, whose anger began to overcome his fear.

"You think you will be safe if you kill me, Sebastian, but you are wrong. There is someone else, someone you do not know about. Whatever you do to me, you are doomed as well."

Sebastian gave no sign that he was impressed by this threat. "I have no doubt that you would say anything to save yourself, Diego, but why should I believe you?"

"Believe what you will," his brother answered bitterly. "I could save you with a warning, but why should I?"

"You will tell me," said Sebastian, "and perhaps I will spare you, though I hardly see how I can arrange it. Still, it is your only hope."

Diego realized all too well that he was playing his last card. Yet it seemed impossible to use it to good advantage. If Sebastian knew nothing about the heir to the castle, he would not take the warning seriously. But once he learned about Antonio, there would be no reason for him to keep his brother alive.

"You ought to know the man I mean," Diego temporized, "since you predicted his appearance."

"I did?" asked Sebastian, touching himself on the chest and raising his eyebrows with such exaggerated innocence that his brother began to fear that the world had no secrets from Sebastian.

Diego was dizzy and stupid from sheer panic, but he had to say something. "Think of a way to save my life, Sebastian, and I will tell you. A fair exchange."

"It sounds like a poor bargain to me, brother, since I have no idea what you are offering me."

"I am offering you your life," said Diego, "or such of it as there is." He suspected that Sebastian might be weakening and pressed his advantage eagerly. "That must be worth something to you."

"A doubtful proposition, brother. I am weary of all this. My work is done and it has been destroyed. Yet there is a life I would spare if I could."

The Grand Inquisitor looked at his brother eagerly. "I knew you would help me, Sebastian. You love to taunt me, but I knew you would not take your brother's life."

A sneer flickered across Sebastian's lips. "If you believe that, brother, then you will believe anything. So be it. Tell me your secret, and I will spare you."

A faint hope grew within the Grand Inquisitor. His sudden reversal of fortune had left him half-hysterical so that he had to struggle to think, but still he understood the need for caution. "How can I trust you now?" he asked. "If I am to die, Sebastian, there will be some satisfaction in knowing that you will follow me. If you want me to speak, you must think of a way to save me."

"I know of no way to save you, brother. I can promise only that I will not kill you myself. Perhaps we will think of something later. But speak now, or you die at once."

"You must swear that you will not kill me."

Sebastian smiled. "What would you have me swear by? Is there an oath I can take that will convince you? Shall I swear by my immortal soul? And what would it be worth if I did?"

Diego's pulse raced and his mind with it. "Not by your soul, Sebastian. Swear by the soul of your wife, by the soul of Gracia, dead these many years. That is an oath I can believe."

Sebastian's dead eyes turned to narrow slits and he rose halfway out of his chair. Diego cringed. His life, like Sebastian's body, hung suspended for a moment. Then Sebastian sank down again and the Grand Inquisitor knew he had won.

"I swear," said Sebastian, as if the words had cost him much.

Diego could have wished for a more elaborate version of the oath but thought it wisest not to press his luck. The issue he had raised was a sensitive one. He watched his brother and gradually began to relax.

"What I have to tell you," he said at last, "concerns a young man called Antonio Manetti, lately arrived from Florence. He is the heir to your estate, and he intends to claim it soon."

Diego waited for his words to take effect, but Sebastian showed no dismay. "The Knight of Cups," Sebastian said, and it was Diego whose face fell.

"He was here not many days ago," continued Sebastian, "inspecting his inheritance."

"You knew of him already?" asked Diego incredulously. "How?"

"I know many things, brother, if not everything I could wish to know. I thank you for your warning, but the young man will not trouble me. Let him spend a night here and he will cease to be a problem. This information is not worth much, Diego. I think you cheated me."

"You swore!"

"Fear not, brother. My oath is good and I will not kill you. But I think you owe me something. Tell me another secret."

Diego looked at his brother quizzically.

Sebastian's voice was as cold as the crypt. "You killed her, didn't you?"

Diego was so startled that his eyes shot up to meet his brother's. His gaze remained there, held by an uncanny compulsion. Sebastian's black eyes seemed to grow, and their darkness was overwhelming. The feeble flame of the candle dwindled away into insignificance and Diego was lost in the depths of his brother's unblinking omniscience. He could not turn away.

"You killed her," said Sebastian slowly. "Not with your own hands. But you betrayed her. Your ambition would not let you rest, nor your jealousy of my happiness. You gave my wife to the Inquisition and thus won favor. You paid for your position with her life."

"Yes," said the Grand Inquisitor. He did not even try to deny it. He could not help himself.

The dark room grew slowly brighter. Sebastian was still sitting quietly in his chair. It was almost as if nothing had happened. Diego wished that were true, but he knew better. He tried to collect his wits.

"You swore," he said, the words catching in his throat.

"So I did," said Sebastian calmly. "I will not harm you. But I had to be sure. And you should thank me. Confession is good for the soul. Do you feel better now?"

Strangely enough, Diego did. The deed he had just admitted had worried him for years, if not because he regretted it then because he feared his brother's wrath. If even this were to be forgiven, there would be nothing more to fear. It was almost too good to be true.

In spite of himself, Diego spoke. "Don't you care, Sebastian?"

"I suppose I should, brother, but it was long ago and I am not the man I was. I am not a man at all. I am a monster and think only of monstrous things. I can hardly remember her."

Diego breathed a sigh of relief. "What is it like, Sebastian? Is there nothing more than what you wrote in the book? I have asked you a hundred times, but still I think that you have never really answered me."

"More questions, Grand Inquisitor?" Sebastian's voice had a hard edge. "Are you never to be satisfied?"

He reared back suddenly in his chair and it fell crashing to the floor. As he stood towering over his brother there was a terrible majesty about him. He was incredibly tall. He seemed to grow until he filled the room.

Diego felt the floor shake. Was this magic? Sebastian seemed a giant, and his brother was afraid he might burst through the ceiling. The whole tower trembled.

Sebastian's voice was an icy echo. "Would you know what I know? Would you see what I see?"

The tower heaved like a storm-tossed ship. Shelves rattled. Cards and chessmen flew through the air. The candle slid across the table on its death's-head base. Diego closed his eyes and gritted his teeth, his hands gripping the sides of his bench.

Then, abruptly, there was silence.

The Grand Inquisitor opened his eyes carefully. The floor was steady. Sebastian had disappeared.

The room was a shambles, but somehow the candle was still burning, its red wax dripping into the eyes of the skull that held it. Beside the skull was a solitary chess piece standing alone on the squares of ivory and onyx—the black queen.

Diego raised his eyes. A woman stood in the shadows. She wore a white dress embroidered with threads of silver. For a moment he imagined that it was Sebastian's wife returned to punish him, but it was not.

It was Margarita de Mendoza.

Diego tried to back away from her and his bench fell over. He crawled into a corner. "You are dead," he whined. "You must be dead."

Margarita advanced upon him slowly. Her legs seemed bound together and he could not see them move. Yet she glided toward him, her green eyes glassy, her red lips fixed in a rigid smile. Her teeth were sharp and he heard them grinding as she bent over him.

"I took no oath," she said.

The Grand Inquisitor whimpered and tried to bury himself in the cold stone wall. Margarita bent down and caressed his cheek.

"Do not be so afraid of me, Diego de Villanueva. I will not kill you yet. There are hours till dawn, and I have no wish for you to die quickly."

19. Three Hunters

THE sun was setting by the time Miguel decided he needed help.

He entered the disreputable Inn of the Golden Cup with reluctance, but not even concern about the dignity of his position could overcome his conviction that Pedro Rodriguez was the only man in the city who would know what to do about the disappearance of Diego de Villanueva.

Miguel spotted Pedro immediately, but the sight was not reassuring. The big familiar sat at the dim corner table, gesturing with an overflowing cup. Seated beside him was the innkeeper, Carlos Diaz. Miguel tried to guess how drunk they were, but he was not an expert in such matters. At least there was nobody else in the tavern.

The young monk made his way across the dirt floor and put a hand on Pedro's shoulder. The corner reeked of wine.

Pedro turned around abruptly at Miguel's touch, then relaxed with a contemptuous smile. "It's the little vicar!" he roared. "When did you get back from your pilgrimage?"

"Yesterday," said Miguel. "I must speak to you at once."

"Well? Speak!"

"I must speak to you privately. It concerns the business of the Holy Office."

To Miguel's relief, Pedro achieved immediate sobriety. He put down his cup, cast a cold eye at Carlos, and gestured with his thumb toward the door to the rear of the inn. Every trace of his former conviviality had vanished. Carlos, looking more saddened than surprised, shuffled away, apparently resigned to the fact that he was not even the master of his own establishment.

"Wouldn't it be better if we went somewhere else?" Miguel ventured timidly.

"You are the one who wanted to speak at once," said Pedro. "One place is as good as another. Sit down."

Miguel obeyed. Uncertain of how to tell his story, he decided to plunge into it at once. Pedro was not a patient man.

"The Grand Inquisitor is gone," said Miguel.

"What do you mean?" asked Pedro, squinting at him ferociously.

"He hasn't been seen since last night. He is nowhere to be found."

Pedro considered this for a moment. "Assassins," he muttered darkly.

"I think not," said Miguel. "I believe he is in hiding."

Pedro looked at Miguel incredulously, but his expression changed to one of rough cunning as he heard the tale of Torquemada and the burning book. Perhaps, Pedro thought, it was time to find a new master.

"What should I do?" Miguel asked helplessly.

"The very question I was considering myself," said Pedro. He drained his cup in a single gulp, but it had no visible effect on him. "Are you sure that Torquemada means to arrest the Grand Inquisitor?"

"I'm not sure of anything," replied Miguel. "I don't even know if I should have told him what Torquemada did. But how could I keep it from him? I'm only certain of the things I saw for myself. Torquemada destroyed the book, and the Grand Inquisitor is missing."

"And you don't know when he left?"

"Not exactly. Sometime before dawn."

Pedro propped his elbows on the table and rested his black-bearded chin on two fists the size of hams. "You should have come earlier, that's for sure." He was thinking furiously. "Now that it's dark, it won't be easy to get him out of there."

Miguel's mouth fell open. "You know where he is?"

"That much was easy. The question is, what are we to do about it?"

The burly old soldier and the frail young monk regarded each other across the table. Finally Pedro spoke.

"We'll have to go after him. Any way you look at it, we'll be better off with him back where he belongs. He should have stood his ground. We'll have to go tonight, whatever the danger. He'll be dead tomorrow if we leave him there. He may be dead already, if he got there before dawn today."

"Where?" Miguel asked in a frantic undertone. "What are you talking about?"

"Look, my young friend. There may be nothing to this business with Torquemada. Maybe it will all blow over. In that case, we need Diego de Villanueva back here so things can go on as they always have. On the other hand, maybe he really is in trouble. If he is, someone will be here soon to take his place. And how will it look for you and me if we let him escape? We'll be taken for accomplices. We must bring him back."

"Back from where?" Miguel asked angrily.

"There's only one place he could be. At the castle, with the ghost of his brother Don Sebastian."

Miguel gasped and heard a similar sound behind him. Whirling, he saw Carlos standing there with a candle in his hand.

"I was just bringing a light for you gentlemen," the fat innkeeper said nervously.

"You were eavesdropping," Pedro retorted. He sprang from his seat and grabbed Carlos by the arm. "Join us," he said. "We have a new recruit!"

Pedro smiled maliciously through his heavy beard while the inebriated innkeeper sputtered a protest.

"Recruit?" he said. "I don't understand you. Let me go!" But Pedro's heavy hand dragged him down to the bench beside Miguel, who only sat and stared.

"You wanted to know what we were talking about," said Pedro sternly, "so you might as well hear it all. You will be one of us. The three of us are going to make an assault on the castle."

"Not me!" said Carlos. He tried to rise, but Pedro held him down. Miguel was equally unenthusiastic, but he kept his seat.

"The pair of you make a fine army," Pedro said bitterly. "A skinny stripling and a fat drunkard. Still, you may serve to distract him for a minute. One good shot is all I need."

"I don't want to go," said Carlos thickly.

"You have no choice," Pedro answered.

Miguel passed a shaky hand across his brow and looked at Pedro. "What was that you said about the ghost?"

"Not a ghost, exactly," Pedro said. "Don Sebastian is a vampire."

The innkeeper's thick features showed only bewilderment, but Miguel turned pale and crossed himself.

"So, vicar, you know what a vampire is?" asked Pedro.

"A dead man," said Miguel, "who feeds on the blood of the living. The Grand Inquisitor spoke to me about them."

Carlos moaned weakly. The others ignored him.

"He told me even more," said Pedro, "because he had to. I was the one who brought Don Sebastian back here after that cannon blew his face away."

Miguel winced. "But how did he become a vampire?"

"Some trick he learned from the Moors, I think. I never heard of such a creature, but apparently those heathen lands are full of them. I don't know what he did, exactly, but when he knew he was dying he found a way to transform himself. I suppose he sold his soul."

"And the Grand Inquisitor let him live?"

"Let him live?" Pedro snorted. "His brother kept him alive!

For nine years! Half the heretics in the Holy House have gone to the field of fire with holes in their throats."

"I'm not going," said Carlos.

"You volunteered when you crept up to hear what we were saying," Pedro said. "You can come with us or we'll leave you off in one of the dungeons of the Holy House."

"I'll come," Carlos said tragically.

"Come on, Carlos, buck up! You may even live through it." Pedro laughed.

Miguel was indignant at such levity. The very foundations of his belief were crumbling. "I cannot believe you," he said. "The Grand Inquisitor could never have tolerated such a creature, not even his own brother. Why would he do it?"

"Why?" said Pedro. He laughed again and brought his hand down on the tabletop so hard that his empty cup jumped into the air. "Why? Who do you think wrote the famous book that caused all this trouble?"

Miguel was too astounded to argue, and Carlos looked back and forth between his two companions as if they were speaking a foreign language.

"Diego knows nothing about witchcraft," Pedro continued, "but Don Sebastian knows everything, and they reached some sort of understanding. But if the book has come to nothing, they'll be at each other's throats at once. There's no love lost between those brothers."

Miguel started to speak, but Pedro stopped him with a look. "No time to argue now," said the old soldier. "We must move at once. I wish I had some better men, but nobody else must hear of this or we'll all be in trouble. You, vicar. What do you know about killing vampires?"

"Nothing," said Miguel.

"Well, the Grand Inquisitor told me a little. Ordinary weapons won't do it. Fire will, or a stake of wood through the heart. But Don Sebastian will be up and about by now and we can't expect him to stand still for that. If only we could wait for morning! I'll have to use my bow. An arrow's made of wood, so it should work. We'll need some crosses. I'll go and get them . . . no. You'll have to get them, vicar. I'll stay here and keep an eye on Carlos. You couldn't hold him. Are you game?"

Miguel nodded gravely. He had no choice, yet he could hardly help wondering whether he was going to rescue the Grand Inquisitor or arrest him.

"Bring three crosses," Pedro said. "And horses, too. You can get the bow from my daughter Teresa. Make sure you ask for the right one. Not the crossbow. Those steel bolts would be no good for this hunt, and besides, it takes too long to load. Get the bow I captured from the Moors, and a quiver full of arrows. Teresa will know the one I mean. It's a heathen weapon, but I know how to use it."

Miguel rose to go.

"One more thing," said Pedro. "I'm worried about my girls. If this night's work does not go well, Don Sebastian may resent it. So make sure you tell them to keep the door barred and not to open it for anyone but me. Not for anyone, do you understand? I don't think he'll be able to get in unless they invite him. At least that's what the Grand Inquisitor told me. Don't let them know where we're going! There's no need for them to learn about things like this. Leave that for experts on evil like Diego de Villanueva!"

Diego lay dead in a stone sarcophagus, yet he dreamed that he was floating down a river. He was stretched out on his back at the bottom of a tiny boat, and though there was no one to guide it, he was not afraid. Above him rose shimmering silver arches. He drifted through them drowsily, his eyes half-shut, and thought of nothing but the gentle motion of the water.

The curved ceiling of light grew lower and he realized that he was in a cavern. The walls dripped with glistening blue phosphorescence—and drew nearer to him. This was less a cavern than a tunnel, and he saw to his dismay that it was closing in on him.

He tried to raise himself but found he could hardly move. The stream below turned turbulent and the boat rushed forward. He slowly raised his head to look around him, then began to panic.

The boat was a coffin, adrift on a river of blood.

He reached for the sides of the coffin. They were wet and sticky, but he managed to pull himself erect. The glowing walls cast cold reflections on the rushing river. He tried to scream, but no sound came. The crimson tide raced toward the end of the cavern and the black pit waiting there. His fingers stretched frantically toward the narrowing walls, but he could not reach them, nor could he stop himself. The void loomed beneath him. With a sickening lurch he dropped into darkness.

He fell, in a long, slow curve that seemed endless. He clutched his knees and huddled in a ball, waiting to be shattered into jelly when his fall was over. His heart stopped.

Suddenly the coffin came to rest. Diego opened his eyes and found himself in a black grotto, its depths hidden by a stagnant lake of gore. This vast red pool was radiant. A light like fire rose from it to touch the towering stones on every side. Diego knew he was dead; yet still he feared the sinking of the casket, as if he knew that something waited in the depths below that might be worse than death.

Thick bubbles rose to the surface of the lake. A hand reached out among them, dripping blood. It groped blindly for Diego. Another hand rose beside the first. Something splashed behind him and he whirled to see the body of his brother Sebastian. Rigid as a statue, it oozed upward from the pool, its face a scarlet mask. It smiled at him.

Diego turned away in horror, but what he turned to face was worse. The bloody hands had clutched the side of his casket and were dragging him down. A head slid up through the steaming surface of the lake, its dark hair thick with gore. The face beneath the streams of red was pale; the eyes were green.

The surface of the lake was alive with hands, hundreds of them, all reaching out for him. Fires sprang up and the lake of blood began to boil. Clouds of smoke obscured Diego's vision, but still he saw a throng arise around him. Dead, dripping faces encircled him, some of them burned and blackened. Dimly he recognized his victims. A mass of crawling corpses weighed his coffin down, embracing him ardently as he sank into the thick crimson. Everything was red.

Darkness streamed into his eyes and awakened him. His dream was done. Night had fallen and he was in the crypt beneath the castle.

He saw his brother bending over him. "Sebastian?" he said weakly.

Sebastian's pale face was expressionless. "You have been dreaming," he said. "Tell me your dream."

Diego made an effort to sit up, but all the strength seemed drained out of his body. He could see nothing but his brother's face and the low stone ceiling above it.

"I am thirsty," said the Grand Inquisitor.

"That will not last long," Sebastian said.

"Why am I so weak?" asked the Grand Inquisitor.

"Don't you remember what happened last night?" asked Sebastian. "Don't you realize where you are?"

Diego glanced anxiously from side to side and saw that he was lying in a low, narrow box. The memory of his nightmare rushed over him again.

"No, no, no," he said sadly. His terror gave him strength and he began to rise. He caught a brief glimpse of the tomb of the de Villanuevas; then his brother's pale strong hand was pressed against his chest, pushing him back into the sarcophagus.

"You remember now," Sebastian said. "You are one of us, brother."

Diego shook his head in denial, but he knew that it was true.

"You would not be here now," said Sebastian, "if Margarita had been satisfied with a quick kill. But she took her time with you. I had no chance to put you in the streets of the city where you belong."

"Margarita?" whispered Diego, his eyes darting back and forth.

"She is not here, brother. She is up on the tower, watching for three friends of yours. They are coming to rescue you, but they are too late and I am ready for them. Yet still you are a thorn in my side, brother. Who would have thought that you would inspire such loyalty?"

"Three friends?" repeated Diego, his mind almost destroyed by horror.

"The Inquisition," said Sebastian. "But you have no reason to fear them. Forget them. They will not take you, nor will I leave you in this sorry state. It is not fit that a Grand Inquisitor should become a creature of the night, prowling through the dark in search of food. I will spare you that, at least, though you have spared me little. I could forgive you everything, I think, if you had not killed my wife. If not for that, perhaps none of this would have happened. You might have stayed a humble friar, and I would not have sought relief in sorcery. You have much to answer for, brother."

The Grand Inquisitor thought of his dream and began to moan.

"I watched you sleeping," Sebastian said, "and you did not seem happy. What did you see while you slept?"

Diego shut his eyes. "What are you going to do to me?" he said.

"I will spare you the misery that I have known," Sebastian said. "But I cannot spare you that which you have brought upon yourself."

The Grand Inquisitor felt something sharp against his chest. His eyes shot open. Sebastian was bending over him, a thick wooden stake grasped in his hands.

"Please," said the Grand Inquisitor. His fingers fumbled at the stake.

"What did you dream, Diego?" Sebastian's voice was almost tender.

"A lake of blood and fire. Blackened hands reaching out for me. Hell."

"What else could you expect, brother?" Sebastian's eyes were dead, but his mouth twitched and grimaced. He raised the pointed stake above his head.

"Sebastian," said the Grand Inquisitor.

"Your dreams will be your destiny," his brother told him.

The stake came crashing down.

The last thing Diego de Villanueva felt on earth was the splintered wood tearing into his heart. The last thing he saw was his blood spattering over his brother's face. And the last thing he heard was the sound of his own scream.

20. The Lightning

MARGARITA gazed over the battlements to the forest beyond. The moon shone with a pale blue light that turned the sky purple, yet already storm clouds had begun to appear.

The last of the water dribbled out between her fingers. She scooped up the embers of the burning herbs in her wet hands and scattered them over the tower in a descending shower of sparks. The incantation was complete.

Her lips moved silently as she watched the clouds boil and multiply until they covered half the sky. The pale moon vanished and the night turned black. One by one the stars were blotted out. She raised her hands to the heavens and was answered by a sullen rumbling. A wind rushed down from the mountains, ruffling her long black hair and blowing the banks of dark clouds toward the forest.

She waited for the approach of the enemy, hoping the coming storm would help. She knew she did not have Sebastian's powers, but any witch could raise a tempest and sometimes direct its thunderbolts. Yet it hardly seemed enough. She was obscurely troubled by the threat to the castle and more than a little doubtful about the impending battle.

The night turned white for an instant and thunder boomed among the mountains like the sound of cannon fire.

She thought of escape. Sebastian had given her the power of flight, and there was nothing to prevent her taking wing to flee from the castle and the men who moved against it. Yet they were her foes, perhaps even more than Sebastian's, and she felt bound to stay.

Still, the mountains tempted her. She had the gift of immortality and could pass it on to others. For all Margarita knew, she and Sebastian were the only ones in creation who had such power. Could she let it die with them? How could she be sure that either of them would survive this night? She envisioned a legion of the undead, spawned by her unquenchable thirst and wreaking vengeance on a world full of perfidy and persecution.

"Margarita?"

Sebastian stood beside her, his crimson cloak blown wildly by the rising wind. She could not face him.

"I thought of running," she said, "but I will stay."

Sebastian put his arm around her. "I wish that both of us could flee," he said, "but things are not that simple. There is nowhere for us to go. We must sleep each night in our native soil, so we dare not venture into France. There might be a cave in the mountains to shelter us. We could live there like animals, Margarita, preying on the villagers till we were hunted down. Perhaps you would prefer it. But this is my castle, and I will not yield it so easily. I will stay and fight. If I can kill them all, perhaps we will be safe."

"I will fight beside you," Margarita said.

Thunder cracked its whip across the sky as she embraced him.

"You will stay here," Sebastian said. "There is no need for you to risk your life."

"But you are weak," said Margarita. "You need blood."

"I am strong enough for them," Sebastian said. "They will be sorry they came here, long before they die."

"And your brother?"

"Dead," answered Sebastian.

The first drops of rain fell upon them and a misty wind billowed over the battlements.

"I can help you, Sebastian. I have magic too. Look at the sky and see what I have done!" Margarita spread her arms and a blue swath of lightning cut across the clouds. "I will strike them down before they reach the moat."

Sebastian traced the line of her cheek with cold fingers. "Do what you will," he said, "but stay in the tower. None of them knows that you are here, Margarita, and they will not hunt for you. Even if they destroy me, you can still escape. They must not find you. I at least have hopes of something yet to come, but you . . ."

"I know," she said, silencing his lips with a caress. "But there are worse fates than oblivion. At least it would mean peace."

He kissed her fiercely and wild breezes mingled his dark hair with hers. His passion drew a drop of scarlet from her lip and he stepped back from her. She smiled at the wound. The blood was the Grand Inquisitor's. A gust of wet wind washed the drop away. The rain rushed down upon them and rattled on the stones.

"Come," he said, "and wait in the room below."

Margarita smiled. "Are you afraid I will catch cold?"

Her dripping hair streamed to her shoulders and her pale face gleamed in the rain. The white silk gown clung damply to her slender body, and her green eyes glowed.

"Leave me here, Sebastian," she said. "I want to watch the storm and to command the thunderbolts."

She reached out a hand to him and he held it for a moment, then he was gone.

Margarita stood alone on the topmost tower of the castle, water running down her cheeks. She turned toward the forest, raised one finger to the sky, then swept it downward until it pointed to an outlying tree.

A ragged streak of lightning ripped the purple sky apart as if it were a piece of paper, and the shattered tree burst into flames.

"Christ!" said Carlos. "That was close."

The proprietor of the Golden Cup stood beside his horse

205

and shuddered. The storm had started only a minute ago, but already he was soaked to the skin. He watched the driving rain extinguish the burning stump of the thunderstruck tree and felt acutely uncomfortable.

Pedro Rodriguez was swearing too, but for another reason. He was wrapping something in his cloak. "Best bow in the world," he muttered. "Even better than the English longbow. Shoots farther. But not if it's wet."

"What did you say?" asked Miguel. The young friar had been staring through the downpour at the forbidding black edifice that lay beyond the forest.

"This Moorish bow. Made of horn and sinew as well as wood. Takes them years to put one together. A fine weapon, unless the water hits it."

"I wonder about this storm," said Miguel. "It was clear enough when we started out, but I've read that a magician can raise a tempest. Could he know that we are coming?"

"It wouldn't surprise me," answered Pedro. "Don Sebastian seems to have a way of knowing things. Tie up the horses here. We won't take them beyond these woods."

"We should take them right back to the city again," said Carlos. The moisture on his fat face looked more like sweat than raindrops. "Are you so anxious to die? You say yourself that he's waiting for us. Who knows what a sorcerer can do? I say we should go back, and to hell with the Grand Inquisitor!"

"Nobody cares what you say," said Pedro curtly. "If you didn't always talk so much, we might have risked leaving you at the inn. But now you're here, so make the best of it. Put this bundle under your robe, will you, vicar? We have to keep it dry."

The innkeeper was becoming frantic. "What do you think we're going to do, Pedro? Just walk up to the castle and knock on the door? We'll never get into the place. You'd need an army!"

Pedro ignored him and peered through the trees at the long stretch of open ground between the forest and the rocks on which the castle stood. He gestured with a thick forefinger. "See those rocks over there, friar? The ones to the left of the castle? That's where the escape tunnel comes out, and that's where we're going in."

"Escape tunnel?"

"It runs underground from the keep. Been there for centuries. If the castle ever fell, it was a way out for the last defenders. Tonight it will be a way in for us. I only hope Don Sebastian has forgotten it."

Miguel finally admitted to himself that he was really going into the castle. His heart sank. Things were moving too fast for him. He no longer believed in the Grand Inquisitor or in witchcraft or the Inquisition. The only thing he could be sure of was that his life was in danger. His faith was failing, and he wanted to run. He tried to pray but heard himself saying, "I am ready."

"Good," said Pedro. "We'll make a dash for the rocks. There's a big stone that we'll have to move to get at the tunnel. It won't be easy, but that's one of the reasons why I brought this fat fool along. His weight ought to be good for something. We'll need you later, friar. For now, just hold on to that cross for dear life. And for God's sake, don't drop my bow!"

Carlos lurked behind them, looking as if he were ready to run back into the forest. "You first," snarled Pedro, grabbing the innkeeper by the scruff of the neck. He shoved Carlos between the trees and into the clearing. "Let's go!" he said.

Carlos stumbled forward a few steps and slipped in the mud. Pedro was right behind him, though, pulling him to his feet and pushing him forward.

They ran. The full force of the tempest hit them as they left the shelter of the trees. Rain lashed their faces and the screaming wind fought them for every inch of ground. Yet Pedro, bulky as he was, moved with surprising speed. He forced Carlos along before him. The innkeeper's shouts were lost in the fury of the storm. Miguel followed them, his black hood flapping in his eyes and both hands clutching the precious bow. He had more faith in that than in the cross dangling from his neck.

They reached the rocks. Carlos, gasping for breath, fell back against a sizable boulder and let the rain fall into his open mouth. Pedro stood with hands on hips and surveyed him disgustedly.

"At least you've picked the right rock," Pedro said. "That's the one we have to roll away."

Carlos and Miguel looked at him in amazement. The job seemed all but impossible, but Pedro was apparently immune to doubt. He stood tall and strong, indifferent to the buffeting of the storm that made the others duck their heads. Miguel was suddenly impressed with him. Pedro might be no Grand Inquisitor, but there were moments when a forthright and determined ruffian was worth any number of scholars. This was adventure, and Miguel began to feel he had been born for it. The wind exhilarated him.

Pedro turned his back to the castle and dropped his heavy hands onto the side of the rock. He pushed at it tentatively, then nodded.

"Come on, innkeeper," he said. "Get up here beside me and put your weight into it. You too, vicar. You might make the difference. Come on now, shove."

Despite his exhortations to the others, it was apparent that Pedro was doing most of the work. Thick legs braced, back bent, beard thrust toward the sky, he struggled forward. Miguel's fingers slipped on the wet rock and his sandaled feet slipped in the mud.

"Push!" shouted Pedro.

"I'm pushing!" Carlos answered. "Anything to get out of this accursed rain!" He grunted and threw himself against the stone. Slowly it began to move.

"Harder!" Pedro said. Veins bulged ominously in his forehead. The boulder tottered on one edge, overbalanced, and went crashing end over end into the clearing.

The three breathless men stood together watching its descent. Then Pedro dropped to one knee to examine the uncovered ground. He scraped some mud away and smiled. "Here it is," he said. "We'll have to pry it open."

"You two do it," Carlos said. "I've had enough." He took a

few paces backward to demonstrate his independence. Pedro ignored him.

Miguel and Pedro squatted together beside the stone trap door. "How could they ever have moved that rock from below?" asked Miguel, raising his voice against the wind.

"This door worked like a sort of lever," Pedro answered. "But it was never meant to be opened from above. Maybe we can pry it up. See if you can get my knife under that edge. Just lift it a bit, and I'll do the rest."

He handed the monk a short, heavy dagger and Miguel slipped its point into a muddy crack. The blade slipped down to the hilt. Miguel looked up at Pedro's face with its dripping beard hardly a hand's breadth from his own face. "Go ahead," Pedro urged him. "Don't worry about breaking the blade. I still have my sword."

Miguel leaned against the hilt, feeling the grating of stone against stone. The trap door lifted and Pedro caught its edge with his fingers just as the dagger snapped in two.

"Got it!" said Pedro. "Good boy!" Miguel might have felt insulted, but he was proud. Pedro heaved the door back, revealing a set of rough stone steps that dwindled into impenetrable darkness.

"You! Carlos Diaz!" called Pedro.

Miguel glanced up. The fat little innkeeper was only a short distance away, a dripping and bedraggled figure standing on a rock and watching them work. He took one step toward them.

A blast of blinding white shot out of the sky and split his skull. His body was alive with light for an instant, twitching spasmodically against a landscape suddenly brighter than day. Thunder rolled down from the mountains and the night turned black again. Carlos fell without a cry and smashed his face against a rock. The rain splattered down upon his broken body. Steam and smoke rose from his sodden clothing.

Miguel crossed himself. His first impulse was to run, but his training overcame it. He moved toward the corpse, intoning a prayer for the dead.

Pedro grabbed his robe, yanked him toward the opening in

the rocks, and threw him halfway down the steps. "Pray later!" bellowed the old soldier. "That was no accident!" He bolted through the hole behind Miguel just before the lightning struck again.

Miguel saw Pedro come tumbling down the steps in the sudden glare and heard the sound of splintering rock. Something fell into the opening above them with a tremendous crash. Miguel listened to a heavy thud and the noise of broken stones rattling down. One of them hit him in the leg, but he could not see it. The tunnel was plunged into darkness, and the roar of the storm turned to silence.

"Pedro?" whispered Miguel.

He heard someone moving. "Pedro?" he called again, his voice breaking.

"I'm here," said a rough but reassuring voice. "And I'm not likely to leave. The last blast sealed the entrance, vicar. I can feel it."

"Where are you, Pedro? I can't see anything."

"Behind you. Reach out your hand."

Miguel groped blindly. There was no light at all. "Are you hurt?" he asked.

"Not much. I got a good crack on the shoulder. How's my bow?"

"I have it. It seems to be all right."

"Good. Hand it over. We might as well get going."

Miguel felt Pedro bump into him and jumped. He had lost his taste for adventure, but now there was no way to back out. He was trapped beneath the ground, with enchanted thunderbolts behind him and horrors he could hardly imagine lurking ahead. He thought of the tons of rock looming over him and imagined them pressing down to crush the life from his thin body.

"You'd better go first," he told Pedro.

Miguel moved into the tunnel and immediately ran into a wall. He reached out and felt for the other, hardly an arm's length away. Both were wet with slime. "It's hardly wider than I am," Miguel said nervously. "And I can't stand up in it, either. I wish I could see."

"You lead the way then, vicar. It's for your own good. If the tunnel is that small I might get stuck in it, and then we'd both be trapped. Just stay calm and move ahead slowly. I'm right behind you. And watch out for snakes."

Miguel felt panic rising within him. He had never been so frightened in his life. He wished himself back in the monastery of Saint Thomas, where there was nothing to face but the wrath of Torquemada. He could not bring himself to take a single step.

Pedro reached out to touch Miguel and felt him shaking. A monk with hysterics would be no help now. He thought of pushing Miguel through the black passage by main force but decided that persuasion might be more effective.

"Go ahead. It won't be so bad. I know it's dark, but the tunnel can't be very long. I'm counting on you, and so is the Grand Inquisitor. We'll be out of this in a minute or two once we get moving. You don't want to stay here forever, do you?"

Pedro's voice was calm and authoritative at the same time, and his last argument was convincing. Miguel wanted very much to be out of the tunnel. Head bent, hands pressed to the clammy walls, the monk moved forward.

There was a foul, damp stench in the tunnel that grew worse with every step. Miguel began to think of suffocation.

"Smells like something rotting," Pedro said, trying to keep up a steady flow of conversation to calm the quivering monk. "Go slowly. It won't be long now. Be careful, vicar. Don't stumble. Something might have fallen down. Just feel your way along. You're doing fine."

Pedro did not mention his own greatest fear, that the far end of the passage might have collapsed. If it had, they were buried alive. His broad shoulders scraped against the narrow walls and he shuddered. His plan had seemed better back at the inn when he was a little less sober. Would this tunnel never end? And what would they find at the end of it?

"Stop," said Miguel. "There's something here."

Pedro's heart sank. "What is it? Can you get past it?"

"I don't know," said Miguel. "I just ran into it. It's on the floor."

Miguel leaned down. The passage was still darker than the darkest night, and he was forced to use his fingers instead of his eyes. He had run into something hard, but now that his hands reached down, it felt softer—a protruding lump covered with rough cloth. He ran his fingers along it until they reached something bigger and softer that seemed to fill the whole tunnel. He touched a piece of wood and something sticky. His other hand touched cold, damp flesh.

Miguel let out a yell and stumbled backward. The two men fell in a heap.

"A dead man!" shouted Miguel. "It's a dead man!" His voice echoed hollowly up and down the black corridor. "Go back, Pedro! Get me out!"

Pedro made a grab for Miguel's flailing limbs and forced him to the muddy floor. He found the monk's mouth and put a hand over it.

"So it's a dead man," Pedro said. "He can't hurt you. You've seen dead men before. We have to keep going. Calm down. I'll lead the rest of the way. I'll have to move him. He's nothing to be afraid of. I'm going to take my hand off your mouth now. Don't shout. Just say yes if you're ready to follow me."

"Yes," Miguel said weakly.

Pedro reached back until he found the bow he had dropped, and he sighed with relief that it was still intact. Only a few of the arrows seemed broken. He crawled over Miguel and put his arms around the corpse.

"Follow me," he said. The floor inclined upward, which he took as a good sign. He was not even disturbed when the body in his arms flopped against a blank wall. "We've come to the end," he said.

Pedro leaned the corpse against the wall and pushed against the low ceiling. It yielded with a groan and Pedro stuck his head up through the opening. The darkness above was less intense; and he could hear rain driving against the walls.

"We're in the castle," he announced. "This should be the keep." He pulled himself up through the floor and hauled the body up behind him. He threw it down beside the trap door and stooped to give Miguel a hand. He was examining his weapons when he heard the young monk groan.

Miguel was pointing at the dead man.

"I thought so," Pedro said. "We have come for nothing."

Sprawled on the stones was the corpse of Diego de Villanueva, his face contorted with agony, a wooden stake protruding from his chest.

21. Two Swords

MIGUEL knelt beside the body of the Grand Inquisitor, yet could not bring himself to look at it. He listened to the muffled thunder. He wanted to pray for the dead, but the only prayers he could think of were for himself. He begged every saint in the calendar to spirit him away from the castle, but when he finished, he was still inside.

Pedro was willing to ignore Miguel for a moment, even though he considered the young monk's display of piety ill-timed. At least it gave the big familiar time to think. He carefully unwrapped his bow and examined it as best he could in the dim light. Determining that the weapon was unbroken, he braced one end against his foot and leaned on the curved bow until it was bent enough to loop the loose end of the string into the notch that held it. Then he chose an arrow and fitted it to the bow. All the while, his eyes darted around the shadowed room, on guard for the slightest hint of motion.

The trap door had opened into an empty anteroom at the bottom of the great tower that dominated the castle. There were no windows, but there was a door—and it was open, which made Pedro uneasy. Against the opposite wall was the first level of the steps that led upward to Don Sebastian's chambers. Pedro, considering the steps, decided they were a trap and a temptation. He felt the same about the open door, through which lightning flashed. He looked down at Miguel.

"What are you doing with that cross?"

Miguel turned to Pedro with an expression that was half insane. His eyes were wide and he was smiling. "I'm going to leave it with the Grand Inquisitor," he said. "He doesn't have one of his own."

Pedro grasped Miguel by the arm and pulled him to his feet. "Are you mad? Hold on to that! He doesn't need it now, but it might keep you alive. I told you about that, didn't I, that the cross will keep Don Sebastian away from you?"

Miguel looked genuinely bewildered. "That doesn't matter now," he said. His voice was like a child's. "Aren't we going home?"

"Wake up, you fool! How do you think that body got into the tunnel? Don Sebastian knows we're here, and we'll have to fight our way out. Do you think you can just walk through that door over there and go free?"

Pedro regretted the words as soon as they were out of his mouth. Miguel took one look at the open door and his eyes went wild. He pulled away from Pedro, rushed across the room, and disappeared into the storm.

"Damn!" said Pedro. He hesitated for a heartbeat, then took a firm grip on his Moorish bow and hurried after Miguel.

A deluge greeted him, rain so heavy he could hardly see, and the water in the courtyard was ankle-deep. "Vicar!" he shouted. "Stay away from that drawbridge! He might be lurking there! Come back!"

Then Pedro remembered the bow. He had to keep it dry, no matter what the cost. A wet string would be the end of him. He ran for the nearest doorway and waited in its shelter, an arrow at the ready. The downpour was blinding.

Rapid footsteps slapped toward him across the courtyard. He almost fired, but the lightning stopped him just in time. It blasted the spot where he had stood a moment before, and in its glare he saw a disheveled figure dressed in black and white.

It was Miguel, racing away from the drawbridge like a man possessed. He barreled into Pedro and knocked him through the doorway.

The room they fell into was not the one they had just left, but Pedro liked it even less than the first. It was awash with lights.

Margarita leaned over the battlements and stared at the empty courtyard anxiously. She could hardly believe what she had seen. Somehow, the two remaining invaders had made their way into the castle, and they had not come through the only entrance she knew of. In fact, she had seen them run out of the keep, directly below her. How did they get there, and where was Sebastian? Did he know they were inside? Could they have killed him? She forgot her promise to stay in the tower. It was impossible to wait there and do nothing. She knew where the men had gone and knew she must follow them. They were only human and should be easy enough to kill. The lightning was useless now that they were inside, but her teeth were still sharp.

"I heard him," cried Miguel. "Out by the bridge. I heard him laugh! And I saw him, too. You should have seen him, Pedro! He is ready for you. You will never kill him. Never! Never!"

Pedro pushed the raving monk away from him to keep his hands free for fighting. There was no time for lunacy like this. Perhaps it was true that Sebastian had waited by the bridge, but that was no guarantee that he would still be there. Besides, Miguel was mad and not to be trusted. It might be better to make a stand here. Yet this room had clearly been prepared for them. Why else were all the candles burning?

They were in the great hall of the castle, a gigantic room where men had met to prepare themselves for battle. A long black table sat at one end, heavy chairs surrounding it. Candles, all alight, covered the table. There was a fireplace across from it, where flames crackled hospitably. This last touch disturbed

Pedro most of all, for he sensed the mockery in it. Above the fireplace was a shield bearing the arms of the de Villanuevas. A red hand severed at the wrist stood against a field of black, the emblem of an ancestor who had lost a limb upon the field of honor. On the wall across from this was a tapestry, a peaceful picture of a knight kneeling in obeisance before his lady.

Pedro kept his bow ready and surveyed the scene. There were three entrances to the hall: the one they had come through from the courtyard, and two others at opposite ends of the room, each leading off into black corridors. Both of these doorways were elevated and short flights of steps led from them to the flagstone floor. The entrances themselves were lost in darkness, and Pedro watched them anxiously.

Miguel sat on the floor and babbled. "He's coming for us, Pedro. He promised me. He shines! You will never kill him. He shines too brightly!"

This talk had no meaning to Pedro, yet it was far from reassuring. He considered killing the crazed monk, if only to stop his wild babble. The man was useless now; he had even left his cross beside the body of the Grand Inquisitor. Pedro's own cross was still with him, hanging from his neck by a golden chain. Its presence comforted him and gave him some pity for the mad Miguel, but if Pedro did not kill him, it was only because there seemed no harm in letting him live.

There was danger enough to consider. Pedro sensed that he was in the wrong place, but he did not know where else to go. Every entrance loomed before him darkly and he turned warily in a circle, desperate to keep the whole hall in view.

Miguel began to laugh. "There is a devil, Pedro. I have seen him! Even the Grand Inquisitor had his doubts, but I have none. He is there, outside the door!"

Pedro spun around to look, his fingers tight on the feathers of the arrow, but the doorway was empty. He listened to the rain spattering down upon the stones.

"He is coming, Pedro, he is coming for us, and she is coming, too! She is beautiful!"

Pedro wheeled around to see the monk crawling across the flagstones toward the entrance near the fireplace. "Shut your mouth!" Pedro told him. "Would you wake the dead?"

And then he spied the figure on the threshold, a woman dressed in white. Even as Pedro turned, she leaped down the steps toward Miguel. Wet black hair was plastered to her head and her eyes were green, like a cat's.

"The witch!" gasped Pedro, and drew his bow. It was impossible that she should be here, but there was no time to think of that.

Margarita had not seen the bow, but suddenly she realized what it was. She saw the long thin shaft of wood and the cold gleam of the sharp steel arrowhead that pointed at her heart, but she had no chance to stop her headlong rush.

The bowstring sang and Margarita reeled across the floor, the arrow buried deep in her left breast. Bright blood spilled over her white gown. Clutching at the shaft, she dropped to her knees, her head thrown back, lips parted in a silent scream. She slumped over on her side and let forth a moan that rose into a horrifying high-pitched wail. Convulsions shook her slender body and rolled her on her back. Then her bloodied fingers slipped from her wound. She was still at last.

As Margarita died, the storm she had summoned died with her. The thunder stopped, and the whining of the wind, and the roaring of the rain against the walls of the castle. Throughout the great hall fell an abrupt and awesome silence.

Miguel heard only the sound of his own breathing and the distant drip of water from the courtyard. He tore his gaze away from the dead woman and glanced around the vast chamber, searching the shadows cast by the flickering candles. The sight of Margarita's death agony had startled him into a semblance of sanity and he was grateful now for the presence of the giant behind him, a soldier who could kill without compunction and who seemed stolidly indifferent to the terrors of the night.

Pedro stood waiting with muscles tensed, another arrow ready, his mind weighing various plans of attack and defense for this battle against demons. They seemed to him as easy to kill as any other enemy, but it was best not to be foolhardy.

A faint sound came from the courtyard, a cold, metallic creak that chilled Miguel.

The noise was repeated and joined with sounds of scraping and clanging. Whatever it was was coming closer. Miguel's fear was of the unexplained, but Pedro, the old soldier, was frightened because he recognized the noises for what they were: the sound of a man approaching in a full suit of armor.

Sebastian appeared in the doorway, clad in shining steel. A black shield emblazoned with a crimson hand hung on his left arm, and he brandished a gleaming broadsword.

"See how he shines, Pedro?" screamed Miguel. "You will never kill him!"

Pedro realized that the monk was right. The old soldier knew it better than any man alive, for he had been Sebastian's man-at-arms and had tested the heavy plate of this very armor years ago when it was new. Arrows would not pierce it, unless a lucky shot penetrated one of the joints, yet there was nothing else for him to do but try. He fired.

The arrow tore through the black shield, for the power of Pedro's bow was great, but it glanced uselessly off the curves of Sebastian's thick breastplate and rattled on the floor.

Sebastian's laughter echoed eerily from his visored helmet as he advanced toward Pedro like some huge machine. Then he saw the body of his mistress sprawled on the floor beside the fireplace.

"Margarita," he whispered. He gave a cry of fury and frustration, then rushed toward the man who had murdered her.

Pedro shot again, but his aim was wild and the shaft shattered on the crest of Sebastian's helmet.

Pedro dropped the bow and drew his sword, wondering whether this weapon would help him. His cross hung from his neck, but he had forgotten it; his fighting instincts were too strong.

"He is coming!" Miguel shouted from the flagstones.

Sebastian's massive sword whirled through the air and whistled downward, but Pedro's blade was there to meet it, and the clash of steel on steel rang through the great hall. Pedro stepped back as the force of Sebastian's blow drove both weapons toward the floor, and he slipped his own blade free. He made a short slash up and out and cut the great black shield in two. Sebastian shook the pieces from his arm and gripped his hilt in both gauntleted hands. Pedro hacked at his helmet. Pedro's broadsword rang and quivered from the impact but slithered off the armor plate, leaving hardly a dent.

Pedro jumped backward, and four feet of fine Toledo steel whirled past him so close that he felt the breeze on his face. He began to panic. He could not pierce Sebastian's armor, and he doubted if his sword could hurt the demon beneath it. He had only a second to realize he was doomed, then Sebastian struck again.

Pedro parried, giving ground with every blow. His breath was coming hard and sweat dripped into his eyes. He held his battered blade upright before him and tried to save himself. Sebastian was driving him toward the fireplace with a hail of blows that increased in intensity as the swordsmen neared the spot where Margarita lay.

The furious onslaught wavered for an instant and Pedro spied an opening. He brought his heavy wedge of steel down with all the power of his huge shoulders and caught Sebastian in the armored joint just above the left knee. The plate was thin there, and it gave. The blade bit through Sebastian's thigh, all but cutting it in two.

Pedro paused for a moment as he pulled his broadsword free, but Sebastian did not cry out, did not bleed, did not fall. Pedro watched in horror as the butchered flesh above the vampire's knee grew whole again. Sebastian's sword was pointed toward the flagstones with an indifference all the more chilling because it was so evidently justified.

Pedro leaped forward with a roar and hacked frantically at Sebastian's chest. Metallic clanging echoed through the room, but that was all. Pedro would have fled, but he was not a coward, and he knew too well what a target his broad back would make.

He flailed wildly with his huge blade until his arms were weary. He was so close to the roaring fire that there was hardly room to run. Sebastian blocked his strongest strokes without apparent effort. Pedro decided he was a dead man, but then he heard Miguel.

"The cross, Pedro! The cross!"

Pedro's eyes dropped to the golden emblem dangling on his black doublet. He felt a surge of hope, but the distraction was his undoing.

Sebastian's sword flashed in a glittering arc and sliced off Pedro's head.

The sweep of the blade sent the head tumbling across the room, and the unsupported golden chain slipped over Pedro's severed neck. The cross clattered on the flagstones and the stump on Pedro's shoulders spewed forth blood like a fountain.

Sebastian's sword was so sharp that the headless man was not knocked down. Pedro stepped forward and his hands reached out. A rain of pumping red fell upon Sebastian and great gouts sputtered as they struck the fire. The bleeding thing advanced blindly and its killer stepped from its path. It stumbled toward Miguel, who scrambled backward up the short flight of stairs behind him. Blood splashed over the monk and he wailed at the touch of it. The dead man struck the first step, staggered, and pitched over at the foot of the stairs.

Sebastian kicked the gory bulk aside and loomed above Miguel. The monk's eyes were mad. He did not try to move.

"I lost my cross," he said sadly. "I left it with your brother."

"Pray," said Sebastian, and Miguel obediently clasped his hands.

The dripping sword rose and fell and the young monk's melancholy upturned face was split in half. Cold steel chilled his fevered brain as he slithered down the steps to land atop the corpse of Pedro Rodriguez.

Sebastian left his sword embedded in the friar's shaven head and turned wearily toward the fireplace.

Pale green mist poured from the slitted visor of the helmet and grew into the shape of a tall man. The empty suit of armor toppled with a resounding crash, and the gaunt figure of Don Sebastian de Villanueva staggered from his enemies and toward the body of his lover.

"You were right, Margarita," he said. "I am weak. I need more blood. There are others who must die tonight. Pedro has not been punished enough. His daughters are living still."

He looked down at Margarita's outspread black hair and staring emerald eyes. He saw the feathered shaft that pierced her heart and the blood that stained the bosom of her silken gown. He kneeled beside her and took her hand. One by one he pulled off all his shining rings and slipped them on her fingers.

"Are you dreaming, Margarita? Or is it only sleep? Whatever it may be, sleep well."

He tried to rise, but found he could not. His strength was almost gone. He twisted his head toward the carnage by the stairs. A puddle of crimson had formed beneath the bodies and oozed across the floor.

Sebastian crawled toward the spreading pool of blood, lowered his head, and began to drink.

22. The Cathedral

TERESA lifted her head when the storm stopped and listened to the sudden silence. "You should leave now," she said.

"Shortly," said Antonio. "You are the cruelest lady I have ever courted. I wonder that you didn't throw me out into the rain!"

Teresa smiled. "I let you stay till it was over, but now you must go, Antonio. It's getting late, and it really isn't safe, for you or for me either. He's bound to be home soon."

Antonio sighed and shifted in the chair he had drawn up beside Teresa's. "Rather than endanger you, Teresa, I will leave almost immediately. But is there still so much risk? You said yourself that you thought your father might be persuaded to give us his blessing."

"Not if he comes in and finds you doing that," she said, slapping his hand gently. "But I think I can win him over. He was quite impressed to learn that you were an heir and soon to be a man of some importance."

"You were impressed yourself," said Antonio. "Sometimes I think you love me only for my castle."

"You are no gentleman, sir," she answered, pushing his hand away.

"If I were a gentleman like some I have known, I would have bedded you already."

"What? Here? With Dolores just upstairs?" Teresa rose in mock indignation.

"Here or anywhere," said Antonio, stretching his legs out before the cold fireplace. "Dolores! She is the most mercenary Rodriguez of all. You should hear her question me about my inheritance!"

"She is only a child, Antonio." Teresa stepped behind him and rubbed his shoulders soothingly. "And certainly somebody should be concerned about the estate. You seem to have no interest in it, or in anything but pleasure."

"What would you have me do? I rode out to look at the castle, but it was hardly worth the effort. A pile of black stones. Not very attractive, and hardly the airy palace I had dreamed about. It made me uncomfortable somehow. I was almost glad I couldn't get inside. At least it's locked up tight enough. The drawbridge was up and a man would need a siege ladder to get over the walls. Still, I want to see what's in there."

"What does the Grand Inquisitor say?"

"The Grand Inquisitor! I've spent the best part of the summer listening to his excuses, and now it seems I can't even have those! I was at the Holy House today, and all I got out of it was some story about the Grand Inquisitor being away. They tried to tell me they didn't know where he had gone!"

"There's something wrong," Teresa said. Her hands were quiet on Antonio's shoulders. "Something may have happened to the Grand Inquisitor. A monk was here tonight, the vicar, in fact; he came to get my father's bow. They have gone to seek some enemy of the Inquisition. I'm afraid."

"Your father! The vicar! The Grand Inquisitor! To hell with all of them!" Antonio jumped out of his chair and stalked across the room to the locked and bolted door. "I'm going back to the Golden Cup. At least the lice are glad enough to share my bed with me!" He pulled irritably at a heavy bolt.

The door creaked open.

"Antonio," Teresa said. "Aren't you going to kiss me good night?"

He looked at her. Her lips were trembling and her eyes shone with tears.

"I'm sorry," she said. "I can't help it. I'm worried, and I don't know what to do. Do you hate me?"

Antonio had grace enough to take her in his arms.

"I didn't mean anything," he said. "It's just that I hate having to wait. But I love you, Teresa. I swear I do. Don't worry about that."

He kissed her tenderly. It was easy enough for him to show passion, as Teresa knew, but this kiss showed something sweeter.

"I don't even care about the castle," he whispered. "I try to be practical, but what is it worth? You are the greatest treasure I have found in this accursed kingdom."

He kissed her again, ran his fingers through her pale hair, and hurried off through the muddy streets.

Teresa held back her tears until the door was closed again. She locked and bolted it, then stood in the middle of the room and wept for joy and sorrow. She kneeled before the image of the Virgin in the corner and prayed as best she could, but the only words that emerged between her gasps were, "Please. Please. Please."

In a few minutes she composed herself. She stood up, straightened the chairs, and washed the two cups she and her suitor had used. When she finished there was no evidence that Antonio had been there, but still she sensed his presence in the room. Even if she had not been waiting for her father, she would not have been ready to climb the stairs to the bed she shared with her sister Dolores. Instead she sat in a chair to dream of Antonio, and her dreams were not as virginal as they might have been.

She was roused from them by a sudden pounding at the door. It startled her for a moment and her heart jumped, but then she realized who it must be.

"Father?"

"Let me in, Teresa."

It was certainly her father's voice. It sounded hollow and strangely sad, but what did that matter? He had come home.

"Teresa. Let me in."

The voice was weak and Teresa wondered if her father might be hurt, but the power of the blows on the door reassured her.

"I'm coming," she said, inwardly thanking Heaven that Antonio was gone. Her hands were trembling with relief and she could hardly hold the key. The bolt was stiff. The impatient knocking never ceased.

"All right!" said Teresa, pulling at the heavy door. "It's open! Come in, and be quiet!"

A man stood in the doorway, wrapped in a crimson cloak. His face and hands were splashed with blood.

It was not her father.

His face, beneath the damp black hair, was as pale and gaunt as a skull, and there was something in his hand.

Teresa stepped back from the door, too bewildered for real fear. Where was her father? She had heard his voice.

All at once she recognized her visitor. She had seen him long ago, when she was a child.

He had been dead for nine years. She stared at him in disbelief, then saw what was in his hand.

It was her father's head.

Teresa did not scream, but she clutched her stomach with both hands and stumbled back against the wall. Her throat made soft, dry sounds.

Sebastian held the dripping head by its shaggy hair and raised it slowly. Its eyes were open and its lips began to move.

"Teresa," it said.

Teresa moaned sickly and looked at the man in the cloak. He was smiling and his teeth were much too long.

"Sleep, Pedro," he said. He tossed her father's head into the street and she heard it slap into the mud. Then she began to scream.

Sebastian's long white hands reached out for her, seeming to stretch across the room. The candles flickered out and the darkness in his eyes was everywhere. Teresa's screams died down to a whimper.

"Teresa?" The sleepy voice came from the stairs. "What's going on?"

Dolores came down into the dark room. Her voice broke Sebastian's spell and Teresa turned to see her little sister standing at the foot of the stairs, rubbing her eyes. Sebastian saw Dolores too. He lunged toward her.

"Dolores!" cried Teresa. "Run!"

Even as she spoke, Teresa realized that there was no one between her and the door. She glanced at the blood-stained monster and saw his hands busy at her sister's throat.

Teresa ran. She heard a short, sharp cry from Dolores and answered it with a heartfelt moan, but still she ran.

She tumbled through the door and fell into the muddy street. Her first thought was of Antonio and she jumped up, heading toward the inn.

What she met in the road blocked her as surely as a wall. Her father's head sat in the mire grinning up at her.

Teresa wailed and spun around. She saw the dead man in the doorway, with Dolores in his arms. Teresa knew she should stop and try to help her sister, but she could not bring herself to stay. The horror on the threshold was more powerful than love or loyalty. She sped down the narrow street toward the public square. Behind her were Antonio, Dolores, and Don Sebastian de Villanueva.

Teresa gasped and groaned as her strong legs rushed her through the dark, deserted thoroughfare. Her mind was with Dolores, but her body had its own will and was bent on survival at any cost.

She looked behind her as she ran and saw what followed her—the image of a nightmare. The thing with the white face bounded along behind her, its long hair streaming, its cloak billowing into the air like gigantic wings. Dolores dangled in its grip like a broken puppet. Its movements seemed supernaturally slow and graceful, yet it was surely overtaking her. Teresa looked away from it and rushed forward.

She dashed into the great plaza that was the heart of the city and there she stopped, the clatter of her shoes on the wet pavements echoing away into silence. The square was vast and vacant, bathed in the cold light of a waning moon. Teresa whirled hysterically, an awful emptiness around her. She saw the buildings spinning past, sanctuaries of the rich and strong that held no hope for her. She would have called for help but could not catch her breath. The dead man floated toward her with uncanny speed.

"Sweet Jesus!" cried Teresa. She turned again and the cathedral rose before her eyes. Its twin towers loomed above her and the spires touched the skies.

She stumbled up the marble steps. The man in black was in the plaza now, only a few steps away. He shouted something at her but she did not understand. Her heart throbbed wildly and her eyes were dim, but her feet moved doggedly up the slippery stairs until she fell against the door.

It was open.

Teresa dropped into the cathedral like a soul falling into Hell. She sprawled on the floor and raised her eyes to the vaulted ceilings. The spaces above her were huge and dark, utterly devoid of life. No one was here to worship and there was no priest. She crawled down the wine-colored carpet that covered the aisle and passed the stiff stone images of melancholy saints, their hands raised in benediction. She thought of their ghastly deaths and waited for her own.

In the light of candles glowing faintly before the distant altar she saw the great carving of Christ in agony upon the cross. She had seen it many times before but had never really understood that it was the image of a dying man.

The tortured face gleamed darkly and drops of painted blood glistened on the brow. Teresa struggled to her feet and tottered down the aisle toward the carving, muttering prayers for herself and her sister. She expected the doors to burst open behind her, but nothing happened. The ghost of Don Sebastian had abandoned her.

To the right of the dying Christ was the statue of a woman, her arms outspread, her robes painted blue. Teresa turned toward her and her compassionate eyes. A deep voice called to Teresa from the plaza, but she would not hear it. She embraced the image of the Virgin and sank dizzily down before it.

Sebastian cast a cold eye on the cathedral. Its twin towers, taller than the ones that sheltered him, were topped by crosses.

He put his boot on the first step, then stopped. The child hung in his arms like a corpse, but she was still alive.

Between the towers and below them was a great round window of stained glass. Its outer rim was divided into twenty-four separate sections, in the center of which was a flower with twelve petals. The flower began to glow, light streaming outward from the central circle.

Sebastian tried to look away.

The whole cathedral shone. The rest of the world he saw was a dull silver, but this was gleaming gold. The radiance spread until the great round window was aflame with it, its multicolored panes alive like some omniscient eye.

Sebastian mounted another step.

This was the place where he had worshiped as a boy, and now he was obliged to enter it again, not as a man but as a monster. The girl who hid within it had to die, or else Sebastian's unnatural life was over. If she survived, the secret of the castle would be exposed. Sebastian pictured himself, helpless in the crypt, surrounded by a mob of pious monks bearing pointed sticks.

He took another step.

The towers of the cathedral reeled dizzily toward the heavens. They were not like the turrets of his castle, though they were nearly as old. The castle was stark and spartan, but these spires were ornate, airy squares of arches and arabesques topped by tapering fingers that pointed toward the stars. The golden glow rippled upward till the towers were dazzling.

Sebastian took another step.

The taste of blood was bitter in his mouth. The child he held was a pathetic thing, but she too would have to be destroyed.

He thought of himself as a child and remembered mounting these steps before. He had held his little brother by the hand and they had laughed and joked and teased each other, indifferent to the emblems of death and resurrection that lurked within the gray walls.

Sebastian grew sick at heart. He shouted for Teresa to come forth, but the words caught in his throat.

The cathedral was as radiant as the gates of Heaven.

He had dreamed of such a night before. The cross had seemed to him a sorry thing, and he never doubted that he could surmount it. The idea that two sticks of wood could repel him was ridiculous; he was not that weak. But this golden edifice was strong.

It was not that he could not enter it but that its presence saddened him. The images of martyred men and women rose before him and he pitied them. He pitied the young woman who had fled from him and the beautiful child in his arms. He thought of Margarita, her body pierced and bleeding, of himself, groveling toward a pool of blood, and he was ashamed.

Sebastian dropped back a step.

He was furious when he realized what he had done. He could not allow this pile of golden stone to defeat him.

"Teresa Rodriguez!" he shouted. "Come forth, or your sister dies!" The sound of his voice was ugly to him, as were the things it said. The unconscious child was heavy in his hands. Yet who was she that he should pity her, and who was her sister? They were the daughters of the man who had murdered Margarita.

He steeled himself and climbed three steps toward his prey. Yet the doors of the cathedral still seemed distant and were alive with light.

The flaming mass that blocked his path was an image of the coming dawn. There was time enough for what he had to do before the sun rose, but the burning spires were an ill omen. He teetered on the marble stairs and his foot slipped down again.

"Come forth, Teresa!"

There was no reply.

The golden gleam was blinding. Sebastian turned his back to it and looked into the soothing silver of the empty plaza. He staggered down the stairs and let his burden rest upon the bottom step. He gazed abstractedly at Dolores and his fingers brushed her blond hair. His head was bowed.

A horror came upon him. His thirst for blood and vengeance had waned, but there could be no turning back now. If he spared Pedro's daughters or failed in his siege of the cathedral, he would surely be destroyed. He sat on the cold marble beside Dolores and put a pale hand to his face. A great sorrow overwhelmed him.

He stepped resolutely into the plaza and whirled to face the golden sanctuary. Its dazzling brilliance stunned him. He raised his arms above his head and let out a titanic howl of fury and frustration. He lurched toward the cathedral, then stopped and threw his hands before his eyes.

A light came on in one of the houses across the square.

Sebastian stooped to gather up Dolores. "I am undone," he told her. "I should have stayed at home and mourned my dead."

Dolores could not hear him and could not see the black wings sprouting from his shoulders.

"There will be another death," Sebastian said, "before the next day dawns."

He rose into the gray sky, the child in his arms.

23. The Castle

TERESA lay huddled at the foot of the statue in an agony of suspense and shame. A hundred times she rose to leave and a hundred times sank back sobbing and groaning. Whatever she did, the sad wooden eyes of the Virgin looked at her with the same tenderness.

Teresa sensed obscurely that she was safe from Don Sebastian in the cathedral, but the thought brought her no comfort, for she had abandoned her sister. She told herself that there was nothing she could have done to save Dolores, but still she felt that it might have been better to stay and die than to hide and feel such overwhelming guilt. She reproached herself for the very pain she felt, which was nothing beside the horrors Dolores might be facing.

Still Teresa could not abandon her sanctuary. And so the last long minutes of the night slipped away, and with them all Teresa's hope. The sky turned pink and pearly gray and the faint light of the coming sun brightened the cold colors of the stained-glass windows surrounding her.

As dawn drew near Teresa's spirits rose. There was no reason for it that she understood, but the promise of day warmed her heart as if the sun's rays had touched it. Light shone through the windows and cast spots of blue and red and yellow on the walls of the cathedral. Teresa stood again and swayed with weariness, but this time she did not sink down. The night seemed an ugly dream. With faltering steps she made her way down the long purple carpet.

She stopped on the threshold, hands on the doors, and tried to imagine what she would see if she opened them. She pictured the dead white face that had haunted her throughout the night, then the face of her little laughing sister. Dizzy with exhaustion, Teresa pulled at the iron rings in her hands and the portals yawned before her.

There was the plaza, just as she had seen it a thousand times before. A faint radiance rose in the east and a few sleepy people trudged across the square. There was no sign of Dolores or of Don Sebastian. It was as if nothing had happened.

Teresa walked giddily down the marble steps. A man passed her and looked at her strangely, but he did not speak.

Teresa crossed the plaza without thinking to talk to anyone. She thought only to reach Antonio. There was no one else left for her. She approached the inn by an elaborate route, carefully avoiding the street where she lived. She had no wish to see what might still be lying there.

Her emotions had exhausted her, as had lack of sleep. Her progress was slow. More than once she stopped to rest against a whitewashed wall. Her odd behavior drew stares from the people in the streets, but Teresa was beyond embarrassment.

At last she reached the inn. The sky in the east was pink and gold, but still the sun was hidden. Teresa collapsed on the barred wooden door and beat on it with slow monotony.

A boy appeared in the entrance and looked aghast at Teresa's appearance. She recognized him as the friend of Dolores who had carried messages to Antonio for her.

"Bring him," said Teresa. "Bring him to me at once. Oh God, please hurry. It's Dolores."

The bewildered boy scampered obediently away and Teresa leaned against the doorway, awaiting his return.

Somewhere bells were ringing. Teresa's eyelids drooped and she nearly fell.

"Please hurry," she said to no one. "Hurry, hurry, hurry."

She staggered in the doorway, but Antonio caught her just before she dropped.

"Teresa!" he said sharply. "What is it?" He was shocked to see her tangled hair, haggard face, and disheveled clothing.

Teresa looked at Antonio through half-closed eyes. He was heavy with sleep and his appearance was not much better than her own, but he was sweeter to her than the statues of the saints who had guarded her through her dark vigil. She went limp in his arms.

"Teresa!"

She would have sold her soul to sink into oblivion, yet she blessed Antonio's insistence. With a tremendous effort she roused herself, to find that she was seated on a bench inside the inn. Antonio held her. She began to struggle against him.

"It's Dolores!" she cried. "He has taken her. We must go at once. He killed my father. Save her, Antonio!"

"What? Who has taken her?"

"Don Sebastian! Master of your accursed castle!"

Teresa was on her feet again, as if her own words had restored her strength. Antonio stared at her in disbelief.

"Don Sebastian?" he repeated. "But he's dead!"

"I know he's dead, but he still walks. I saw him, Antonio! Don't argue with me!" She pulled him up from the bench, her hands working frantically. "Must I show you my father's head in the street?"

Antonio did not understand, but he could hardly doubt her. He was suddenly wide awake.

"My sword," he told the boy. "Bring it to the stable. And be quick about it!"

He ran into the street, Teresa right behind him.

"Where could he have taken her?" he asked. "To the castle?"

"I don't know, he could be anywhere, but we must try the castle. Oh God, Antonio, I know he meant to kill her! I think we are too late!"

"When did it happen?" asked Antonio.

"Hours ago, it seems. What must you think of me? I hid from him in the cathedral, and I was afraid to come out. I abandoned her."

"Thank God that you at least are safe. What could you have done against him? And what manner of man is he, to walk abroad years after he has died?"

"He is not a man at all, Antonio. He is a ghost, he is a demon, he is a monster! You should have seen him. . . . No. Stop. You should not follow him. He will kill you, too."

Antonio stopped outside the stable and looked to the east. "The sun is rising," he said, "and these spirits are strongest in the night. I will stop him if I can. Besides, I cannot have trespassers on my estate." He almost managed a smile. "Where is that boy with my sword?" He stepped through the shadows to the stall where his horse waited.

"What is a sword to a dead man?" Teresa asked. "I should never have told you! Don't go!"

Antonio calmly saddled his horse. "Wait here for me," he said, for all the world as if he were not afraid.

"Wait?" shouted Teresa. She almost slapped him. "I'm coming with you. It's all my fault, and I will not be left behind. Antonio!"

"I have only one horse," he said, taken aback by her passion.

"Then I will ride behind you," declared Teresa. "But hurry!"

Had Antonio reached the forest sooner, he would have seen two figures among the trees. One was a tall man dressed in black; the other was a small blond girl in her nightgown. Shafts of golden light broke through the leafy branches above them, but the dark man avoided these, skulking in the deep green shade. The child was crying.

From time to time he pointed out dead sticks of wood to her and she dutifully picked them up. Her arms were filled with fuel, and rotting bark darkened the front of her white gown. He bent over her and whispered in her ear. Her lips trembled with every word, and tears streamed down her cheeks.

He kneeled before her in the shadow of a great oak tree, his dead eyes level with her own. His hands touched her shoulders and his words came rapidly. She did not turn away from him.

Birds sang in the forest, heralding the dawn. The sun struggled up behind the purple mountains and cast its beams on the black towers beyond the forest.

The man stood up and put one arm around the child. She was all but lost in the folds of his crimson cloak. Together they walked through the trees until they reached the rocky clearing between the forest and the moat. They struggled up the stony path, the girl bent by the weight of her burden, the man lowering his head before the warm rays of the sun.

At length they reached the castle. He took some of the wood from her and helped her arrange the pieces into a circle.

Then he leaned down and kissed the weeping child.

The sun rolled majestically up into the sky, but the shadow of the castle fell upon Dolores and Don Sebastian. Trembling, they embraced.

Antonio lashed the reins mercilessly against the neck of his gray stallion. The beast responded nobly, but it could hardly gallop through the thick forest, such efforts as it made serving only to punish its riders. Low branches whipped Antonio's face into a mass of cuts and bruises. Behind him, Teresa wrapped her arms around his waist so that his body helped to shield her, but more than once a springy bough slapped out at her. Their progress was maddeningly slow.

Antonio cursed the trees, his mount, and the woman who clung so feebly yet still screamed exhortations upon him.

"Too late! Too late!" Teresa shouted. A branch struck her shoulder and nearly threw her from the horse.

Antonio pulled up his mount and turned to look at her. "I will leave you here," he said. "We are almost at the castle, and I will make better time without you."

"Damn you, Antonio! Ride on! We will be there in another

minute, and now you would leave me behind!" She hit out at him with both hands, her eyes wet, her face wild.

Appalled at her ferocity, Antonio made no answer but to spur his steed.

Near the edge of the forest, where the trees grew thinner, rocks rose up from the ground to bar their way. The foaming stallion leaped over some and stumbled over others, but the two riders kept their seats. Finally, they broke through the outlying trees.

They saw the bleak black castle, its towers silhouetted against the rising sun, its dark bulk looming majestically against the purple ranges of the Pyrenees. Antonio reined his horse against the very sight of its grim strength.

Teresa screamed in insupportable anguish.

Antonio turned his head to look at her and saw a face hideously distorted by misery and pain. Turning back, he saw what he had missed.

A fire burned before the castle, just outside the distant moat. In its scarlet flames a body writhed.

Antonio turned sick and dropped his reins. Teresa groaned, unclasped her hands from his waist, and slipped off the stallion to the rocks below.

Antonio dropped down beside her. He feared for his mount, but the beast apparently had no wish to approach the castle. It stood shivering among the stones as Antonio knelt at Teresa's side.

She lay in a sobbing heap upon the ground, flailing her arms against sharp stones.

"She's dead, she's dead," Teresa cried. "Everyone is dead!"

Antonio reached out toward her carefully, almost afraid to interrupt her grief. He glanced toward the castle, thinking for a moment to drag the burning body from the flames, but he knew he would be too late. It was better to stay with Teresa and comfort her as best he could. He gathered her up and rocked her in his arms.

As they huddled together on the outskirts of the forest, Antonio saw all his dreams destroyed. The wailing woman in his arms was suddenly a stranger; the estate he hoped to claim, a mausoleum.

A shadow fell over him.

Antonio looked up and saw a figure standing dark against the sky. Its hair was wild, its arms outspread.

It was Dolores—tear-stained and bedraggled, but certainly alive.

Antonio choked and gasped and tried to speak, but for a moment no words came. Teresa, her face hidden on his shoulder, had not seen.

"Teresa," he said weakly, then again, "Teresa."

When she did not answer him, Antonio spun her around until she faced her sister. He shook her fiercely. "Look," he croaked. "Just look."

Teresa opened her eyes and fainted dead away.

Antonio held Teresa and stared at her sister. Her face had changed; she was not the child he had known.

"Help me with her," said Antonio. They propped Teresa up against a boulder and brought her back to consciousness with shouts and slaps. "We thought you were dead," Antonio told Dolores.

"He let me go," Dolores said.

Teresa stretched her hands out to Dolores and drew the child down to her. She held the little golden head against her breast, and the sisters wept together.

Antonio felt lost at the sight of their communion. He stood aside to let the sisters cling to each other and raised his eyes to the black towers.

"Don Sebastian!" he said. Spurred by some impulse he could not have named, Antonio ran toward the castle.

"What happened, Dolores?" asked Teresa.

"He killed himself," Dolores answered solemnly, "and he made me help him. He said he was already dead. He was very sad."

"Poor Dolores."

"He said it was a penance, that I should gather wood for him. He meant to kill me, but he changed his mind. He said it was enough that father died. Is father dead, Teresa?"

"Yes."

Dolores was silent for a time. She craned her head to see the castle and the fire that burned below it.

"I saw him once before," she said, "when he was alive. Why was he still here?"

"I don't know, Dolores."

"He didn't like it, being here. He said to tell you he was sorry. He would have killed us both, Teresa, but you stopped him when you hid in the cathedral. He said you saved me when you did that."

"Oh God," said Teresa, and she crushed her sister in her arms. "Oh Christ. Oh Jesus."

"He said he would confess to me, since there was no one else. He told me things, but I couldn't understand them. Then he said it didn't matter."

"What did he say, Dolores?"

"I don't know. I don't remember. I don't want to know. He made me pray for him. I was scared, but I was sorry for him. Then he stood where we had piled up the sticks, and he lit them with his fingers. He just stood there and caught on fire. I ran away then and found you. I want to go home."

"Oh, Dolores," said her sister, "what home have we now?"

Antonio scrambled up the rocky incline and stopped before the wide gray walls of stone. From there he watched as his dead kinsman died again.

Don Sebastian did not die like any ordinary man. He was not chained or tied, and there was nothing but the strength of his own will to keep him in the fire. His body was bathed in flame, but still it stood erect. The crimson cloak blazed behind him and the black velvet suit smoldered.

Sebastian saw a dim image of the young man who ap-

239

proached his funeral pyre. It was his heir. Then smoke filled Sebastian's eyes, and the golden flames before them turned to molten silver.

Awestruck, Antonio stared as Don Sebastian was consumed. The dead flesh boiled and blistered, and the long hair turned into a torch. The dark eyes bubbled in their sockets and ran down the blackened cheeks in bloody streams. The skin dropped away in dusky strips until the bones were bare. The blaze wavered and the stripped skeleton gleamed and glowed. Its bones shone like some precious metal.

The naked skull still glistened, but the ravaged corpse did not collapse. It gestured to Antonio with a desiccated arm.

Antonio stepped back in horror.

The grim jaws gaped and the long teeth glistened as the dead thing spoke.

"Here is your castle," said Don Sebastian.

The hot spine snapped and the silver skull dropped into the flames. Bones tumbled down behind it, and their weight put out the fire. As the flames sparked and sputtered out, they sent the bright skull spinning from the embers of red and black.

The dead grin rolled toward the dark walls of the castle and the head of Don Sebastian de Villanueva sank with a splash into the waters of the moat.

Black smoke floated up above the towers and was lost in the bright blue of the heavens.

24. The Cannon

THREE days later, French troops crossed the Pyrenees and occupied the castle. This maneuver was part of a series of minor border skirmishes arising from the conflict between France and Spain over the control of Naples. The French were driven back, but not before cannon fire had shattered the walls of the castle, toppling its great tower.

Antonio Manetti fled back to Florence. With him went the daughters of Pedro Rodriguez. There they lived out their days in peace, if not in plenty.

The castle fell in a few hours. Torquemada took two years to die, and Columbus was carried back in chains from his third voyage; but the Inquisition endured for another three hundred and thirty-eight years.